Dear Reader:

It is indeed my pleasure to present *There's Always a Reason* by William Fredrick Cooper. In his first novel, *Six Days in January*, readers were introduced to William McCall; a young man whose outlook on love showed that men do indeed love deeply. Now the wonderful, charming character is back and this time he discovers that love is more about giving than receiving. When he meets Linda aka Lucky, during a period when everything is his life seems to be falling apart, not only does he quickly realize that things can be worse but how truly blessed he is. Not only is he blessed to have met Lucky but he is blessed to be given the "experience of loving her."

I first met William at a writer's conference several years ago and was immediately taken aback by his honesty about life and his passion for writing. I knew before I even read a single word of his writing that it would be outstanding. Why? Because the emotion was there and emotional writing is generally the best writing. William is a trooper and fans and booksellers alike seemingly adore him, and for good reason.

This book brought out so many deeply rooted feelings while I was reading it. I found myself laughing and I found myself crying and in the end, I found myself praising this novel as I am now doing so to you.

Thanks for giving William's novel a chance and I am confident that you will enjoy it as much as me. Make sure that you check out "Dear Zane...A Lust Letter from a Fan" also penned by William and which will appear in my first nonfiction title, *Dear G Spot*, in July 2007.

I want to thank those of you who have been gracious enough to support the dozens of authors I publish under Strebor Books International, a division of ATRIA/Simon and Schuster. While writing serves as a catalyst for me to release my personal creativity, publishing allows me the opportunity to share the talent of so many others. If you are interested in being an independent sales representative for Strebor Books International, please send a blank email to info@streborbooks.com. Also, visit my blog at http://myspace.com/zaneland.

Blessings,

Zane

Publisher
Strebor Books International

ZANE PRESENTS

WILLIAM FREDRICK COOPER

THERE'S ALWAYS A
REASON

SBI

STREBOR BOOKS

NEW YORK LONDON TORONTO SYDNEY

Strebor Books
P.O. Box 6505
Largo, MD 20792

There's Always a Reason © 2007 by William Fredrick Cooper

ISBN-13 978-0-7394-8179-0

Cover design: www.mariondesigns.com

Manufactured in the United States of America

ACKNOWLEDGMENTS

"Only when you have been in the deepest of valleys can you ever appreciate how magnificent it is to be on the highest mountain."
Richard Milhous Nixon
August 9, 1974

It's funny how words spoken at one person's resignation can galvanize the spirits of another. Thanks, Richard.

I want to first and foremost apologize for the delay of my second novel; Lord knows, I didn't mean for it to take such a long time. However, to say real life got in the way is an understatement. I lost my everyday job and couldn't land another one for almost two years. Eviction notices coming left and right, lights and heat going out occasionally, warding off depression, it got rough for a minute. Then upon landing one, my boss took flight, leaving the responsibilities of running a growing department, and many nights and weekends in the hands of eighty attorneys. Deadlines came and went, and ultimately, it came to the "now or never" point to release this novel. Sometimes truth is stranger than fiction. However, through the process I learned so much about faith and mental toughness, some of which I hope I conveyed in this effort. If not, then readers, I tried. And will keep trying.

Bianca Carrion: At time of publication, I don't know whether you'll be here with me, or home with your Father. I'm praying you're around for my first U.S. signing. One of the things many of us could learn from you is how strong the will to live is, the ability to smile during grinding times, and to live life with unconditional love. Bianca, words cannot describe my thanks for everything. I love you and you will always live within me, no matter where you are. Whether you are here or in heaven by the time this hits the shelves, don't hurt nobody (you know what I'm talking about!!!) Darryl Franklin: You are, by far, the best dancer I have ever known, but more importantly, an even better man. Your sacrifices regarding Bianca inspired this story of love, and I am grateful to know your courage.

I never had the opportunity to express my gratitude for all those in the U.S., Canada, England and other places that went into their pockets and purchased my first novel, *Six Days in January*. When hearing how some people drove three hours to purchase the book, and others waited as long as two weeks for it to arrive abroad, that made me feel special. To those who gave indication that it was 1) very different from what's popular, 2) very refreshing and special, and 3) provided emotional therapy, it let me know that I accomplished what I set out to do.

Somehow, making a difference means more to me than anything else.

Additionally I am appreciative of the many tough reviews I received. Black Expressions members—I appreciated our love/hate relationship. Thumper: your review was not used as toilet paper. In the alternative, every time I lost confidence in my writing, I pulled it out as motivation to prove you wrong. Call it a basketball player's mentality. When you go the paths less traveled, you know you're not always going to win fans accustomed to the norm. Many of us prefer to escape from reality, but sometimes we must THINK. Everyone is not going to like what you do, and though it can be tough to accept negative critique, (Do you know how many authors want to say "Screw you. You sit down, learn how to put feelings on paper in a way that may save lives, make tremendous sacrifices in your personal life, and hold their tongues?)" It's a necessary evil in the development of our craft. So keep those coming as well.

There are many people to thank. Anyone who looked at the last acknowledgment I wrote knows I am long-winded. But I don't want to forget a soul, as many have touched my life. God, thank you so much for the journey, as well as the determination to see things through the eye of another storm.

When you have a purpose for someone, you navigate them through many storms so they can deliver your messages. All things are not possible without you, Big Guy. Eyvonne Wilton, Elaine McCormick, Deacon Anthony Nolen, Sr. and Allegra Maple: Your stories are ones that are profiles in courage, and I only hope that I captured some of your bravery in this novel. To the family of Luther Vandross: the singular voice of hope and love that kept me from falling too far down, and I am so grateful. I sure do miss him.

Ms. Audrey T. Cooper, thank you for being so understanding about my financial woes when I was unemployed and not dragging me through the legal system, as well as holding it down like a trooper. Lastly, I want to say thank you for raising our daughter to be a queen. I know that if anything were ever to happen to me, Maranda would be okay, for she has a treasure in you. From the bottom of my heart, I say thank you for being a blessing from above. Maranda, if there's anything I want you to inherit from your father, remember that he's not a quitter. Life throws us curveballs sometimes, but the tests are there to make us stronger. Use every clip in the chamber of knowledge to get through. I love you so much. Daddy's so proud of you.

Cheryl Faye Smith: Thanks for everything, baby. You are incredible, and I love you very much for all you have done to help me strengthen my writing in every way possible. (That night when you told me to prove it when I said "I want to be the best" stands out.) I couldn't have done this without your demands of excellence from me. We make a hell of a team. You wanna know why? Because I know a man with the power of "Who Do."

Zane—what can I say that already hasn't been said? I love you like a sister, and though I piss you off sometimes with my enigmatic ways and delays in submitting my stuff (the perfectionist in me), I truly hope that I represent Strebor in the best way possible. Charmaine Parker, you are priceless. I appreciate everything about you. Rick Parker—Take better care of yourself, please. A brother loves your humor. "T.Q." —you are the man!

Man, there were so many people that helped me through my literary tour and struggles, from all over the place. God definitely gives you what you need when you need it. Sarah Oyango ("Black on Black" CHUO 89.1FM— Ottawa Ontario) and my Kinkii Ladies of Ottawa, Canada: I really love your support, and can't wait to see you ladies again. We gotta go dancing again. Sarah, you have a heart of gold. To think: it all started with a simple Black Planet post. From the bottom of my heart, I want to say *Thanks*. To Neil Armstrong (York University Radio—Toronto), Milton Thompson, Carrie Mullings (my condolences on your father) and Gary (your last name escapes me, but I love you.): as per your requests I won't change my writing style for anyone, eh? To Sean and Michelle Liburd, owners of Knowledge Bookstore (Brampton, Ontario): I simply can't wait to see you guys again. Thanks so much for taking a chance with me when the other bookstores wouldn't because I wasn't... You know the deal. I'll never forget the love.

Many book clubs looked out for a brother, and I have been truly blessed. To Judi Belle Raines and the Sugar and Spice Book Club: I love the realness of your family. Circle of Sisters (Kalamazoo, Michigan), Mahogany Book Club (Far Rockaway), Sisters in Spirits, Imani Book Club and Nubian Sistas (Miami, Florida): you ladies are incredible. Joy Farrington, Kris Hollis, Patricia Louis: Thank you ladies, for being you. Gwendolyn Ames and the Amigirls: I can't wait to return to your Retreat. Lord Knows, it was tons of fun dancing the night away. Alicia Latimer and The Sisters Sippin' Tea Book Club (Tulsa, Oklahoma): That "Man Up" conference was incredible. Thanks for including me in the program.

Carla Carter, I really enjoyed staying with you whenever in Maryland. Thanks for looking out, and being a real friend even when I didn't understand. Sonya Allen, you are amazing, a real sweetie. Tell your sis I said WHAZZZUUPPP! Angela Ray—thanks so much for being you when I was touring in the Carolinas, but I expect nothing less from a Delta. Carol Blake, you are, and always will be my creampuff. Girl, you helped me with money, T-shirts, your wisdom, photocopies, and did so with love. I cannot begin to tell you how much you mean to me. God bless you and Bermuda Press! Karen Butler-Brock: thanks girl, for being there for me. Joyce Adewumi: You were right: we are humans living an experience. Lisa Solomon-Jackson— Always a positive word, whenever I needed it. Rhonda Lawson—I wish that I could have reached out more, but a brother was going through some serious shit. You are one of the sweetest people I have ever met. Melonne—You know what's up! Okay, I admit, I cried when Jerome Bettis and the Steelers went to the Super Bowl, for I believe in perfect endings. Please kiss that wonderful son of yours. Tell my ladies in Cleveland Whazzzzzupppp!!! To Susan McNamara, Brian Sachs and Michael Stonberg—the temp assignments were right on time. Jason Bernstein: How does it feel to look in the mirror? You are incredible, and I enjoyed working for you.

Now I realize that other sorority members might put down my book with my next words, but I want to say that the unity and love each unit represents is a mandated necessary in the black community. To the Crimson and Cream, the Delta Sigma Theta Sorority: Everywhere I have turned, from the God-mother of my daughter (Josephine A. E. Tucker), to close personal friends (Brenda Woodbury, Danielle Spears, Gail P. Carr, Pardiece Powell-McGoy) to Literary Aides and Inspirations (Jackie Perkins, Linda Battle, Victoria Christopher-Murray) and women that touched my soul (Staci Shands—Congratulations Ms. New York!!!, Joy Tyler-Hill: You are so crazy!) you queens have given me fortitude. I only hope Linda Woodson represented in print how to make a man stronger, as you ladies have done for almost a century. Give a brotha an honorary Ooo-oop.

David McGoy, my childhood friend and editor: That seventh-grade water gun fight in front of Tad's door has turned into something, huh? (Thank goodness for Martha Smith—LOL!) I don't know how you deal with my emotional nature, when writing these books. But I know that I can't do this without your uncanny critical/nurturing spirit. I love you.

My boys: Allen Brown, Askia Farrell, Allen Brown, Stacey and Tad Spencer, Daniel Marks, Bobby Moore, Christian Davis, Baruti, Steve (Randall—wink) McGoy, Hector Gonzalez, Iscom Jones, B.K. Simpson, Anthony Lopez, Jesus Hernandez, Darren Hunter, James Bethea, Memphis Vaughan, Jr., Roger McLean, John Fleming and Michael R.D. Cooper: No matter where I go with this, know that our friendships stand the test of time. You guys have looked out in so many ways—from dinners when you knew I was down in spirit (I never opened my mouth, but you guys sensed my troubles) to insulating my daughter within a positive village whenever I go into my writing zones—I can't possibly repay you all for the deeds done. God Bless Each Of

You Guys. Grandma: Thank you for keeping a roof over my head and teaching me that three dollar chicken and noodles recipe. I make it pretty good, you know? Ma: Thanks so much for passing along the energy to help in any way I possess, as well as the talent of transforming meditations to paper. You have a natural gift of expression that can touch lives. You need to write something. Pop—You know how we do. I love you, man.

My brothers, Adrian, Jeff and Gerald: You guys are my soul. Thanks so much for just being there to listen and love. My sisters, Janessa and Stephanie: there's a winner in each of you, but sometimes, you must reach deeper than you realize to uncover it. Cassandra Solomon, Albert, Kenny and Ingrid Morgan, Katrina Spicer, Michele Wilson, Nathasha Brooks-Harris, Joyce Powell, Anita Turner, Rosalyn Lewis, Alicia Martinez (my cyber lover—LOL) and Andree Michelle (take care of my big brother for me—wink): Thank you so much for keeping me sane. I love you ladies so much. JoOna Danois: Read the message in the novel carefully. I hope you get it.

Nancey Flowers, (Another Delta) thank you so much for teaching me how to navigate through the literary madness. You never find out who your friends are in this industry until the shot clock winds down. Thank you for being there. Vincent Alexandria, when it's all said and done, this industry, no, our community, will realize that to whom much is given, much more is required. I am honored to be your left hand with Brother 2 Brother, and more than honored to be a friend. I love you, man. Tracy Grant: I miss you. Do the damn thing in California.

Nancy Gilliam and Denise Spiller: you ladies are awesome. Tina Brooks McKinney: that critique meant a great deal, as it made me buckle down. Is there any more drama comin'? Allison Hobbs and Jessica Tilles: If I accomplish what you ladies have, I'll be grateful. Allison, your words of encouragement meant more than you ever realize. Eric Pete: You know how we do. I'm so proud of you. I studied "Don't Get It Twisted' carefully, and combined it with my own femininity and tried to nail it. Thanks for showin' me the way with a wonderful blueprint. Chet "C. Kelly" Robinson: You are an incredible writer, one of my favorites. I only hope I did you and Timm McCann proud. Donna Hill: You're admired more than you realize. Gloria Mallette:

If I weave a tale like *The Honeywell*, I'd feel happier than if I saved money on my car insurance…You get it. Tracy Price-Thompson: We've come a long way since Atlanta. I love you, little sister. Karen E. Quinones Miller: You know that I love you, girl. Evelyn Palfrey: Thanks for having me amongst the Marvelously Mature. Kashamba Williams: You are my girl!!! Darren Coleman: I have always admired your work, and that you think I'm one of your favorite writers means the world to me. We have got to collaborate. SOON! Wow, I'm actually someone's favorite writer. Roy Glenn: That plane ride to Houston was so much fun. You only deserve the best. Carl Weber— Without you, there'd be a lot of people doing negative shit. Thanks for saving some lives, man. My Strebor Family: I wanted to name all of you, but our galaxy of stars has gotten rather large. I want you all to know that I admire each of your talents, and hope that all of you realize that it takes the sum of us to make this thing happen. Each of your success is my own. There's no "I" in team, so it's up to us to follow Zane's selfless lead. Talent without humility means nothing, ya feel me? Kerry Wagner—I needed that kick in the ass, and I love you for it.

I want to pause with the authors for a tick and give thanks to the homeless shelters I visited before penning this book, as well as "my friends." Trust me, your stories of survival can make a book on its own. I will help, don't worry. To my sexy nurses Karen Spencer and Sarena Morris: your insight and information proved more valuable that you ever imagined. Karen, your trailblazing experience galvanized me. I believe in breaking ground with the hopes that I can make a difference. That means more to me than any best-seller. Cheryl (Luckee) Tanksley: That nickname, as well as our friendship, means more than you can possibly imagine. You are a great woman who I am hoping receives a King.

Lynette Holloway (*Ebony* magazine): Thanks for allowing me to contribute to history. I am truly blessed to know you. Carol Mackey (Black Expressions): Can you clone yourself? Just teasin.' Thanks for having faith when I was sleeping on office floors, trying to become self-published back in 2001. To my spades partner, Tee C. Royal: Thanks for supporting me from the go. Geoff has a hell of a woman. Heather Covington (Disilgold): Your selfless spirit is infectious. He must host another awards show together. —LOL Charene Thornton: I love you, big sister. It's amazing how a simple e-mail in 1999 triggered all of this. If this literary thing takes me far, then it's all because of you. I am here, because you were there. I love you.

My Court Family: Ruthlyn Charles, Barbara Reaves, Lenny and Larry, Diane Howard Ruiz, Edwin Ruiz, Rafael P. Valdez, Yvette Wilks, Tracy Motley, Doris Harrell, Antoinette Anderson, Michelle Lumpkin, Caprice Cummings, Alice Hall, Ruth McLean, Karen Shuman, Renee Hill, Ann Davis, Lynn Little, James Bouyer, Wilson Kenney, Robert Scott, Dave Brantley, Dawn Marie Goins, James Libson (AMAG), Octavia Richardson and Camille Jacobs: thanks for being my guinea pigs. My Seyfath Family: Cathy Hernandez, Lydia Ravnikar, Jennifer L. White, Carolyn Ylagan, Patricia Simmons, Angela Wilson, Cleo Hall, Sandra Gonzalez, Alfunso Batista, Jerry Montag (thanks for pushing me), Jennifer White, Michelle Duerr-Condia, Susan Riccio, Amy Nill, Martin Villoda, Carol Valdez, Newt Newton, Roy Robinson, Edward Rodriguez, Ray Anderson, Bradley White, Andrew (DJ Dru-Tiz) Ortiz, Tara Smith Williams, June Daniels, Pamela Hackett, Elizabeth Schrero (my prayers are with you and your family): You guys are incredible and I thank you for your support. Darryl Milner, thanks for being so cool and keeping me sane.

To my Black Singles Connection Family: You guys are incredible, and though I'm not on the site anymore, you are all with me in spirit. Now, if you guys can only talk some sense into Tasha about renewing my membership...LOL!!! All Of You: Adareau, AfroAngel4U, Sirinity, Alicia1951, Zorab, ASultryMD, Joyfullady, Atrsylady, Smooth595, BlackButterfly06, Bspeciallady19, Bttra, Caramelsolace, CatAJazzFan, Catwoman1, SuperNatural, Classyladie, Coalblack, Daiyaah, Desiree6, DMD357, Godessjaye, Iregal, JCwings, Juan1, Big Coby, Dparline, Mark Anthony, E-Z Mark, Tylisa, Natural2Unique, Dhampt (From your boy Coopizzle) BlushingBeauty, RareLuv, Libbi4U, Maxee, MissJazz, Missunited, Penumbra, Prettywoman, Queen34234, Redbutterfly05, Shaystang, Shenda47, Snoopylov2, Soulfuljoy, Starch, Sunrisesmile, Taliah2, Txlady, Peanut, Waitingforyou, AAA247, Afroasian, Charlesthegreat1, D. J. Webb, DarkCinnamon, Detroit Red,

Dion, Jericho, Kelvin, Larry 0517, Lightsaber, Merkwerke, Mr. Dotson, Felicia517, Foxylady, Oinpharoah, OneLuvand Peace, Prepaidman, Rufio1, Saukretees, Siera153, TheLoftyOne, Uarenotalone, Veggieman, Litesun_1, Letsdolunch90703 and Smooth 595: This love thing is not easy, but if I refuse to give up, neither can any of you!!!

To Leah and Courtney Floyd: Each of you ladies has a beautiful future ahead of you both, but you must focus on good, and what has substance. Make your mother proud. To Larry (Papa H) and JoAnne Hardison: You guys will always own a special place in my heart, continue teaching Generation X how love is supposed to be. Robert and Robyn Hardison: You opened your homes to me when I was at my lowest, and I am so grateful to both of you. Jan Forney: Thank you for allowing me to be close to you. Sometimes we need tough times to see the beauty that lies within us all. To Mommy: You saved my life. That's all I can say. Though this "Thank You" may seem little, you know it means so much more than you can imagine. I can't begin to tell you how much you mean to me. You are a treasure, a diamond that floats above murky waters. Thank you, Mommy, for being you. Always, Daddy.

Well, I think I got everybody. If not, then you know my heart, which means that I won't forget you the next time. To my readers: In terms of writing, I'm only hoping that you appreciate the substance I try to write with. So many are out there making a difference with the many stories we tell. But my hope is that you take something away from each tale that can help us, as Black people, grow together as one. The problems with us are many, but with a little love from us all, they can become few. We need to show love towards one another, because in our struggles we need each other. Authors, readers, and community, a little love is all is takes. A little love is all we need.

I'll see you guys in another three years.

I'm out like Captain Kirk.

William.

"Love has nothing to do with what you are expecting to get—only with what you are expecting to give—which is everything."
—KATHARINE HEPBURN

ONE

"Yes! Yes! Don't stop. It feels so-o-o good!" the woman screamed as the sound of her flesh slapping against her chiseled lover reached a crescendo.

"That's right! Take all this dick!"

Over the past year, he had survived numerous trials that would have broken the spirit of most men, but somehow he'd brought a semblance of order to a world that, for him, could be described by the acronym FUBAR: fucked up beyond all recognition.

The genesis of it all still tortured him, however. Recalling the recollection of that life-altering memory, the mind-blowing moment still shattered his senses like a sledgehammer blow. His bald head throbbing intensely, all attempts to still the headache had been futile, prolonging his plaintive state.

A year later, the torment of the nightmarish day remained.

Riding across the Manhattan Bridge on a crowded "Q" train in a punch-drunk stupor, still unsure of his surroundings, William McCall stared at the downtown skyline of New York City through red, sleepless eyes.

While the Freedom Tower project was in its embryonic stages, the hub of concrete skyscrapers lacked a familiar accent without the Twin Towers. This particular morning, the majestic view seemed even emptier, for if anything mirrored the loss of the magnificent World Trade Center, it was the gaping hole in his heart.

Rolling the dice of love for the umpteenth time, once more he had crapped out. All his dreams of a future with Anna Daniels—his exclusive, exquisite love, the woman he would grow old with—were shattered by an unforgettable sight.

"It's all yours, Baby…"

"That's right! This is my shit here!"

The x-rated scene seemed on an unending loop; the sound of the lovers' lusting banter and physical exertion reverberated between his ears.

"Ooh, I love it when you do it that way…"

"Do you want it harder?"

"Yes, Baby, yes," Anna screamed. *"Harder, dammit! Harder!"*

Her explicit words giving direction, commands and encouragement to continue the animalistic activity echoed in his mind as if it happened yesterday.

It wasn't supposed to happen again. He thought he'd figured the damn thing out; the crazy masculine force that embodied strength, yet made men vulnerable to the desires when surrendering to that special woman. Praising love and its workings during its prosperity, he refused to allow the jaded world of contemporary dating to bring about negativity.

Acknowledging and correcting mistakes of yore, his past demons were in the rear view mirror of distant memories, having been replaced by confidence and restored trust. Coming of age, he reached the stage in his life where wisdom met self-worth, adding to substance. Someone would come along who would appreciate his virtues, aid him in strengthening his character to build him up as he would her, and their love would conquer all.

What he witnessed made a mockery of his personal growth.

"Does he hit it like this?"

"No…he…doesn't…mmph."

He watched as Anna's sinuous back arched like a jungle cat as she succumbed to the powerful sensations of the man's fluid movements. Squealing as she churned against his abdomen, her hips rolled and her backside wobbled as she met her lover's vicious thrusts with equal vigor.

"That's right. You better cum!"

Repeatedly replaying the scene, *she never responded to me like that,* William thought. Lovemaking with Anna had always been pleasurable; exciting and ecstatic, spellbindingly sensual. Loving the way she cried, "take me there," when he explored each curve and crevice, every single pore of her copper skin, *her orgasms always drenched our sheets.*

Remembering how he religiously brought her to nirvana, he enjoyed investigating her core with his mouth, face and nose. Licking her labia like a starved cat, then tickling her triangle the way Ray Charles tuned the ivory, his singular purpose after midnight was to make her chest hurt from the ragged breaths of a climax. Then, as she recovered from his oral performance, he pleased her with the tempered thrusts and seductive stirring of his rigid tool. Taking delight in the fact that she'd purse her lips or clench her teeth in response to his meticulous care, living for the sigh of contentment that came from her sexual surrender, *there was no equal to the loving I gave her,* he believed.

Assumptions can be a motherfucker, he now realized. His performance paled in comparison to those five minutes of unscheduled voyeurism.

"Baby, let me suck you. I wanna taste you."

"Damn, girl, you're out of control," the baritone announced as Anna swept her tongue along his erection. Pumping her head like a piston, up, down, and all around on his oiled steel, she proceeded to seal her lips around the meaty spot where shaft meets head, and sucked relentlessly. Connecting with the male version of the G-spot, her lover's knees sagged ever so slightly.

"Damn, Baby, you got skills!"

Peering upward from his groin, Anna's expression was of a famished woman willing to do anything to please.

"You like that? Do you like the way I suck your dick, Baby?"

"Oh, hell yeah!"

The memory of her begging to fellate him would never leave him, nor would the grunts, growls and groans of the shared lasciviousness.

Witnessing the woman you love stick her tongue out to capture another man's release in her mouth can devastate a man; especially when watching the events with an engagement ring in hand. The simultaneous loss of your love and your livelihood, and the recollection of such however, can rob him of his sanity.

The approach of midlife had matured William. A couple of years before his world collapsed, his responsibilities as a Managing Clerk at Goetz, Gallagher and Green quintupled when the New York-based law firm merged with smaller ones in Seattle, Philadelphia, Chicago, Dallas and Los Angeles. Having complete confidence in his abilities, Mr. Gallagher, the senior principal of the country's third-largest law firm, met with William and other partners from the additional cities and recommended he oversee the implementation and progress of various computer databases in the newer venues.

The promotion was not without resistance from an elderly, seventy-something Dallas partner.

"Are you sure he's the best man for the job?"

Although singed by the heat of corporate racism, William stared indifferently into the pupils that tried to bore a hole of intimidation through his chocolate countenance.

Surprisingly, Gallagher's response was immediate.

"I wouldn't be too concerned," he announced. "I can assure you that Mr. McCall is the best man for the job."

"I must say, his credentials stand out," the Seattle partner added.

"But he doesn't have a bachelor's degree," the Dallas attorney countered.

William thought of Vivien Thomas, the brilliant surgical technician who, despite pioneering the treatment and cure of "Blue Baby Syndrome" was not properly acknowledged for his natural abilities and experience because he lacked a college education.

"At this point, I don't think that has any relevance," stated a Chicago partner. Fifty something, he was the only other black face in the meeting. "I mean, his track record in the New York office speaks for itself."

Philadelphia agreed.

"I think he's the right man for the job," the partner boomed.

"He'll need an assistant to supervise the New York office in his absence," Gallagher added.

"I'm sure I'll find someone," William uttered.

"Okay, then it's settled. Congratulations, William," Gallagher said. He was promoted to managing supervisor on the job, a position that would utilize his expertise on the numerous court and legal database systems prominent to efficient filing and monitoring court cases. The opportunity to travel as he spearheaded the training of subordinates in the various offices was one he embraced, and the significant raise in pay was appreciated.

Seventy grand a year. William beamed. *That's a long way from the twelve grand a year I made doing messenger work back in the eighties.*

"Gentleman, I assure you that you've selected the right man for the position," he boasted.

Now it was up to him to find a suitable assistant.

He thought he'd secured such in Markham Chandler. Well-dressed, articulate, ambitious and athletically built, the chestnut-complexioned man the Robert Monroe Agency sent reminded William of himself at thirty.

The interview was conducted over a steak dinner at Houston's, a swank midtown restaurant located in the Citicorp building. Noticing and admiring his confidence from their initial handshake, both had been born in Brooklyn's King's County Hospital, had come from large families and attended college at NYU, without graduating. Additionally, Mark, as he preferred to be called, had his rough dues in his occupational field, a point William noted while surveying his resume.

"So, I see you're presently working for Reliable Clerical Services, Mark," he observed.

Mark nodded. "I enjoy working with…"

"Juan Roldan?"

"Do you know him?"

"Very well. He's like a brother to me and I try to support his endeavors by sending him my legal business for the other offices. You know, like out-of-state document retrieval, filings, and service of process. I'm very proud of him. He's come a long way." William paused. "Since I know everyone who's employed by him, I find it rather odd that he never mentioned you."

For the first time, he saw a tiny crack in the veneer of Mark's self-assurance.

"Mr. McCall, I'm always busy, handling his court work in Westchester, Suffolk and Orange counties."

An awkward moment ensued, during which William fought confusion. A novice at conducting interviews, he wanted to construct a link of completeness; to be professional, yet easy-going and approachable. Unlike his interactions with superiors who fancied their reputations as taskmasters, his fancies were to be a *cool boss*, one that can chill after hours with his employees, yet be able to maintain the bridge that separates managers from subordinates.

The process would start with a simple request.

"Mark, please call me William. Whenever I hear Mr. McCall, I look over my shoulder for my father."

Seeing the relieved smile from across the table, he eased the pressure that came with the attempt of leaving an impression.

"Are you familiar with the local and federal rules?"

"I sure am."

"Can I give you an exam?"

"I'm ready whenever you are."

"Okay then. Let's count the days on state court pleadings. Can you do that for me, Mark?"

"Sure. On a summons with notice, its twenty days from the date of personal service that a defendant must serve a notice of appearance and demand for complaint. A summons with the complaint, if personally served, a defendant has twenty days to answer. Am I correct?"

Smiling, William remained silent.

"I guess you want more, huh?"

"Yup."

"If served in any fashion other than personal, then the defendant has forty days from the completion of service to answer or file a motion."

"What constitutes a completion of service?"

"Service is perfected when the proof of service has been filed with the court."

"That's correct, Mark. Now, what are the state rules with regards to counterclaims?"

"You reply to counterclaims that are made in a defendant's answers, and you have twenty days to reply, twenty-five if the answer was served by mail."

"The state rules for discovery in New Jersey?"

"Superior court?"

William nodded.

"Thirty-five days for production of documents, sixty days to respond to interrogatories."

He's an excellent candidate, William thought as he nodded approvingly. Spending the next half-hour quizzing him further on the rules and regulations, Mark never faltered as his answers continued to be immediate and accurate. Dazzled by his prospective employee's zeal, William remained reticent with his findings. After discussing the firm's benefit package and incentives, he shifted to a lighter dialogue.

"Come to think of it, Mark, you do look familiar."

"I've seen you play basketball," Mark noted as he sipped from a cola.

Nothing like talking sports to raise an eyebrow.

"So you ball, huh?"

"Very well," he responded.

"Our firm's team could use help at shooting guard."

"I play the point, William. I love comin' down, shakin' the crap out of a dude with a killer crossover, and laughing at him as I score."

"But will your team win? All that matters to me is the *W* at the end of the day. And that comes from making your teammates better."

"I *make* my team better by scorin' buckets."

Smiling, William couldn't help but notice his arrogance, not to mention his eloquent speech slipping into street vernacular.

He'll learn a lot from me if he can suppress the cockiness.

"See, now with that attitude, you couldn't play the point here." William laughed. "You get everyone else involved first. Only when necessary do you take over games."

Smirking, the competitor in Mark surfaced, albeit slightly. "I take it you're the point."

"Yes. I've been the lead guard for years now."

"I remember you torching some teams in the corporate league games. You also played for Team Dynasty in the Dyckman league on 204th and Nagle, right?"

"That was many years ago. I'm kind of old now."

"But you still have a great first step. That championship game at Baruch College, in the Lawyers' League last year, you hit about thirty, right?"

Smiling, William nodded. "I hit a lot of jumpers that night. You know, the 'chip' will be in the Garden from now on."

"I heard. So I guess the new point guard will take the firm there," Mark announced.

Shooting him an *oh really* look only hardened competitors recognize, William yearned for the steamy asphalt of a summer blacktop beneath him, as the spirit of a gym battle surged into his bloodstream. In his youth, the pill would've already been at the table, and just a whiff of conceit from an opponent would be sufficient fuel to still the tongue of any trash-talker.

But he was older now.

"I guess so," he sighed, making a concession to Father Time.

"C'mon, you mean to tell me you don't keep track of your points?"

"That's for young guys. When you near forty, all the individual stuff becomes irrelevant."

They argued the point for the next five minutes: Mark, from his *And-1* mix-tape point of view and his prospective employer, from the "been there, done that" perspective. During the banter and the ensuing back-to-business conversation, William smiled. Reminding him of an impetuous little brother, he relished the opportunity of being a mentor, as a previous authority, Michael Garvey, had done the same for him.

That his skin was bronze and his origins were of the same impoverished roots he'd risen from only strengthened the bond. In loving his fellow black man, he made a pact with his Maker that whenever the opportunity presented itself to be his brother's keeper, his actions would be swift.

No further candidates would be interviewed, no background or reference checks, for he trusted his brother. The next day, the office manager made Mark an offer of forty-three grand a year—*more than I ever made as an assistant*—and he had his running mate, both professionally and socially.

Having a pupil, he recalled, *meant letting him know he was appreciated.*

Acting on those thoughts, he always sprung for dinner during the after-hour training sessions, as well as drinks whenever they ventured to The Den, an always crowded Harlem nightspot that satisfied all sweet tooth cravings with its assortment of chocolate and eye candy.

"What about Perk's or the Lenox Lounge?" William contended, referring to historical Harlem watering holes.

Markham smirked. "Man, those spots are A.P.O."

"A.P.O.?"

"Yeah, man. A.P.O. All played out."

"Oh, I knew that."

"Yeah, right."

Together, they chuckled.

They would find that same chemistry in the Lawyer's League skirmishes. William found his desire for basketball rekindled by his younger, more gifted backcourt mate, and together they led their firm to consecutive seasonal championships. Acknowledging the skills of his colt-like partner, he relinquished the point guard position and flourished in a lesser, complementary role.

A year later, he was still rewarding his pupil; they watched Yankee games from first base box seats and endured *what are they doing here* stares directed at token minorities seated close to the historic playing field. One particular evening, the fabled Pinstripes had opened up a 12 to 2 can of whoop-ass on the hated Red Sox.

"Yo, this game sucks," Mark announced as A-Rod launched another lame fastball from Curt Schilling toward the right-field bleacher bums. "The Yankees are puttin' that head out."

"Tell me about it," William responded, scanning the historic landmark. Hundreds of fans headed toward the exits as they too cared not to stay for Frank Sinatra's "New York, New York" victory serenade. "We're outta here."

Leaving the house that Ruth built, he dialed his cell.

"Hey, Baby. I know it's late, but do you want me to come out? Cool. I'll see you later."

Mark sighed. "Are you still dealin' with that crazy chick? I keep telling you to leave her alone."

"Man, what do you know about women?"

"Man, I have a K.I.S.S. philosophy."

"K.I.S.S.?"

Mark nodded. "The 'keep it simple stupid' philosophy. No woman's pussy is worth more than my dick, William."

Sliding his Metrocard through the train turnstile at 161st Street, William understood Mark's resentment. Five years earlier, Mark was engaged to his high school sweetheart, Clarissa Stevens, and found out that Douglas, the three-year-old boy he thought he fathered, was the child of Stan, an older brother.

Distraught over the revelation, he almost landed in jail because he pummeled his sibling so bad. Clarissa was left to fend for herself from that point forward. Even attempting to recoup the monetary support given from his heart in judicial proceedings, Mark's efforts were futile when the judge dismissed the case.

He might have fared better had he not beaten up his brother, William thought. Seeing a remorseless stare in his eyes every time his assistant recounted the events that damaged his heart, he removed the employer hat.

"Sometimes, they're too young to appreciate a man with good qualities," he argued. "Most women in their twenties are still finding themselves. Having not yet experienced life, a lot of their actions are selfish and self-centered, for they're self-absorbed. It's an 'all about me' stage they grow out of with maturity." Hearing his own tone reminded him of the many times Steve Randall, his old Delaware buddy, had tried to fill his head with similar logic when it came to his dating beliefs. "Have you healed completely?"

"Yeah, man. Fuck these bitches."

"They're not bitches, Mark."

"You should be saying the same thing. Anna guarded her heart for a year before submitting. How do you know she's worth marrying? The times we watched pay-per-view fights at her house, she seemed rude to me, like she doesn't respect you."

Having crossed the line, William's response to Mark was stern.

"You should stick to resolving your own issues. I got this."

"I sure hope so."

One year, 365 days. And if you crave an additional day of sordid memories, try leaping to 366. Although time passes in a blur, negative events seem to unfold slowly, so that the stinging aftermath tortures you longer than the experience itself.

His two-year relationship with Anna Daniels was not unlike any other relationships, full of peaks and valleys. Recalling their introduction, *it was at a Wednesday night birthday party.* The Big Apple was injected with spring fever, and William decided he needed to be around his own people before making the long trek to a lonely Brooklyn apartment.

Venturing to Perk's, he remembered spotting her, above the clouds of congestion, sipping a glass of bubbly in solitude at the bar. A gray ice bucket on the counter nursed a bottle of Moet, the source of her revelry.

In actuality, she noticed him gazing at her. Blushing, as if caught with his hand in the cookie jar, familiar feelings invaded his bones.

After all these years, he was still bashful.

Damn, she's too attractive to be alone. What's up with that? I wonder who sent her the bottle.

His answer emerged through minutes of observation. She was with a girl-friend, simply chillin'. A few men attempted to get her attention, but she ignored their advances, saving her attention for the bald-headed chocolate brother who went beet red in the face.

As William waged an unnecessary war with his nerves, she simply awaited his arrival. And when he finally mustered the courage to stand behind her, she called him over.

"What kept you, sugar?"

"I don't know, actually."

There would be another bottle of champagne that evening, plus stimulating conversation. Anna Daniels was seven years older than he at forty-four, and a mother of two. After fourteen years as a driver for the New York City Transit Authority where her hours changed on a bi-yearly basis, she obtained a degree in business administration and transferred to the corporate offices as an assistant manager in the payroll division.

Her youthful facial features belied her years, and her smile possessed enough electricity to illuminate Harlem. Gorgeous hazel eyes, matching her fitted olive dress, glowed with attentiveness, and captured William's heart from hello. Her ample bottom, healthy thighs and gymnast calves turned the heads of many in the establishment, but all of her faced William with an interest that surpassed polite pleasantries.

The resident deejay must have felt their heat, for R. Kelly's "Home Alone" broke up their discussion.

"Let's dance," he said.

The chemistry issue now resolved, they shared another interest, a rhythmic one. Closing the place down with their brand of fancy footwork, they exchanged digits, and their first date would occur a week later.

Greeting her with two dozen red roses on a sunny Sunday afternoon—*thank goodness for those ten dollar boutiques on Eighth Avenue,* William recalled—he thought of the Long Island Railroad ride to Freeport where she resided, the movie *Collateral* they'd enjoyed, and the ensuing dinner at Cornbread and Caviar, a soul food establishment in nearby Baldwin.

"Why isn't there a special someone?" he asked while sampling roasted chicken.

"I'm hopeful," was Anna's response.

Before William's heart could feel like it belonged, her candor doused his fires.

"But I'm in a physical relationship. We meet for sex every now and then."

"Why isn't there a total commitment?"

"He's in a relationship."

A distinct, metallic sounding tone from William's gut spoke loudly.

Enjoy the wonderful time, and forget about her, it screamed to his brain, with the hopes that possible synchronicity might cause the male mass of skin, bones, water and weakness to heed the warning.

"I don't understand. Why are you wasting time?"

"It's easier to live life this way."

"I went that route, Anna. It didn't work for me. At the end of the day, I felt empty, like I was using someone or being used."

"I can separate the two."

"So you rather detach your emotions?"

"Men do it all the time."

"Anna, men who do that are running from pain, or commitment. That 'happily single' shit preached on the radio is a nice way for men to justify their reasons for not stepping up. It's like saying, 'I'm scared to give my heart completely, but I still want to have sex with you.'"

"So, what's wrong with that? Everyone has needs, and some of us can separate the two."

"Anna, the booty call unions end when someone develops feelings. That always happens when the sex is too good."

"So what does that make me, William, a whore?"

He paused. "No. You're a woman hiding behind her fears. Moving from one liaison to another just because you want to continue having sex doesn't make things right. Don't you feel empty afterwards?"

Seeing Anna shake her head "no" made that initial feeling punch him in the stomach.

Enjoy the wonderful time, and forget about her.

Despite the echo in his head, somehow, the thought was in conflict with William's compassion.

"Anna, why are you driving a used car when there are Ferraris in your driveway begging for a test run?"

Sighing, then pausing, her pouted lips frowned as her body language shifted from confidence to uncertainty. Eyes downcast, fretful fidgeting, both were telltale signs of a woman used to men in a bad way.

"Sometimes, I wonder if love is emotional propaganda to keep everyone from jumping from rooftops," she continued.

William couldn't fault her cynicism, not after hearing about her journey down a tortured path: a physically abusive husband and a dysfunctional twenty-something son; passionate pledges from men that produced disappointing results; failures which left her abstinent for years after the birth of another son; then the opposite extreme complete with momentary diversions, booty calls and quick fixes on company property. Finally the fear of following in her mother's footsteps as she grew older: antidepressants and alcohol to soothe her loneliness haunted Anna. Having been frequently burned, she was fiercely protective of her heart, and for survival's sake she compromised her need for companionship, opting for temporary maintenance whenever necessary.

"I'd rather not have the pressure of a relationship. They're too much of a struggle," she repeated.

"So I guess this date is a waste of time, huh?"

His bluntness brought a sad look, then, a resigned sigh from his date.

"William, I'm hopeful."

"Well, I'm not here for option status. Nor am I here submitting a 'fuck buddy' resume."

As if to prove his point, he dated her for six months without ever mentioning sex. Mindful of her feelings, he sent cards which expressed his feelings and initiated simple, 'how was your day' phone calls to let her know he cared. Exotic dinners were prepared for an additional plate at his apartment, and classic DVDs were viewed at her home between affectionate pecks. Gentle and romantic, he treated her to foot massages, sent love letters via e-mail, and on numerous evenings he cradled her in his arms as she pressed her head against his heart in a serene slumber.

Having dealt with aggressive men who oozed sexuality from their pores, Anna wasn't accustomed to the honeyed handling William provided.

"He's responsible and reliable," she told her mother, who lived in a Baltimore suburb, over the phone. "Very busy socially, yet always making time for love. Everybody loves him."

"He might be different," the matriarch responded, "but be careful."

Innately understanding her issues and hesitance because of his own days of mistreatment, William was patient, hoping she would view him as a positive exception as opposed to a negative rule with regards to men.

Whenever the sex topic surfaced, he uttered three words, "Look, I'm good."

"I can't wait to find out," she responded after being greeted with lilies the day the negative results of their HIV examinations came back.

Anticipating the moment where their bodies would become one, a tingle at his groin served as a reminder that he wanted her.

Moments before consummation were as heated as the act itself. Make-out sessions at her home progressed gradually, from the couch, to her kitchen, then to her bedroom after she sent the kids away to Suffolk County for a weekend at her sister's lavish Brentwood home. Engaging in a deep lip lock, then sucking on pointed nipples like a newborn infant craving formula, William's smile shined through the darkness.

"Sex is supposed to be intense," she argued.

Not when you know a woman is in over her head.

When that moment arrived, all Anna could say was, "Oh my god." William matched her energy with his own ravenous recklessness. Melting her lips with tender kisses, then exploring her fleshly folds creatively each night they shared the same bed, kitchen counter, or other places, the pulse of his tongue had her climbing walls. Nibbling on thick vaginal walls, he feasted on her clitoris like it was his favorite entrée, delightfully dancing within her until a multitude of magnificent explosions escaped her.

Unaccustomed to a man enjoying her so much, *Anna's orgasms were so strong*, he remembered. Her free-flowing eruptions had frightened many a partner, so she found it shocking when she actually heard him gulping.

"Mmm, tasty," he revealed.

When penetration was requested, William parted her skin with an erection wanting unconditional love by day, and unadulterated lust by night. Searching her pupils as he eased in his tip, then full shaft in her pleasure place, his strong steady strokes were measured, meaningful and majestic. In and out, up and down, in slow circles and calypso-like swerves, he demanded tremors every time, and received never-ending moans on call. Playing her sex spot as if born to, he never stopped moving inside her goodness until he saw the glassy-eyed stare of euphoria.

The recipient of love in every conceivable way, for the first time in her life Anna was introduced to a man sensitive and secure, attentive and affectionate to her every need. Still, she was mired in deliberation, wondering if he was too good to be true.

William's frustration with her fears of flying increased daily. Having exorcised his own demons years ago, he wanted her with him in that special place.

The water's warm, Baby. Please join me in paradise.

His leniency with her ceased completely when she received a phone call from a former suitor. Joe, a former fling she described as well-endowed, called while they were making love one Friday evening, wanting her company on an Atlantic City gambling run. Upon hearing the bass voice invade their moment, William's tenderness turned into hours of territorial barbarianism.

"You were in rare form last night, a little rougher than normal," she announced on a Manhattan boat cruise the next evening.

"You should turn your answering machine down."

A pregnant pause followed.

"I still get offers, William, but I was with you."

"Have you made him aware of the man you're dating?"

Her failure to respond revealed that she was still protecting her heart.

By the time she deemed herself ready, singing Brian McKnight songs on their anniversary en route to work, William was ready to move on. A year had passed and while leaving the door ajar for her declaration, he'd begun fielding overtures from potentials.

Incensed, Anna confronted him.

"I'm a person that thinks love through," she announced through tears. "I've endured so much."

"Sometimes, you have to take a chance, Anna. Love isn't logical. It's not something you think about. Either you feel it or you don't," he countered. "Do you feel me?"

Peering deep into his loving brown eyes, she nodded.

After this meeting of the minds, he assumed all commitment issues were resolved, so for the next year he focused on taking the union to the next level. Although his occupational promotion caused him to be away for extended periods, he made sure she was always cognizant of his affections. Bubble baths, and helping her teenage son with his schoolwork replaced the novelty infatuation, and Sunday park strolls after church hinted toward permanence.

Though a sincere effort was made on her end, every now and then disenchantment still reared its ugly head.

"Sometimes, being with you is like being alone," she said.

"Honey, you have to sacrifice today for tomorrow," William uttered repeatedly.

Unbeknownst to him, the future he spoke of did not include him.

❧❧

He shopped out of state for an extravagant, yet affordable two-carat engagement ring, and planned a low-key presentation upon his return from the Philadelphia office. Having a key to her beautiful, modern deco home, the fateful Thursday night was the only night he'd ever shown up unannounced. Hearing the loud lyrics of Marvin Gaye's "After the Dance" as he pushed down the metal door handle had him thinking she was longing for him. Surprisingly, the house alarm went silent. Noting the dim living room lights and not hearing the hum of an Xbox upstairs, William smiled.

She knew I was coming directly to her tonight, so she sent her son away. Perfect.

Pulling the velvet blue jewelry box from his suit pocket, excitement raced through him as he anticipated the moment where dreams come true for any man.

No more bullshit, just the beginning of forever.

William McCall was ready for marriage again.

The vows would not start on the wedding day; but on bended knee this quiet summer evening. Promising to love her faithfully, he would dry her eyes and permanently erase all of the sorrow she experienced when unsure of a man's love, and cling to her with all his might through seasons of pleasure and pain.

Tonight is the beginning of the rest of our lives.

Passing the living room, the music drowned his footsteps. Assuming she was in the kitchen he veered right, saw an empty wine glass and half of a steak on her electric stove. His palms sweaty with anticipation, anxiousness caused beads of perspiration to escape pores on his bald head.

Yet he never felt more confident.

It's not like I'm asking her to marry me in public.

Turning back, William started down the corridor leading to the bedroom. His loving smile disappeared quickly as he approached the doorway.

Closing his lids tight, then lifting them, his eyes threatened to come out of their sockets. His head throbbing with hurt, his nostrils twitched and his feet froze in place. Paralyzed and demoralized at once, the sight ripped the affection from his heart.

Jimmy Swaggart had had a better time when he watched.

Seeing Anna with another man was like a dagger piercing his soul. An excruciating feeling clenched his jaws as the sharp tip entered his chest.

His mind abuzz in bewilderment, panic-stricken thoughts entered his brain swiftly; stupid, desperate thoughts.

We can work through this. We'll get past this.

The faint ember of hope was extinguished with the next image. More hurt filled him as the couple, so engrossed in mutual pleasure they failed to see their observer, changed positions. Her lover's eyes were screwed shut as he went personal. Kissing her passionately, he assisted her to his groin and encouraged her to perform fellatio.

His woman obliged hungrily.

As she took his erection in her mouth, the man's facial features mixed pleasure and pain as he strained to fight his release.

The terror that punctured William's chest cavity produced confusion. His throat burning, the muscle in him that loved so deeply stiffened and grew cold. Rigor mortis set in, causing the death of his benevolence and compassion.

If he were friends with Smith & Wesson, there would have been three explosions.

Her head.

Her lover's.

And, lastly, his own.

Three lifeless bodies for the local news.

Resisting a natural ballistic urge, William refused to allow the rage within to take over, even as the visual worsened. Only after watching Anna down his milky solution, then collapse upon him in breathless bliss, did he speak.

"Are you two done?"

Before she could shower him with awkward words and feebly defend the indefensible, he was out the door, on his way to his Brooklyn apartment.

Home was a necessary refuge till dawn, when unknowingly, the curtain rose for Act Two.

Arriving to work an hour early, he made a beeline to the Human Resource department to talk about job-related matters and was met with a response from the office manager.

"They've been expecting you in the conference room," she announced.

What's this all about?

The bad dream wasn't over.

Seeing the partner from Dallas wearing a look of vindication on his face upon entry, he immediately sensed something was amiss.

Seating himself at the head of a long, oval table, William bravely smiled.

"I didn't know we were having a meeting."

"I had the other partners fly in last night," Mr. Gallagher announced.

"I just got here," the elderly twang added, knowing damn well he was lying.

The partners from Seattle, Philadelphia, Chicago, and Los Angeles remained eerily silent as Gallagher opened a manila folder.

"Mr. McCall…"

I was William during a phone conference yesterday.

"Is this your signature on these vouchers?"

Sliding the folder along the brown table, William reviewed the documents. The looping, straight cursive looked a lot like his inscription.

"It resembles my penmanship, but I don't ever recall signing these requests." There were fifty in total over a period of four months, the net sum adding up to just over thirty-thousand dollars.

"Do you know what the money was used for?" Gallagher asked.

William shook his head, indicating he did not.

"But you signed these requests," the Dallas partner added. "Where are the receipts?"

"Gentlemen, there seems to be a misunderstanding here. I've never seen these documents before today. I never signed them."

"But it's your handwriting," the partner from Seattle declared.

The brother from Chicago cast his eyes downward at the brown table, never making eye contact.

"I can get to the bottom of this," William coolly assured. "I'm sure this is a mistake."

"That won't be necessary," Gallagher said. Pausing, there was a callous stare. "You are terminated from your position as managing clerk at Goetz, Gallagher and Green, with no severance pay. If you attempt to file for unemployment benefits, we will have you arrested on embezzlement charges and prosecuted to the full extent of the law." Measuring his anger, he continued. "That you conducted yourself in an unethical fashion after everything we entrusted in you shows a lack of appreciation of your progression. Consider yourself lucky that you're not in jail."

Lucky? Lucky? After everything you've done for me? Are you kidding me? I earned every promotion I received through hard work and long hours, by traveling all over the country for you, teaching your respective staffs how to utilize their legal software. And this is my thanks? This is bullshit!

When declaring his innocence verbally, he was far more diplomatic.

"Gentlemen, I didn't do this. Have you looked into this further?"

"We exhausted every angle, Mr. McCall. And your fingerprints fit the crime," the old Texan announced. Unable to conceal his frustration, "For crying out loud," he taunted. "Stop telling falsehoods and admit the truth."

William's agitation escalated.

"The truth is I had nothing to do with this! Where's Markham Chandler?" he inquired.

"That's not a concern of yours anymore," Gallagher retorted. On cue, two burly white men draped in undersized blue blazers entered the room. "Security will escort you out."

Returning to his office to retrieve his belongings, to his amazement, the possessions were all packed up and ready to go.

Even the Enron people had thirty minutes to leave.

Like many who'd experienced loss by way of Katrina, the winds of change dramatically altered the life of William McCall. All his dreams of contentment crashed and burned, causing restless nights of anxiety. His life in the legal profession was over, just like that. Blacklisted wherever he turned, many New York City employment agencies wanted no dealings with a bad seed, so they stopped submitting his resume to other law firms. One particular instance, he saw a recruiter toss his credentials into a trashcan.

Trembling badly when recalling the fact that his 401K earnings were spent on the engagement ring and outstanding bills, he found false comfort in marijuana, puffing and hoping for the expiration of brain cells that triggered sweat-filled depression, and sleepless, sheet-drenching nights of tears.

Five months later, his savings were depleted as well. Falling behind in his bills, a humiliating progression began. The cable went off, then Con Edison. Showering in cold water and shivering through the winter while burning candles for light and heat, he grew desperate. Applying for jobs everywhere, he was overqualified for places like Staples and Subway, for they feared his departure upon immediate hiring. Taking and acing the civil service tests were no problem, but the waiting lists for occupation at the post office, transit or sanitation were over two years long.

He fell several months behind in rent, and was served with eviction notices and court appearance papers at his Brooklyn apartment. Somehow, he lost all petitions for extensions.

The judge had given him thirty days to move.

Desperate for a place to live, he turned to family. His father, Wilford, had recently returned from Norfolk, Virginia, and found love with Tonya, a woman twenty-five years his junior. Together, they lived in a Bedford-Stuyvesant brownstone with her three kids. *No room there.* Edith Hall, his eighty-one-year-old grandmother, sent him money whenever she could, but she had adopted two kids who now occupied the bedroom in her Bushwick home that was once his. *Strike two.* His mother, Eunice, had relinquished the West Brighton apartment where she'd raised her six children and moved into a cramped one-bedroom in the Todt Hill Section of Staten Island. *I can't go there.* His brothers were either out of state, incarcerated, or had large families of their own to take care of.

William had no place to go.

Placing his property in storage and living on food stamps, he became an inner-city nomad, spending time sleeping on the subways and "bathing" in terminal or restaurant bathrooms. Three pairs of black slacks, each worn in the seat, and a couple of dress shirts were the clothing for interviews, and dingy blue Levi's and a maroon polo shirt were for Saturdays and Sundays.

Finally, near the end of his rope after two months and with nowhere else to turn, he moved into a Brooklyn homeless shelter until he could find any type of employment that would allow him to put enough money aside to get his own place again.

Fighting to maintain his dignity, the mere fact that he hadn't put a bullet in his temple was no small feat. When the manager of a Times Square McDonald's asked him when he could start, it was restraint from an unseen force that prevented him from grabbing the man in a bear hug and thanking him for saving his life. His job would entail mopping floors and removing garbage, but William was simply grateful for the opportunity.

Donning the traditional uniform complete with a black, golden-arched embroidered cap for the first time, the achievement, albeit small, was significant in its message; he had weathered the storm. It was a long way from black pinstriped suits and interacting with legal minds all over the country, but the uphill climb would start here.

The depths of endurance exacted a heavy toll on his spirit but it paled in comparison to the agony gripping his heart. In an effort to harness the migraine that surfaced whenever the vision of Anna in heat with another was relived, William closed a fist at his side.

It's amazing how a single moment can annihilate one's faith in love, he reflected somberly.

At that point, as he rode the train en route to work, he overheard a trio of well-dressed black women questioning the substance of their male counterparts and their whereabouts.

"Girl, I'm tired of waiting for lazy-ass brothers to get their acts together. If I can succeed in this world, get my own home and car and have a successful career, then so can they. I'm sick of their excuses."

"Where are the real brothers who give up their seats on trains?" one of them chimed in, looking left, directly at William. Her gaze meeting the eyes of an emotionally devastated man struggling to put it all back together, this woman, dressed in a maroon Donna Karan suit, added more attitude to the next question posed. "What are you looking at?"

Trying to ignore a confrontation, William averted his attention.

"Don't look at Ronald McDonald. He can't afford a real woman," another one added.

"Hold the lettuce, hold the pickle, so that you could save a nickel," she taunted, bringing howls from those nearby.

Pain seeping from his heart, William's experiences with women passed quickly before his eyes. All those rejections in youth because he wasn't cool; the days he'd been ridiculed because he wasn't getting any; the time he escaped the clutches of teenage peers and ran away when they were trying to get him laid on a project rooftop; the gay accusations because of his sensitivity; loving the wrong girl in his twenties and the emotional repercussions that left him mortified; the infidelities that destroyed a solid marriage; the conquering of all insecurities and fears through self-introspection; and lastly, the horrible chain of events that returned him to this familiar place.

Boo-yah! All of these moments flashed by quicker than an ESPN sports highlight. Rising, something in him snapped as he approached his tormentors.

"Let me see your left hands, NOW!" he demanded.

Three ringless digits shot out immediately.

"Now, you see," he stated condescendingly, "it's selfish, sophisticatedly dumb women like you three who don't appreciate decent, hard-working brothers. Instead of looking for solutions that might help you maintain a decent relationship with a man, you moan about the problems with having one. It's women like you who are looking for men who don't exist. It's bitches like you three..."

Pausing, he collected himself and reined his anger in, but not before removing three quarters from his pants pocket. Hurling them in their faces, he could care less if he bloodied them. "Look, do us all a favor. Make up your minds, decide what it is you want from a man, and buy a damn clue!"

The train doors opened and William got off at the Rockefeller Center station. Hearing applause from people in the subway car who were moved by his rant, there was no consolation in this display of solidarity; he felt worse than he had prior to unleashing his wrath. Reentering a recognizable state of gloom, gone again was the energy of positive passion that had taken six years—a lifetime in the world of love—to recover. Dark clouds of ambivalence and apathy toward women; bitter, cynical feelings he had thought were buried forever, had resurfaced with a vengeance. Disheartened, even nauseated by the thought of sharing and caring, he wouldn't revert to days past where he released his pain by way of emotional mistreatment.

Hurt people, hurt people, he thought. At forty, he was still strikingly handsome. The bald head remained, however, his smile—once having possessed so much wattage when eager to please—had received a death sentence, destined to shine never more. His brown eyes, formerly soft, warm and inviting were indifferent, moody and suspicious. The taut six-pack owned a half decade earlier had been sacrificed for long hours in the office, then eventually, the will to carry on. Only his hyper-metabolism and the stress of the past year had kept him from pinching more than an inch. Tired legs supported the extra ten pounds of age, but his chest was still moderately built, a by-product of a daily regimen of push-ups. His full lips were not ruined by his weed binge, but a smooth, chocolate countenance was lined with cynicism. His body definitely exhibited telltale signs of the struggle, but his heart had been destroyed.

Feeling like Willie Mays must have in 1973, stumbling under routine fly balls in Oakland, or an aging, battered Ali in Las Vegas, or Michael Jordan struggling with the Washington Wizards, William realized that he'd lasted too long in the game of love and was tired of making a fool of himself. If he needed a further reminder not to reenter the *meat market*, all he need do was would pull out the engagement ring.

I got ninety-nine problems, but a bitch ain't one. Anymore.

TWO

The ritual was like clockwork: wee-hour awakenings in her flat in Jersey City Heights, the dull pains in her back and stomach, a trip to the bathroom for Tylenol or Advil to cure her ills, and the clutching of a pillow on her olive-colored living room sofa while watching *Woman of The Year*, one of her favorite black and white movies, until the pain subsided and weariness wiped her out once more.

Alternately restless and fatigued, her beautiful, blemish-free countenance, filled with a lively copper-brown shade throughout the day, became ashen and colorless. The sharp twinge made her whole body hurt for an instant. Then, as rapidly as the sensation arrived, it departed.

It's bad nerves, she concluded. There would be no more doctors, no more sonograms or clinical appointments producing bad results; the surgical incision at her abdomen and the clammy sweat a hormonal furnace produced through the years aided her memory. Adopting the mentality of a soldier, Linda Woodson would grit her teeth and bear the uneasiness.

Every now and then she reached out to her sorority sister and closest friend, Josephine Smith.

Tonight was one of those nights.

"You're just lonely, Lucky," she assured her. "Why don't you call Emerson? You know you miss him."

"Josie, you need to wake up your husband and give him some."

"Please girl, we already handled our business. Carl's down for the count. I had him whimpering like a puppy."

"What else is new?"

"I should have asked for a fur coat while I was laying it on him. He would have been like, 'Yeah, Baby, whatever you want, it's yours.'"

"I know, right?"

They giggled.

"Seriously, Lucky, you should call him. He'll hold you."

"It's been over between us for a few months now. And you know I don't go backwards."

"Are you telling me that you feel nothing for the man you saw as your husband three months ago?"

"Once upon a time."

"Lucky, you don't expect me to believe that, do you?"

Grimacing, "Ouch," Linda groaned as another rush of agony moved through her.

"Lucky, you want me to get dressed and come over?"

"No. I'll be okay."

"You need to call that man."

"At two in the morning?"

"You know he'll come over. He still loves you."

"Yeah, I guess you're right. Maybe I'll do that."

After hanging up, Linda held the soft head support tighter while curling up in a fetal position. Unable to live the lie, the mere thought of it, coupled with Josie's humor or a Sunday stroll to nearby Hoboken come daybreak, always helped her through.

This early Sunday morning, however, seemed more difficult than most as the agonizing sensation lingered longer than normal. The steady sway of her five-seven, size-twelve frame providing little comfort, lonely tears cradled her eyes as she rocked and reminisced.

She'd thought Emerson Perkins was the one; her perfect soul mate in every way. He was tall—six-four to be precise—dark and distinguished. His brown skin matched her chocolate hue; a set of full, sensational lips fit the oval shape of his head, gorgeous round eyes and the smooth bald shine of his dome. Intelligent and gifted, Swahili was only one of the seven languages this wine connoisseur spoke. At fifty, his resume of accomplishments first as a criminal prosecutor, then an executive investigator, was full, and his life seemed complete with her by his side.

And at forty-seven years of age, many of them spent in the wilderness of dating games, Linda Woodson thought she had weeded through the midlife dating madness and found him.

That is, until he dropped Hiroshima on her spirit.

"Lucky, I want to start seeing other people," he announced over a spring Sunday brunch at Londel's in Harlem.

Stunned, Linda saw the green dumpster containing her devotion being emptied. They'd been together for three years. Running a trembling hand through a bushel of salt-and-peppered culture locs, a tender glow faded from her eyes. Crushed and compacted, her soul was driven to and discarded in the waste area where jumbled, confused and broken hearts go. Wanting to yell, scream, to take him to task for the homicide of her emotions, the numbness of the stinger had her mute.

Trying to accept this new abandonment would be difficult.

"Why?"

"I met someone."

Disillusioned and dejected, she winced as her brain registered the image, then swelled with another heartbreak headache. Like cutlery, her instincts sharpened when recognizing a deeper, unspoken truth. Linda immediately realized he'd omitted the real reason for his sudden change of heart. Only three months removed from looking at Poughkeepsie homes together, her eyes watered at his change of heart.

"How long have you been seeing her, Emerson?"

Arms folded together, the concert of veins in his neck tightened, as if he was on the verge of exploding. Unable to look at her, his gaze was distant.

"About six months."

"But we were looking at homes upstate!"

Linda felt the volcano of emotions churning. Threatening to bubble over in the form of lava-laced obscenities, graphic things that are said when the shock of betrayal sets in, she gripped the back of her seat to steady her nerves.

Relax, Lucky. You have to calm down, or the next few minutes won't be pretty.

Regrouping quickly, one of the questions swirling around in her mind escaped her lips.

"You were intimate with this woman, no?"

An awkwardness that screamed "no way out" filled the area as Emerson exhaled deeply.

"Last night was the first time."

"Is she fertile, Emerson?"

His pause increased the tone of her persistence.

"Is she fertile?"

He never answered. Reaching across the table, his large caramel mitts offered feeble consolation.

Linda pulled away.

Staring at the restaurant's hardwood floor, she willed away the nausea choking her insides, then returned her face to his.

A brave smile stopped her disappointment from running wild.

"I understand." She sighed.

Those two words were air escaping her lungs; they were used so much. To Emerson, they were the language of positive encouragement to pursue a dream. However to Linda Woodson, they provided a cloak of strength, a combative shield to the wretchedness that accompanied a familiar feeling.

It had happened again.

My Arms Are Cold and Empty

My arms are cold and empty
My ears will hear no cries
No baby smiles or pleasant coos
For a dream of motherhood dies

My womanliness is a contradiction
A purpose met a cruel end
No swollen womb, nor fulsome glow
No life beckons from within

No innocent laughter will touch my ears
No kisses will I taste
No fluttering heartbeat or morning's unease
Child-bearing hips gone to waste

My arms are cold and empty
My ears will hear no cries
No baby smiles or pleasant coos
For a dream of motherhood dies

No fingers reaching for earrings
No gentle fist like clasps
No suction on nipples by hungry lips
No tumbling body grasps

No pre-school nerves or adolescent angst
Nor prom or graduation's pride
No Mother's Day Cards or Chocolate hearts
All dreams and desires have been denied

Mother, Mommy, Mama, Ma
Are words I'll never hear,
No tear-stains to witness 'I do' from a son
Or a daughter that's always near

My arms are cold and empty
My ears will hear no cries
No baby smiles or pleasant coos
For a dream of motherhood dies.

Twenty-five years marked a silver anniversary to those in heavenly bliss, but was a quarter century-long nightmare to others warring with an agonizing truth.

Such was the case with Linda Woodson.

The horror show started at twenty-two years of age, at the onset of senior year at SUNY New Paltz. A moment of lust at her off-campus apartment with Larry Reynolds, her college boyfriend, was interrupted by the pain above her pleasure zone.

"Baby, you're hurting me," she said.

"I'm close, Baby. I wanna cum."

"It hurts, Larry. Please stop."

Coitus was interrupted, much to his annoyance.

"Baby, I'm sorry."

Larry caught his breath, but not his displeasure.

"Yeah, right."

"I'm sorry that you didn't finish."

"The hell you are," he responded.

Reaching for his clothes, Larry was bathed in their passion, yet unfulfilled.

"Are you screwing someone else?"

"Of course not, Baby. What would make you think something like that?"

Pausing, his tone was an aggressive one. "Then why do I hurt you all of a sudden?"

"A girl can only take so much loving." Linda chuckled as she rubbed his chest. "C'mon, Baby. Come back to bed. I want to hold you."

"Tasha, you never complained about me before recently."

Linda's brown eyes widened. "Tasha?"

Rubbing a hand through his curly hair, Larry winced.

"Tasha?"

Still, there was no response.

"You're still seeing her, aren't you?" The inquisition continued. "Are you still fucking this woman after I gave you a second chance?"

His silence gave her the answer she could barely take.

Finally, he spoke. "You're always in class."

"That's my crime, being ambitious?" Staring into his eyes, she saw more. "You're not telling me everything, are you? Are you?"

He said nothing; his silence revealing a truth that she didn't want to acknowledge.

"Is there anything else, Larry?"

"Shit, Linda, I wasn't happy with our sex life. You've been complaining all the time that it doesn't feel right, that your pussy hurts all the time."

"It's not my pussy that hurts, you asshole! It's my stomach!"

Finally relenting to angry tears, the rejection that overwhelmed Linda muffled his screaming and pleading.

The college puppy-love was over.

The memory of it all wouldn't be as easy to ignore, for the discomfort below lingered.

He was big, she thought initially and dismissed it as the pleasure/pain sensation going hand-in-hand with good loving.

That notion disappeared when she gained weight, as well as early morning vomiting.

Don't tell me I'm pregnant.

Her schoolwork suffered because of the anxiety, as did her joining the Delta Sigma Theta sorority. Having failed in a previous attempt at crossing the line, she began her senior year knowing this might very well be her last chance to follow in her mother's footsteps and pledge undergrad. Her focus unwavering despite her maladies, all anatomical problems would be addressed once accepted into "Crimson and Cream."

She'd barely made it over. Limping throughout the initiations on thick, heavy legs, the morning of her special service, she'd nearly passed out. Immediately, she'd called her mother, Mamie, a librarian by profession in Greenville, South Carolina.

"What's happening to me?" she asked.

"You might be pregnant, honey. Did you use protection with him?"

"His condom broke once."

"He didn't stop?"

"Who does, Mama?"

"Will you tell him if you are pregnant? Are you gonna keep it?"

Silence.

"Linda, you have some tough decisions to make. Are you ready to be a mother? Or do you want to finish school?"

"I think I can do both. I don't need that asshole to…"

"Remember who you're talking to, Linda."

"I'm sorry, but he made me so mad."

"Linda, do you remember the five 'R's? You're supposed to relax, recover…"

"Reflect, resolve, then, resume." Linda paused. "You told me this so much that I'm like Pavlov's Dog."

"That means I've done my job, Baby."

They chuckled.

"Mama, my body still doesn't feel right. I've been having really bad stomach cramps."

"It's probably the stress of unplanned parenthood."

"I think there's something else going on."

"Then go to the doctor and get it checked out, Lucky. I'm sure it's nothing."

Although her maternal, Southern-rooted tone was soothing, Mamie Woodson prayed that her own misery wasn't inherent; a horrible curse passed on.

She called her only child Lucky, for Linda was a walking miracle. Years ago, while eight weeks' pregnant, she too experienced pains in her lower region. A trip to the gynecologist brought earth-shattering news. What she thought was all baby was in fact an abnormal growth.

"You cannot carry this child full-term. It will not survive. You will not survive," the doctors said during a sonogram.

"I am having my child," Mamie said calmly.

Her determination was forged by tragic circumstances. Just a month earlier, her husband of two years, Julian, an undercover cop, was murdered in a drug deal gone haywire. The tragedy occurred the very day her pregnancy was confirmed. Nearing their Spartanburg home with chardonnay in her blue Buick LeSabre that fateful winter night, she decided, would be the last night she would have her favorite wine.

Gleefully approaching the entrance of her Simpson Street dwelling, she saw two black suited officers at her doorstep, and the flashing red lights of a familiar salt-and-pepper-colored vehicle in the driveway.

What are the county police doing here?

Their facades were expressionless as they approached her and the words they uttered sent her world spinning as his legacy moved within her. Screaming loudly, she collapsed in their arms. Sweat from cocoa-complexioned temples and mortified drops of pain met at her chin.

A widow and single mother, simultaneously.

The cruel irony devastating, the potential to make a life was realized as the breath of a man who found joy in loving her was taken away.

"I am having my baby, even if it kills me," she repeated to the doctors.

Her dreams of motherhood were recognized, barely. Suffering through massive bleeding during childbirth and two strokes from fluid loss, she lay in a coma, playing a dangerous game of blackjack with God. After three weeks of touch and go, the second card was turned by the faint sound of a daughter's cry.

Twenty-one.

"Where is she?" she whispered as her eyes opened. "Where's my baby?"

A few minutes later, Linda was brought to her. Her full, precious smile resembled Julian's.

The tears flowed as she cuddled her; this time, beads of joy. Lucky Linda revived her life with a reason to recover, then, resume.

Years later, when speaking with her lifeline, Mamie Woodson prayed daily, hoping with all she could muster that her painful history would pass her daughter over.

❧❧

Originally deciding against childbearing after her mother revealed her trial by fire, having worked each summer as a supervisor in a local youth program reversed Linda's thinking. Establishing a connection with the teenagers during retreats, when lecturing about abstinence, drug and alcohol abuse as well as life's everyday struggles, the warm union she shared with mother stood on her left shoulder, beaming proudly at her initiative.

Wanting that same connection, Linda would keep her unborn while maintaining the course. Less than seven months from completion of the requirements for her bachelor's degree in Political Science, she was determined to graduate and move to the Big Apple, where the LSAT exam, then law school awaited her.

First things first, however: would she be going alone or with a family?

Making a trip to the gynecologist, Doctor Davis Malloy confirmed her expectancy and initially assumed the persistent twinge she was experiencing was overcompensation of her lower back muscles, a product of her sudden weight increase. But to be safe, he did a vaginal exam and sonogram.

"Everything will be fine," the doctor assured.

Easing her tension with his good-natured charm, Davis Malloy was more than the overseer of her body. Throughout her college years, he'd served as a sounding board of wisdom, having guided her through trying times with his humor, insight, encouragement and, on occasion, money when necessary.

"I'll pay you back," she always offered.

"If you get your degree and your juris doctorate, the debt will be satisfied," he always responded.

Perhaps his benevolence was due to the fact that he was a widower at forty, having lost his wife, Emma, to cervical cancer. Having no kids with her, her death served as motivation for him to further his knowledge of the female anatomy. Completing medical school and with practitioner's license in tow, he became a model of excellence to his patients. Believing that a transferral of energy and love improves the quality of health and life, many of his peers viewed him as a non-conformist.

Many of the women he treated, however, thought of him as a father figure, especially when dealing with the complexities and delicacies of their life-producing organs.

"If properly nurtured, they are the ultimate source of strength and power," he always said. "However, if neglected or mismanaged, they retaliate by becoming weak with diseases. And we don't want that."

Expressing these words with wisdom and warning, Dr. Malloy was prophetic in most cases. He could tell, just by the examination, whether a woman treasured her body as if it were a temple or, in the alternative, had little regard for her health. Having stressed this to Linda, she followed his advice in all instances.

That's why upon receiving the undivided attention of a technician, he grew silent during the sonogram.

"Linda, you need to take a look at this," he quietly said.

Turning the monitor toward the examination table so she could see it, he pointed to a large, unrecognizable mass above the uterus.

"Am I having twins, Doctor?"

Directing her attention to the lower left corner of the screen, Dr. Malloy showed her the location of her nine-week-old child, then redirected her attention to the center.

Naïve and confused all at once, Linda was perplexed. "If that's not my baby, then what the hell is it?"

"What we're looking at is a very large tumor," the doctor answered soberly while rubbing his speckled goatee.

Linda wanted to flee the room, as well as the questions hemorrhaging her psyche, questions that couldn't be answered yet. The pit of her stomach churning, she gave the man she entrusted the well-being of her temple a menacing stare.

Faultless, forgiving of this natural reaction, yet feeling the tension, the doctor excused himself to consult another doctor, leaving Linda and her jumbled emotions with the technician.

"What does the tumor mean? What does it mean?"

By now the look on the assistant's face said the impending news was bad. "Miss Woodson, do you have any children?" she asked.

"This is my first."

The technician sighed.

"Miss Woods…"

"You can call me Linda."

"Do you wish to have any?"

Why is she asking the obvious? "I want to have this baby I'm carrying."

Again, the technician inhaled deeply.

"Okay. Linda, from the appearance on the screen, the tumor will cause problems. You might not…" Gathering herself, she sighed again. "The doctor will tell you more when he returns."

On cue, Dr. Malloy returned, this time with another gynecologist, Dr. Wilton, for an on-the-spot consultation and second opinion. Both began asking about her medical history.

"Did your mother experience problems giving birth to you?" Dr. Wilton asked.

Making no effort to hide her tears, Linda nodded yes, then doubled over, sobbing.

"Everything will be fine, Linda," Davis comforted. "Everything will be fine." The unenviable part of his job was now beginning. Whenever he delivered bad news concerning the creation of woman, he thought of the fateful day, years ago, when Emma turned his own life upside-down.

Sympathetic yet unsparing, Davis became Dr. Malloy once more.

"Linda, you will not be able to carry this baby to full-term. Any attempt to do so would jeopardize your health." Seeing the quizzical look through her tears, he continued. "You would not live through the pregnancy and your unborn child would not survive if you didn't survive."

More silence.

"I would…I would…die?"

Both practitioners nodded slowly.

Disoriented, opaqueness filled her soft eyes. Weeble-wobbling in vertigo, her thoughts barely filtered the doctor's observation.

"The tumor inside of you is feeding off the increased estrogen your body is producing, and growing rapidly. You need to have an abortion as soon as possible."

Despite the fact that her choice for life was removed, she waited an additional two weeks before the inevitable course of action. Shell-shocked, she first informed Larry, hoping he would help pay for the operation.

His words were typical in their insensitivity. "Well…whose is it?"

Why is this fool questioning my morals?

Because of his infidelity, their relationship had deteriorated to the point where they couldn't even be friends. That he added to her despondency made her all the more livid.

"Larry, go fuck yourself! Unlike you, I don't sleep around," she snapped.

"Linda, wait… Maybe we can fix this. Maybe we can fix everything."

"The only way the problem can be solved is by abortion, Larry. The longer I carry this baby, the more my health is threatened."

Reading the defiance in his eyes, for some strange reason, her words failed to register.

"Can you wait a couple of months to see how things go?"

"Are you even listening to me? I can die if I don't act now."

"Well, I don't believe in abortion, and I think you, and your doctor, are full of shit!" With that, he stormed off, never realizing the depths of his desertion! Further pouring salt in her open wound, he called her the next day, reiterating his unsupportive stance.

"Goodbye, Larry," was her only response.

Hanging up, she immediately dialed her only source of rescue.

"He didn't help you, Lucky?"

"No, Mama," Linda responded. Sobbing once more, the journey of her sadness came from her toes, traveling through her medium-built frame, liberating itself from her instability through quivering lips.

"Baby, don't cry. Don't cry, Baby."

"Mama, are all men like this?"

"No, Lucky. During our short time together, your father was the sweetest, kindest, most caring man I've ever known. Julian never left me wanting in any way." She paused. "Linda, other than your textbooks, do you read novels?"

"Yes, ma'am."

"Some of them are good, right?"

"Yes."

"And others are awful, am I correct?"

"Yes."

"Men are the same way, honey. In your lifetime, you're going to run across a bunch of lousy books that leave you feeling like you wasted your time. Those men are misguided, intimidated by your strength. But for every Larry, there is a classic read, a decent man that deserves all the love you can muster. Some may be well-to-do, and exude confidence in whatever they do. Not a lot of work is necessary for this type of man.

"Other diamonds, however, may be in need of polish. To see the full luster of their power, you will need to be patient, and nurture them until they find their way. What I'm saying, Lucky, is not to allow this one experience to jade you, Baby. Love all men the same and if they don't appreciate you, then be on your way and harbor no resentment. The ones who are receptive to your positive spirit, you work with. The others will put those '5 'R's' to the test."

Sensible and caring, the right words always came to Mother Woodson when it came to Lucky Linda. It would take all the love in her reservoir to help her daughter survive a reality whose mere mention conjures the rawest of emotions.

❦❦

Conducting another sonogram on Linda, Dr. Malloy was stunned by his revelation. Spreading massively, the tumors had swelled in number and size, growing outside and within the muscles and tissues of her uterine walls. Two of them obstructed the baby, which would make the operation more difficult than a simple abortion procedure.

"Is everything okay?" Linda asked.

The look on Davis' face masked his concern. In all his years of practice, he had only seen this voraciousness once before. Praying silently as he processed her question, a former patient, Karen Moss, came to mind. Her tumor growth had been so abnormal that further examinations were expedited.

The results had been devastating to her.

Remembering her face as he delivered the prognosis, he would never forget her wail of despair, nor the enduring bitterness from the experience. Making a pact within the confines of his practice, he would exhaust every resource when dealing with one of his favorite patients.

"I have to run more tests."

The process of ending the life of a child shattered Linda, causing her to bawl after the doctor told her he would have to put her under anesthesia to remove most of the tumors as well as the fetus, then keep her overnight for observation.

Before going under, she instructed the doctor to call a new friend.

"How do you feel?" Josephine Smith asked while driving her home the next morning.

Still groggy and weary, her meek response was filled with pain. "Weird. A life was scraped out of me."

"You'll be okay. Just make sure you rest."

"He put me on the pill, with the hopes that it might reduce the remaining tumors."

"I hope they work."

They didn't. Over the next three months, her flow became heavier and heavier, causing Linda to use two tampons and a pad simultaneously. Then, on a couple of occasions, she experienced double periods, causing absenteeism from classes and incapacitation.

Not only worried about her timely graduation and public embarrassment by way of accident, Linda had more grave concerns. Fearing she was at risk for toxic shock syndrome, she continued to battle dizziness and nausea, as well as pelvic inflammation and bladder problems.

She was falling apart emotionally, as well as physically.

Valiantly, Dr. Malloy did everything within his power to salvage her options. The last thing in the world he wanted to do was remove the purpose of someone so young.

However, the result of this last series of tests forced his hand.

"You need to come in and see me tomorrow," he said to her over the phone.

The inflection of his tone, while calm, told Linda that she was going to need support.

"I'm on my way," her mother said after a brief chat.

Driving up Interstates 85 and 95 doing eighty-five with a lump in her throat, Mamie Woodson shaved two hours off the twelve it would normally take to reach the north. Trying to protect your only child from potential devastation does that sometimes.

Upon their arrival at the doctor's office at noon the following day, the only person they saw in the waiting area was a beautiful young woman. Full-figured, cocoa brown and wearing a colorful scarf on her mane, sadness and fear was in her eyes as well.

"I couldn't let you go through this alone, soror," Josephine announced.

Even in life's darkest moments, sisterhood found its shine.

"I'm going with you into the doctor's office, Lucky. I need to know what's going on," Mamie said.

"I'll be okay, Mama."

"Lucky, I think you're going to need me in that room."

"If I do, I'll have him call you in," Linda said as she left them.

The corridor lights, burning a low-lit yellow, seemed dimmer than normal. The nurses and technician, leaving a staff meeting, were solemn as she passed them by. One of them, a middle-aged black woman, lowered her head after eye contact.

Dr. Malloy greeted her at his entrance.

"How are you, Linda?"

"I'd be better if I lost some of this excess weight."

"That'll happen soon enough."

"Doctor, whatever the results are, please don't sugarcoat them. I'm a big girl," she uttered while seating herself.

Pausing, then sighing, Dr. Malloy gathered himself. "Linda, there are two tumors in your ovaries growing at an unusually rapid rate. Further tests indicate that you have leiomyosarcoma, a rare fibroid."

Leio-what?

Growing numb, things became blurry in a hurry for Linda as the doctor continued.

"Those tumors are malignant, but we detected them in their earliest stages, so you won't need any radiation or chemotherapy treatments."

Did he just say radiation and chemotherapy?

Total darkness.

Fear.

Hysterics.

That's what this type of bulletin brings.

"However, in order for the cancer…"

Cancer? Cancer? I'm only 22.

Her life was about to be turned inside out.

"I have cancer? Am I going to die? I don't want to die, Doctor."

"You won't, if we act swiftly. In order to avoid the cancer from spreading, I recommend that you undergo a total hysterectomy as soon as possible."

A major part of Linda was destroyed. Just like that.

Trembling nervously, she covered her mouth as her eyes welled with tears. The part of her brain that produced sound shut down as she rocked in shock.

Instinctively, Dr. Malloy stepped into the hallway and motioned to the elder Woodson.

Within seconds, Mamie stormed the room and hugged Linda as the sounds of devastation finally came.

"I knew she didn't need to be alone, but she tries to be so brave," her mother said, cradling her daughter.

"Being stubborn is a good thing. Not in this instance, however, Mrs. Woodson."

"That's Ms. Woodson to you, Doctor. What did you tell my baby?"

"The truth, ma'am."

"And that is…"

"Mama, I won't be able…"

Linda remained unthawed to her fate. Her sudden, tragic truth was unmentionable.

Softly, yet straightforward with a slow nod, the news was confirmed by its bearer.

"Is there anything that can be done to prevent this from happening? I mean, she's so young," the elder Woodson pleaded.

"I'm sorry, Ms. Woodson. She has cancerous tumors in her ovaries."

Waving her hand at him, Linda's mother could barely take the prognosis herself. Her tears, silent yet filled with strength by way of her own trials by fire, went unnoticed by her daughter as she comforted her.

"Oh, Baby, I'm so sorry. I'm so sorry."

Recognizing the need for the two to share the grief alone, Dr. Malloy excused himself.

Branded a survivor by God, Mamie Woodson overcame so many ordeals of her own to raise a beautiful daughter. Refusing to wallow in self-pity and moving forward with elegance and grace, an enormous dose of fortitude moved within her small, bow-legged structure. She knew her own resolve lay in Lucky as well.

Like her, the joy that wept uncontrollably in her arms had been dealt a cruel hand. Teaching her how to play it would be the most difficult thing she would ever do.

Somehow, she found the words.

"Linda, please look at me, honey."

"I can't."

"We'll get through this together. It can be done. You know I experienced something like this."

"But your operation came *after* you had me. And your tumors weren't cancerous."

"The doctors told me I wasn't supposed to have you and I went against their wishes. But you already know that."

Finally summoning the courage to peer upward, Linda inhaled a breath of her mother's resiliency as she listened.

"You know, when the doctors told me I wouldn't survive if I gave birth to you, I knew everything would be fine, for inside of me was my blessing from God. I walked in faith, even though it meant staring death in the face with the hopes it would blink first.

"Nothing since has proven me wrong. For everything I endured to bring you here, you made worthwhile with your good heart. You will survive this, just like I had to live life without your father. You will go on."

"It's one thing to decide not to have children," Linda retorted. "But I'm being told that there is no possibility for me to bring life into this world. I have no choice, Mama. *No choice!* What are men going to think when I tell them I can't have children?"

"You can't concern yourself with what you can't control, Linda."

"Mama, how do you think I'll feel when I see other pregnant women? How do you think I'll feel at baby showers? Or when I see strollers? How about mothers with daughters in hair or nail salons? They'll be no recitals, parent-teacher conferences or a son or daughter graduating from college like I'm about to do, no weddings to attend, or grandkids for you, nor I. I feel like less than a woman."

The sniffles resurfaced, then, another meltdown followed.

Her mother reinforced her support.

"You will carry on, Linda. It will be difficult, but you will go forward. Let God take care of you. Walk in faith and He will help you find four things: something to hope for, something to believe in, something to do, and someone to love. For me, He provided those four things in you.

"Watching you grow into the woman you are has been such a joy. And knowing from the blessing that you've become, I know you will receive the same."

Bravely, Linda smiled as she regrouped.

"Well, Mama. At least I won't drive anyone crazy with a biological clock."

"Your sex drive will be stronger because you'll feel free. I'll have to introduce you to people as my hot-in-the pants daughter."

It was a poor joke, but one that induced a smile from both parties. Somehow, someway, Mamie Woodson knew her daughter was going to be fine.

🐛🐛

My arms are cold and empty
My ears will hear no cries
No baby smiles or pleasant coos
For a dream of motherhood dies

But my soul will carry on
With help from the Lord above
Who blessed me with the courage of a mighty queen
And the strength of a mother's love

Remembering her mother's words twenty-five years later, Linda Woodson carried on despite lacking an essential part of being a woman; but not without an immediate struggle. When Dr. Malloy returned to the room that winter morning, he delicately explained the type of operation she would undergo, how he had to remove all of her reproductive organs, and the aftermath of it all, both physically and emotionally, the latter presenting more of a challenge than the former. Linda would need steady rest and support from friends and family, for she couldn't lift anything heavy for six weeks. Also receiving knowledge of taking pain medication, antibiotics, testosterone and estrogen, and the critical gauze-changing technique, Mother Woodson, assuaging her daughter's pain with another embrace while choking back tears once more, fought with the vulnerability as well.

The day she signed her consent form and other pre-operation documents, Josie literally had to force a pen into Linda's trembling hand.

After the procedure, she felt hollow and unattractive, often finding herself in bed in the same blue nightgown for days. Mamie Woodson took a leave of absence from her library position and stayed with her throughout the recovery period. Additional support surfaced when the older women of the local sorority chapter fixed meals and aided with nurturing words.

"Life goes on, Baby," they encouraged.

Nighttime would prove difficult. Awakening in the middle of the night in a cold sweat, often times Linda found herself crying at the drop of a hat. Feeling listless and lethargic, she wondered if life would ever return to normal.

"It'll pass, Baby," mother consoled.

Dr. Malloy, ever the noble gentleman, would bring flowers to her and her mother every time he visited. Mamie Woodson, enamored with his charm, not to mention the fact that he had pledged Omega Psi Phi in college, always had a hearty meal waiting upon his arrival.

Linda, noticing the deepening attachment, felt the magnetic sparks between the two when together.

The energy in the air was that of soul mates finding the missing link, she recalled.

"Mama, are you falling in love again?" she asked one evening in February.

"Hush, child. The man needs to eat. Don't you see that?"

"I can't believe you. This man done looked at every part of me, of every woman here upstate and you…"

"It's just dinner, honey."

"Yeah, right, Mama. I'm going to have a stepfather that examines other women's…"

"Child, please." She paused, then giggled like a schoolgirl. "You have to admit, Lucky. He sure is handsome."

Twenty-five years later, she still prepared dinners for the retired gynecologist. Davis Malloy recognized the character of the elder Woodson during this emotional stretch, and his heart kicked into a trot. For the first time since Emma, that feeling of flying amongst the clouds had returned.

"I'm never letting your mother go," he bragged to Linda.

By year's end, they would be in Spartanburg together, madly in love. Spry, still vibrant and happily retired from their professions, years later they were the most loving seventy-something couple in the world. Continuing their communication, nary a Sunday would pass without an hour-long phone conversation, sometimes two whenever Linda had man troubles.

"I wish there were more old-school lovers," Linda exasperated.

"Your day is coming, dear," her mother constantly retorted.

Every time Linda ventured south for a visit, she would see a crystal vase in their old-fashioned living room filled with a dozen, long-stem red roses, compliments of Davis. That, or in the alternative, her mother dressed in a leopard print nightgown.

"Big Daddy loves this," Mama cooed proudly during her last visit.

"Oh, Mama, you need to stop."

"I should have married a gynecologist years ago. They sure know every part of a woman's body and how to..."

"Mama, that's too much information!"

"Lucky, you're forty-seven. How do you think you got here?"

"I arrived by stork."

They laughed.

Something good came out of it, Linda reflected.

As far as finding something to do, her lack of maternal decisions with a biological son or daughter dramatically altered her career course.

"I have to work with children," she said to her mother the minute she had her Masters.

Employed as a caseworker for Children's Services in lower Manhattan, Linda championed the cause of the abused and neglected. Where the faces of many of her colleagues thinly veiled fatigue and frustration of an emotional workload, she seemed immune to the tense challenges that came with her silent observations of clean or messy homes during visits. Poised and unflappable when analyzing the many signs of abuse on children, she possessed a dynamic, take-charge mentality when called for; every move concerning the future of the kids made with a delicate mixture of maternal love and maintaining a family structure. Although poised on the exterior, her insides were forlorn whenever she recommended removing an emotionally abandoned child from the unstable homes.

Some of the tenacity she saw in the faces of mothers desperate to regain custody of their children moved Linda. Silently admiring their fight while undergoing the infuriating and demeaning process of getting their offspring home, for every step they took in terms of mental and emotional rehabilitation, she took two toward them. The parents on repented paths and maintaining and restoring family structure gave her something to believe in.

Fighting through the lingering annoyance causing her whole body to hurt, Linda redirected her attention to the high-definition screen to Spencer Tracy and Katharine Hepburn. Comfortable and confident both as professionals on screen and lovers off of it, Linda felt the deep affection and admiration that was apparent to all, and watched their nine movies together religiously. Whether it was an alluring look from Katharine, or a resounding slap on a tender part of her anatomy by Spencer, *you knew these two were soul mates from the minute their eyes locked in this, their first movie together.* Reminding Linda of what her mother and Davis possessed, something strong and powerful, their unique chemistry also served as something hoped for.

The more she focused on the movie this particular morning, Linda's eyes knew the one thing that would make the picture complete. Lord knows her efforts were valiant. Heeding every word her mother said, she gave many a man a chance and a half, only to be disappointed repeatedly. Yet gracefully, she always took the high road, silently working through the denial, anger, guilt and shame by thinking good things. Accepting each fate for what it was, the words of her mother rang in her ears.

It's more productive to remain positive than it is to waste energy being bitter.

And at forty-seven years of age, it was too late, way too late to restructure her philosophy. Did she really want to? One evening, while watching a rebroadcast of a BET special concerning down-low brothers, she viewed a female spewing venom on another man that let her down.

"PAIN," she mumbled as her sister in the struggle raged on. "Positive alterations internally needed."

While understanding this fifty-something sister's inhabitation in a painful prison, she questioned her healing approach.

When failure happens once or twice, you can blame another person. But when it becomes a pattern, a check-up from the neck up is in order. She needs to ask herself these questions: Am I doing something that attracts the wrong type of man? Why am I not recognizing substance? Do I know what real love is, or am I still enthralled with images as opposed to character? Why am I allowing my negativity to swallow me whole? Finally, she concluded that it may be "too late" for this woman to make changes.

Her hopes, however, remained undeterred. *But has love passed me by?* Asking herself this question the day Emerson Perkins decided that he wanted children, finding someone to love for Linda still proved daunting. The pangs of discomfort that ran through Linda were long gone, but the salt of dry tears stained her cheeks as she turned off Spencer and Kate.

THREE

"Thank goodness for the Cingular family package and free weekends," Steve Randall said to his lifelong friend. "You need a way for people to contact you."

"I really appreciate the fact that you looked out, Steve."

"Black," Steve said, calling William by their mutual nickname, "I don't know why you didn't come to me sooner for help."

"You know I've never been one to burden anyone with my struggles. I figured sooner or later, this too will pass."

"Save the 'I'll go through my struggles alone' rhetoric. How long have I been in your life, man?"

William sighed, then, as if programmed by a Microsoft computer chip, recited history. "We've been friends since the summer of '78 when I played kickball in front of your building in the projects."

"Pride comes before a fall, Black. Don't you think you've fallen far enough?"

Still the voice of reason in William's life after nearly thirty years, Steve Randall was stunned to hear of his adversity. Having moved from New Castle, Delaware to Oklahoma City, Oklahoma, he was on a trucking route east when he decided to call William in the hopes of hooking up after years. Surprised when learning that his home phone was disconnected, he was more amazed when he returned home to a letter from his boy chronicling the events of the past year.

William received a Federal Express package containing a five-hundred dollar money order and a cellular phone the next day. Accompanying these generous gifts was a note: *Use the phone after seven P.M. when the free minutes kick in. Steve.*

"You need to move out here with me," he continued.

"Steve, you've done enough, man. I have to get it all back on my own. Right here."

"Not working at Mickey-D's you won't. Tomorrow you'll be promoted to fries, right?"

Only your boy can get away will such cruel humor.

"Nice one, Steve. Actually, tomorrow is Sunday, my day off."

"Seriously, you know how we do. My door is always open."

"You know I appreciate that. Listen, the shelter coordinators need help serving dinner."

"Help yourself first, Black."

"I am, but you know me…"

"I know, I know. Always trying to save the world before yourself. Holla at me soon."

"I will."

Hanging up, William counted his blessings as he moved into the dark, dingy mess hall of the old hotel turned makeshift shelter in downtown Brooklyn. Sharing a warm smile with his roommates in the struggle, to them his presence in the facility served dual purposes; he was an inspiration to some, and a poster-child of caution to others. Acting as an unofficial counselor, he listened to their stories, offering wisdom to the sane who maintained hope for better days, and politely encouraging the insane to find a method to their madness.

The supervisors at the shelter respected William as evidenced by them giving him unheard-of responsibilities for a resident when he asked how he could be of assistance during his stay.

"How was your day, Ms. Watson?" he asked one woman while piling beans, sliced frankfurters and cole slaw on her plate.

"Well, I heard from my son today. He's sending me money later this week."

"That's good. Put some of it aside for a rainy day."

He should be trying to get her out of this place, he thought. *Some kids are so selfish that they won't even help the mothers who gave them life.*

"What's up, Mr. Jackson?" Taking a deep breath, he ignored the pungent odor of urine and grime coming from the man while praying for once, that this elderly, unkempt man would make sense.

"He told me I'm crazy but the captain said I wasn't. Together, we're gonna save the world, young man."

"And you will, Mr. Jackson. You will."

With every interaction, William realized he wasn't the only one warring with ups and downs.

Some survive the storm, others just lose it.

"Ms. Carter, how was your day?"

"Absolutely divine," the woman stated. "And yours, you handsome, positive brother?"

"Absolutely divine as well, ma'am."

Full of wisdom and love, Alvina Carter was a mother figure to many of the residents. A member of the Black Liberation Army in her younger days, throughout her adulthood she'd been labeled as uppity, argumentative and too troublesome because she spoke of truths many in society never wanted to hear. Over her bed in this residence was a poster of Malcolm X, which had immediately captured William's attention. Though mellowed in her frail, gray-haired seventies, her conscience still burned with anger.

"Four hundred and fifty years and the games are still being played," she muttered one day to no one in particular.

William was right behind her that day.

"Tell me about it," he agreed. From that simple reply, a connection deeper than merely understanding the torrent of everyday problems was forged. Sharing discussions about the history of the Black Panther Movement and the Nation of Islam in the sixties, they talked through many a night over cheeseburgers, sometimes echoing the sentiment of Malcolm, who, before his pilgrimage to Mecca, had preached total segregation as opposed to integration.

"I bet it was cool to see productive, black-owned businesses flourish in Harlem," William said one day after a long day at work.

"It was something to behold, young brother. We were turning over revenue within the community and everyone was taking care of each other. And Brother Malcolm gave great speeches on the corner of 125th and Seventh Avenue, always speaking of the worldwide unity of Africans."

"I can imagine. Today, many of us still look for approval from the master," William joked. "It's either that, or we accept their negative traits dictated to our culture."

"And the cream dilutes some of the things we do by pushing negativity in our communities as positive," Alvina responded. "Everything from the beer that pollutes our insides to the stupid videos on the idiot box and street books being read by all these teenagers teaching them self-hated. Heaven help us if we start enhancing our intelligence by actually thinking."

Many times William wondered what unfair catastrophe had brought this profound spirit to this state of affliction. No one knew. And out of respect, he never asked.

"Come by my room later, William. I want to talk with you."

After dinner, he went to her. Tapping on her partially opened door at nine-thirty that evening, he asked, "Ms. Carter?"

"Come on in, Baby. Please, call me Alvina."

The years of a rough life seemed to take its toll on this lioness, for her caramel face wore war stripes brilliantly disguised as weary wrinkles. Also experiencing breathing difficulties through emphysema, her eyes, normally tired-looking, became alert and attentive at the sound of William's tone. Feeling the sunny rays from his positive glow, somehow she was always invigorated by his presence.

William took his customary place on the floor at the head of her bed.

"You know, you never told me how someone so intelligent, thoughtful and good-looking wound up in a place like this."

"It's just a bad season, Alvina," he stated with a forlorn sigh.

"William, I think something very special is about to happen to you. That's why you're going through all this. He's getting you ready."

"Well, I hope whatever it is doesn't include a woman. There's a bunch of Jezebels out there that bullshit you as well as men."

"They've had good teachers. However, you don't strike me as the type who gives up."

"There's always a first time." Bitterness and frustration filled his voice as he continued. "If I were an alien just arriving on earth in search of a black woman to love and watched all the sitcoms, listened to all these talk radio shows, and read all the literature and periodicals geared toward their emotions, I would think they are the only ones facing odds when it comes to love. Yet many of them are so angry they are hurting men.

"Fear governs that crap. Fear of opening up. Fear of disappointment yet again. Fear of looking in the mirror and having to do the work to be respected by men. Fear of accepting their friggin' mistakes. Fear of learning to love again. I'm sick of hearing the vent when some of these heifers are doing the same damn things to men they cry about. I'm just tired of all the bull…"

"Tell me what happened, William."

"What makes you think something happened?"

"C'mon, what do I look like, an old fool?"

Her blistering truth induced more brooding.

"I really don't want to talk about it," he said with a frown.

"What, you have somewhere to go?"

"No."

"You got something better to do?" she sternly asked.

As his head hurt with the memory, William poured out his soul; the pain of a heartbreaking history and the root of his present mentality.

He was drained after the unbearable recitation and expected to receive some type of sympathy or understanding in the least. But she, to his surprise, simply stated, "I know what your problem is."

Unable to suppress the look of skepticism he felt in that instant, William remained silent, waiting to hear what this matronly woman had to say.

"You make bad choices."

"I didn't choose to fall in love with a woman who would stab me not only in the back but also rip my heart out!" he angrily decried.

"Of course you did," she calmly countered.

His ire taking control, William began to rise. "You don't know what you're talking about."

"Sit your behind down, boy!"

"Who do you think you're talking to?"

"Do you see anyone else in this room? Now sit down and listen to someone who knows a bit more about life than you!"

"Look, Ms. Carter," he began, reverting back to a strict cordiality. "I really don't want to talk about this right now."

"Sit down, William, and stop living in denial. You can't always run away when someone is telling you something you don't want to hear."

Reluctantly, William returned to the floor, but this time he put distance between them, leaning now against the opposite wall.

"Life is tough, sweetheart," she tenderly began, "but everything we do, feel, believe is by choice. God, in all His infinite wisdom, gave us free will. On any given day, we make the decision to either be joyful or sad. We decide whether we want to make the most of the little bit we have, or complain because we don't have more. We decide who to let into our hearts, and who to keep out. We make the decision to listen when our heads are telling us to run, or stay because our loins are throbbing with desire. You just sat here and told me when you met this woman. After listening to her views on relationships, your head was telling, no, *begging* you to forget about her. But did you? No. You made a choice to ignore your gut instincts and try to create something meaningful with someone unworthy of the goodness you were offering her. When good intentions are misunderstood, emotional abuse usually follows."

"That's what I get for trying to play Captain Save-A-Ho," William cracked.

Alvina breathed heavily.

"Now was that necessary? You sound as immature as her actions. And that's not to say that she, for all intents and purposes, is a bad person; she's probably just a product of her upbringing. She has no self-worth. You can't give that to a person. Why would you try to build a relationship with someone who thinks, from the outset, that relationships are too much trouble? You're setting yourself up for failure, and if you can't see that, then, Baby, you need to change your glasses."

"I just thought she needed the right man to show her what she could have," William sadly explained.

"You can't fix people, honey, especially someone who doesn't want to be fixed. That woman is comfortable in her dysfunction. In her small world, she's happy chasing materialism, am I correct?"

William nodded. "I remember being at her house, and a group of people from her job were arguing about where to place a crystal chess board in the living room. When I asked if anyone knew how to play chess, the room grew silent. No one knew how to play it. My thought was 'why have it for show, if there's no meaning, or substance behind it?'"

"No substance, William. You just answered your own question. She doesn't know anything about giving love because she doesn't even love herself. So, she pacifies herself in things like the accumulation of possessions, and temporary sexual happiness. She can't give you what she doesn't have. No one can. And why do you feel you don't deserve better than someone who's incapable of returning your love?"

"I don't feel like that. I know I don't deserve what she did to me. I did everything in my power to make her happy, to be all she needed," William argued.

"But why would you pursue someone who doesn't want the same thing out of life that you do?" Alvina tenderly asked.

Pausing, William couldn't answer that, but it gave him plenty to think about. And since they were being so open and honest with one another, he felt it was the perfect opportunity to inquire about how she'd come to live in this place.

"Why are you here, Alvina?"

"You mean, what happened to me that I ended up in this God-forsaken place after living on this earth for seventy years?"

William suddenly felt as if he was intruding and began to take the question back.

"A man is what happened."

Unsure of whether he should probe further, William remained silent for the next few seconds to see if she would continue.

She did.

"Albert Newcomb was his name. Albert and I had a love-hate relationship from the start."

Feeling comfortable, her speech slipped into that of a generation ago, an unselfish, bond-establishing age far removed from the immediate, I-want-it-all-now-on-my-terms generation; a group that discouraged the impatient, minimum-input-expecting-the-maximum-output-from-love craziness of today.

She proudly continued. "He was with me in the struggle; you know, the movement meetings, Woodstock and the war protests."

"You listened to Jimi Hendrix and Janis Joplin?"

"Chile, my favorite song is 'Somebody To Love' by Jefferson Airplane. Anyway, will you let me finish my story, please?"

Smiling like an eager kid, William complied.

"Albert and I knew each other since our early twenties and despite the fact that I knew he was no good, I loved him anyway. He was like a drug to me. There would be long stretches—years—when I wouldn't hear from him and didn't know where he was, but whenever he showed up, I could never turn him away. Now that ain't to say we never had any good times. Oh..." She laughed reminiscently. "We used to have a ball. Albert and I used to go to the clubs and we'd dance all night. We'd go on trips—I've been all over the world with that man. He was a hustler—shot pool, played poker, craps, whatever. If it wasn't for the fact that I was making decent money as the personal assistant for the president of one of the city's largest banks, we would've been living in a place like this years ago. I don't know what it was about that man, but I could never refuse him anything he asked of me. Gave him my money so he could gamble; paid for most of the trips we went on, too."

"Sounds like you had it bad," William quipped.

"I sure did, honey." She shook her head as she recalled, "He was somethin' else, Albert was, but I loved him. I loved him bad, Baby. He was into drugs, too, in the later years, anyway. When we were marching back in the day, we were totally against all that stuff. Then we started experimenting and that was that. I can't blame him for it, because I got hooked up with the cocaine myself. It was like I had to, just to keep up with him. I used to have a pretty expensive habit, but somehow, by the grace of God must be, it never affected my work and I don't think my boss ever knew. I retired about five years ago. I had a little bit of money saved, but when you're spending more that you're taking in, savings don't last too long. Then last year, Albert died.

The little bit of money I had left, I used to bury him. Lord knows I didn't know funerals were so expensive. Cost me close to ten thousand dollars. I didn't have any insurance on him, and since he didn't have any legal income coming in, he didn't have anything to leave me. I'm just glad we never had any kids. Can you imagine where they might have ended up with parents like us? Anyway, that's what happened to me."

"Wow," was all William could say.

"But I ain't bitter about it. I made the choice to put up with Albert and stay with him for all those years. I can't put that blame on nobody else. That's why I can tell you about choices, William. Everything we do, whether good or bad, is a choice. I'm glad that I've learned in my old age to put my trust in God, though, 'cause now everything I do, I ask Him first. I've had a good life. Had some good times with Albert and have some great memories. I choose to let the bad things in my past, stay in my past. If I were to die tomorrow, I think I'll be welcomed in heaven. Least I hope so," she said with a good-hearted laugh.

"I'm sure that you will, Alvina."

Reaching for him, the frail woman clutched his hand. "You're a good man, William. Your heart is there for everyone to see. Your kind spirit is so giving, and so beautiful. These are things God took into account when He placed you here. There are people in this shelter that need you. Life is a constant struggle, son. Trials come and trials go. Some can hang, and others fall by the wayside.

"Somewhere, in the midst of it all, there are heroes. Not of the red cape variety, but ordinary, everyday people. We need heroes, for it gives us faith that tomorrow will be better. Heroes help us learn from the errors of our ways, and show us, through example, what the human spirit can endure, and give. Have you ever wondered why the women of today have so much anger? All that eye-rolling is a defense mechanism. Here, let me show you."

William's eyes widened as he helped her into a sitting position, and watched Alvina flick a transformation switch. Into the closet went the senior citizen, and out came the defiance of a new millennium woman.

"Back in slavery, when we fought to protect their families, they created a scene with what you know as 'the attitude.'" Pausing to catch her breath, she placed her wrinkled hands on her hips, swiveled her neck, then, wagged a finger in the face of a man thirty years her junior. "It was used to get the attention of the slave master, and draw it away from the male slave. Sometimes it worked; most often it got them whipped."

For a minute she did this, until her vigor-robbing ailments broke that closet door down and recaptured her body. Returning to a resting position, she continued. "Now, through years of conditioning, my sisters use this as a form of strength to lift themselves; a shield over the gentleness we so desperately want to give our black kings, our heroes.

"Black women today need heroes, William, men that still believe in chivalry, who'll protect them from the evil everyday workings of cynicism, to show them, and their families, unconditional love. Sad to say, brothers today don't understand this; that's why they get such a difficult time. Black women feel compelled to become their own heroes, holding out faith that one day, they might happen to run into one hero humbly dressed as a black man." Winded, her voice was full of conviction. "We need heroes. People like you, son."

Mouth agape, William did a double-take.

"Me? A hero?"

"Yes. Think about your presence here. This place needed a hero, and you were chosen. You bring energy to the hopeless, and your words of encouragement keep them going."

"It keeps me going, as well."

"There's a reason for everything, son. Sometimes we don't understand His methods, but I strongly believe there are no coincidences in life."

"Like this conversation, Alvina." Rising, William reached over and embraced his mother in the struggle. "Thanks. I needed the kick in the butt."

"Anytime."

"Listen, since tomorrow is Sunday and I'm off from work, why don't you and I get up, put on our best Sunday clothes, and find a church to go to."

The old woman's stubbornness returned. "Don't get me started on churches. The women in there are lonely, and some of those preachers and deacons are the biggest whores around."

"No, they're not!"

"They are!"

"They're not."

"They are!"

William made no attempt to conceal his laughter.

"Alvina Carter, you of all people should know that you don't go to church to pass judgment on who's there. You're going for the message God is delivering through them." He paused. "Besides, it's been a while since I've had the honor of going to listen to The Word with someone beautiful."

The matriarch's caramel complexion went flush.

"Well, since you put it that way, come by about eight-thirty and help me get ready. I don't have much to wear."

"Neither do I, but He doesn't care what we look like."

"Are you sure you want me to come? I have shortness of breath…"

"You didn't sound like it earlier, when you were putting me on blast."

"William, my hips and knees ache, and I walk real slow…"

"Will you stop it already? You sound like me, with all those excuses."

Rediscovering her youth in a sweet way, Alvina had a twinkle in her eyes.

"Goodnight, William."

William's rest was peaceful, and pleasant. Awakening at the onset of dawn, he smiled as he reached into his blue duffle bag. Out came an old blue King James Bible, and a remnant of his former prosperity, a small bottle of Derek Jeter's Driven cologne.

Dressed in blue jeans and ready to go, he went upstairs to check on his other half. To his surprise, he found her room dim, cold and empty. Gone was her poster of inspiration; and the blue flowered sheets that covered her mattress lying on the floor. Next to it was her favorite quilt, a thick, brightly colored one.

Disappointed and distressed, peace turned into a puzzled panic as William ran downstairs for a supervisor.

A burly bald man was found.

"Where's Alvina? We're supposed to be going to church this morning," he blurted out.

"Ms. Carter is no longer with us," the attendant responded coldly.

"What do you mean 'no longer with us'? I just left her room at eleven last night."

Hearing the commotion, another supervisor, a white female no older than thirty, intervened. "William, she's gone."

"Gone? What do you mean gone?" His throat burning with confusion, William's emotions were now in complete disarray. Pain and hurt flowed through his veins as his body trembled. "I was just with her last night!"

The attendants, fearful that an emotional commotion might be interpreted to others as an angry rant, ushered him into a nearby office and into a seat. There, they administered the final blow.

"One of the night attendants heard a sudden thud from her room, and rushed upstairs," the woman calmly stated. "We found her sprawled on her back and her eyes shut. By the time the paramedics came…she was battling so much… a bad heart, kidney failure, shortness of breath… I'm sorry."

William didn't move. His top teeth biting his lower lip, tears welled up and overflowed from sad eyes. Shaking his head, he muttered repeatedly, "Gone."

"Are you gonna be okay?"

"Yes," William answered with a quivering voice. "Can I go back to her room one last time?"

Begrudgingly, the attendants nodded yes.

Numbness filling his soul, he didn't feel the steps he climbed, nor the mourners walk back to a place that had been filled with spirit and life hours earlier. William reentered Alvina's room and wrapped the comforter around him as he sat on her bed.

Well Alvina, I guess God decided to grant you entry into those pearly gates sooner than you expected.

The regular Sunday service at Brooklyn's House of Baptists was a personal wake for him, a two and one-half-hour bereavement period. Silent, sullen and somber as he listened to the choir sing and the local bulletins, all composure was lost when the local pastor spoke of reasons for everything in life, even death.

"The strength of our forefathers lives within us all, and we keep them alive with our actions," the booming voice from the pulpit declared. "This doesn't mean we won't face adversities while doing so, especially being black with so much against us from birth. Sometimes we feel as if the ocean of life is drowning us. Arms flailing, our limbs thrash as troubling waves slap us, then pull us underneath seas of burden. Sometimes we don't know which way is up as we fight to break the surface of pain. Blinking, trying to focus, nothing positive is on the horizon, for we are surrounded by nothing but despair. The sparkling sands of mental, emotional and spiritual help seem so far away, especially when the waters are infested with killer sharks, people with negative energy trying to rip your positive soul apart with spirit-eating teeth. Each row in their mouth means a certain type of adversity: the first row might be violence, the next racism, then treachery, deception, hatred, and so on…

"But know this, beloved: the word of God is the ultimate life preserver, one that will lead us to safe shores. We may be troubled on every side, yet not left without answers. We may be perplexed, but never left in a muddy, murky lurch," he announced. "We experience many problems, through job loss and the death of those near, through homelessness and other ills, but we are not forgotten, nor forsaken. You will never be left, for He heals all wounds, and provides all things for all people. There is a reason for everything in life, and we must never forget that."

Bawling unashamedly, at the end of service he was surprised when rising to leave, a total stranger hugged him.

"Your time for happiness is coming, brother," the woman, an attractive salmon-colored queen with round brown eyes testified. "Just keep the faith."

"Thank you."

Outside, William's eyes burned as the sunlight of midday hit them. Wanting to get away from the city, he remembered a particular autumn morning, when unemployed and having no money, he had jumped a PATH train turnstile and discovered the peacefulness of a place that opposed the legal minds of midtown and the busy Wall Street financial area, the fish and vegetable markets of Chinatown, and the eclectic bistros of SoHo, Tribeca, and the Lower East Side.

He needed the waterfront in Hoboken, New Jersey.

Arriving shortly after one, he strolled around the pier, noticing lovers sharing pecks of affection while holding hands, as well as a festival complete with food and Italian bands stationed in a nearby parking facility. Pausing briefly, he stood against the railing and gazed longingly at the New York City skyline and the gray miles of water that separated occupational burden from after-hour bliss. Loving the splendor of the view, it also served as a reminder of the pain he experienced in her borders.

A middle-aged couple stood nearby, canoodling publicly. The bearded man, heavy with European features, dressed in black denim jeans, a yellow golfing shirt and brown boating shoes, and the full-figured West-Indian-looking woman shared a slow, easy kiss; their steam igniting the sensuality of passers-by.

Familiar feelings of loneliness invaded William as he played voyeur once more. Hearing a symphony of purrs and groans escape her, the beau licked his lips, a la LL Cool J.

Soon, those vacant feelings of craving love left him, taking with it his admiring smile. The sun-dappled skies were suddenly eclipsed by the dark clouds of a recurring nightmare.

"Where do you want it?" the lover haunting William's mind asked Anna.

"In my mouth, Baby. I want to taste your kids."

A little over a year ago, the sight of it stripped away his armor of confidence, making him feel confused and inadequate. For a split second, the memory of it all had made him want to leap into the Hudson River and drown himself.

This Sunday, however, the strength of the horrible memory was diminished by resolve. Fortified by the combination of Alvina's and the pastor's words, positive feelings fought with his internal demons, then cast them out of his brain, thus restoring a broad smile to his countenance.

"It's good to see two people in love," William said to the couple. Then as a precaution, he left their side.

Continuing his pensive meandering, he found himself parallel to a bike path, lined on one side with a street named for Frank Sinatra, and on the other with benches facing the waterfront.

Looking around for a resting place, he saw the strip was full of activity.

There were bicyclers, runners and folks young and old, enjoying the summer breeze and peaceful atmosphere. Kids were dangerously playing on a path of boulders leading to the large body of water, seeing who could throw their rocks the farthest, and parents and other elders stood nearby, hoping none of them slipped and fell.

Taking his eyes off that precarious sight, William peered left and suddenly his attention was arrested by the motion of a firm backside swaying seductively to the music of an MP3 player. Fluid with her side-to-side motion, the melon-colored Bermuda shorts hugged her bottom with a familiarity that comes from a lasting relationship. Her shapely legs exhibited a penchant for exercise, her upper body resembled Angela Bassett's. The white tank top she wore appeared painted on as it outlined her torso exquisitely and exposed her muscular, yet fully feminine arms. That she had decorated her left shoulder with a small one-word inscription made her all the more appealing. The crimped culture locs, resting midway down her back, gave her an artsy bearing.

As she moved to a nearby bench, curiosity got the better of him. Pausing a few feet away, he leaned against the rail just above the shoreline. Absent-mindedly watching the seagulls as they landed at the water's edge before gracefully soaring away after capturing the children's attention, William didn't have a view of her face, but noticed the small ethnic earrings she wore. He wanted to see her eyes, but the sister was wearing shades and a pair of wraparound headphones. Her head bopping fluently, she was in her own little world; whatever she was listening to, she was genuinely pleased by it.

Remaining on the periphery of her vision so as not to disturb her groove, his inquisitiveness to her choice of music was satisfied when he heard her crooning, albeit, off-key, the lyrics to one of his favorite vocalists.

"A chair is still a chair...even when there's no one-un-uhn sitting there... but a chair is not a house, and a house is not...oh. Oh, yeahhhh...you can kiss goo-oood ni-i-i-i-ight. Oh oh, oh, oh yeah, yeah..."

Singing terribly, no one could have mistaken her for the next "American Idol," but you couldn't have told her that. She was in the zone.

Impressed, William couldn't suppress his smile.

God, I miss Luther.

Recalling the day that the singular voice of heartbreak and hope had left for heaven, *it was a month before it all went bad for me*, he thought. In those last days in his Brooklyn apartment, William remembered blaring Luther's genius full blast, sometimes high off the burning bush he smoked, singing all his songs while on the precipice of losing everything he worked for. Feeling his remarkable mixture of sadness, celebration, joy, and reassurance when pertaining to the energy known as love, he treasured the uncompromising sincerity of his tone, the power of his words.

They were sung with love for us all.

Wanting to hear more, despite the fact that she couldn't carry a tune in a tote bag, William took a seat on the opposite end of the bench. Tolerating her howl, he shook his head while wanting to say the words it seemed her body and soul needed to hear when she sang "I Who Have Nothing." He wished that he was having dinner with her at Sylvia's through "Nights In Harlem," swaying back and forth while dreaming of being her remedy during "I Can Make It Better," and longing to satisfy starved desires when she barked, "Let me hold you tight, if only for one night."

After a while, the singing ceased. Silence of a few seconds passed before he said, "I see you're a big Luther fan, too."

"I'm sorry, I didn't hear you," the woman responded after pulling an earpiece away from her head.

"I said, I see you're a big Luther fan, too. I was listening to you sing."

Removing her sunglasses and revealing beautiful almond-shaped brown eyes, the woman blushed.

"I'm sorry. I was just…kind of in another place."

"I feel you. Luther does that to you."

A wide smile touched her lips. "He was one of my favorite artists. I really miss him."

"So do I. I feel like he's going to come out with something new any day now."

"You know it's funny. I was thinking the same thing as I listened to these tracks. I feel like he never left us."

"He hasn't. He's left a body of work that's nothing short of amazing," William stated.

"Tell me about it." She sighed. "Well, at least we still have Prince, Stevie Wonder and Michael Jackson. They're the musical trinity of substance as far as longevity is concerned."

"We've got to keep the little boys away from Michael, though."

The woman frowned.

Instinctively, William suddenly sensed her displeasure.

"My bad," he immediately responded. "Are you a big Michael Jackson fan?"

"No. It wasn't the joke. It's something else I thought about. I love Michael Jackson. I grew up with him."

"So his trial didn't scare you away?"

"No. I just wish he would have focused on making good music."

"Maybe he'll make a comeback, like the pretty-boy, light-skinned men these comedians keep talking about."

"Michael ain't light, though, he's chalky. Besides, I like my men chocolate, thank you very much."

Together, they chuckled, but suddenly, a laugh escaped William as if it had been released from bondage.

"It wasn't *that funny*," the woman said.

"You have to excuse me, but I needed to hear your approval."

"As handsome as you are? You can't be serious."

"You sound like John McEnroe when you say that."

"He was a great tennis player back in the day. I loved watching him serve and volley. Today, they all play from the baseline."

"Wow."

"What?"

"A woman who has sports knowledge. Now, that's an oddity."

She nodded her head. "Yes. I do. Football is my favorite sport, then baseball, followed by basketball, tennis and boxing. I used to watch them all the time with my mother. She's a huge sports fan." She paused. "I wish there would have been some professional teams in the area where I was raised."

"So, you're not from here?" William asked.

"No, I'm from the South."

"I didn't hear the accent."

"It only comes out when I'm around family."

"A Southern belle…from…"

"Spartanburg, South Carolina. Ever hear of it?"

"The only Spartans I ever heard of were…"

"The Michigan State Spartans, right?" Seeing the amazement on William's face encouraged her to go further. "I was a big Magic Johnson fan, also, since his collegiate days. The Lakers were my team when I was in grad school."

William smiled like he hadn't in months. "Magic and Kareem, what a team. My greatest moment watching sports was back in '85, when the Lakers beat the Celtics in the Boston Garden after all those years of failure."

"Mine, too. Especially since Magic screwed up in the finals the year before."

Coolly, the woman raised her hand and William enthusiastically completed the high-five.

"You really know your sports, um…I didn't get a name, Miss."

"Lucky. You can call me that."

"I guess I am lucky, huh?" William extended his hand only to meet air.

"That's not necessary. The high-five was as good as a handshake. But you could give me a name."

"William. William McCall."

"No middle name?"

"No."

"Interesting," she said confidently, giving him an inquisitive look. "What is your astrological sign?"

"Gemini. I was born on May twenty-first."

"Gemini," she said thoughtfully. "You're very intelligent, but you're restless, have a short attention span and lots of energy, but I'm sure you've heard all of this before."

William nodded in agreement. "What about you, Lucky?"

"I'm a Virgo. August twenty-ninth."

"That's the same day as Michael Jackson's."

"That's another reason why I like him."

"You know, I can dance like him."

"Are you serious?"

"Sure am. Look, I'll show you."

Rising, William stood in front of her.

Embarrassed, Lucky covered her eyes only to have her hands removed.

"C'mon, I need your help," William insisted.

"How in the world… Do you know me?"

"No, but I want you to sing for me."

"You're serious, aren't you?" she asked incredulously.

"As a heart attack. C'mon."

Humming the opening, then belting out her unique rendition of "You Rock My World," Lucky could barely suppress her laughter as she watched this man do his thing; a triple spin, then freezing on the toes of the front of his shoes, side-to-side, then a backwards moonwalk, seductive hip wiggles, and a salsa step to boot. His dancing garnered the attention of a few couples passing by who applauded after he completed his minute-long routine.

Breathing heavily, sweat trickled from his brow as William returned to her.

"I can't do it like I used to. So, did you like?"

Composing herself, Lucky smiled. "I must say, you do have talent. But you know what I also thought while you were trying to impress me?"

"What?"

"I think, at some point, William, you have to go from the short pants of a kid to the long slacks of a man."

Removing a jovial grin, umbrage appeared on his face. "Lucky…"

"Linda. My real name is Linda Woodson."

"Linda, if I embarrassed you, that wasn't my intention. I just figured we were having a nice time and all…" Rising once more, insecurity ran through him. "Listen, it's been a pleasure talking to you. I'm sorry about the intrusion." Turning to walk away, his progress was disrupted.

"Are you giving up that easily?" Linda asked in a soothing tone.

Turning to face her once more, William saw a smile with the wattage that would have had New Jersey competing with the lights of the city across the water had nightfall been upon them.

"I don't know," he responded. "I thought I did something wrong."

"No, you didn't. I was just kidding." She patted the bench seductively.

"Why don't you sit back down and tell me how you learned to do all of that?"

"You don't want to know all of that," William said, shifting nervously after he revisited the seat.

"Really, I do. I need to know the origin of this madness."

"Are you sure you want to hear this?"

"Spill it," Linda ordered with a warm smile.

"Have you ever heard of a group called the Force MD's?"

"They made that song 'Tender Love,' am I correct?"

William nodded.

"Well, back when... Are you sure you want to hear this?" he asked a third time.

"Spill it," she repeated.

"Okay. Well, back in the day when Michael Jackson was a hit machine with the *Thriller* album, they had dance contests all over the city. One of the singers from the group, Jesse, would win them all. But it always seemed like I would go next-to-last, while everyone was chanting, 'We want Jesse.' Linda, I must have done the Motown 25 dance routine hundreds of times before him, and I would always hear 'You're better than Jesse,' and still," he continued, shaking his head while chuckling, "Jesse always took home the cash prizes. I remember once I almost beat him at a hometown club on Staten Island called the Island Room, but because they knew him, they gave it to him."

"I wonder whatever happened to the Force MD's."

"A lot of them died suddenly and tragically," William said sadly. "They were guys that went from singing in front of my project building on Staten Island to touring with New Edition. They reminded me of the Temptations."

"They're another one of my all-time favorites."

"Mine, too."

"You look too young to remember them."

"How old do I look, Linda?"

"About thirty."

William smiled. "C'mon, you don't see the gray in my goatee?" Moving closer, he inhaled the scent of her. "L'air Du Temps, hmm, not bad."

"You know fragrances, I see."

"I try."

"Well, how old are you?"

"I just turned forty."

Linda arched an eyebrow. "You look much younger."

"Good genes, I guess. How old…"

"Don't even think about it. You'll never get that from me. You weren't even supposed to ask."

"Not even a clue?"

"Let's just say older than you," she answered flirtatiously.

Her deep voice breathed endearing, encouraging warmth. Somehow, the tragedy of the morning seemed distant to William, that is, until he saw Linda grimace before rubbing the curvature in her spine.

"Are you alright?"

"Yes, William, I'll be okay."

After a sip of her Poland Spring and a few deep breaths, she appeared so.

"You seem to be in a lot of pain, Linda."

"It comes and goes, but I'll be okay," she answered, forcing a grateful smile. "This type of pain comes after you turn forty-five."

"I thought you weren't going to tell me how old you were?"

"I didn't. You just know that I'm over forty-five." Pausing, she conceded. "I'll be forty-eight next month."

"I never would have known. Those locs make you look younger than me."

"That's an awfully nice thing to say."

"So where is he?"

"Who?"

"You know who, the dude who let you out of the house all by your lonesome on this beautiful summer afternoon. Why isn't he with you? You know us Northerners can be strange people."

"I know. My mother told me to watch out for 'those crazy Yankee men that dance like Michael Jackson' in the park," Linda joked.

"Touché."

"I thought you'd like that one." She got serious. "Normally, I come here alone to enjoy the peace of the waterfront, and to get my mind off of things."

"Things like what?"

"Things, that's all you need to know for now." She paused momentarily before adding, "But since you went there, what about you? I don't want to get jumped by a harem of green-eyed monsters while I'm sipping on my water. What brings you here today?"

"The death of a friend. She and I were supposed to…" Feeling as if he were giving away too much information, William halted his speech. His countenance now troubled and defensive, gone was the warmth of minutes ago. A knob had turned in his mind, dismissing the obvious chemistry between the two, and a wall of anxiety was constructed in record time.

"I'm sorry, William."

"It's cool. Listen, I've taken up a lot of your time. I better get going. I'm sorry to cut this short, but I have some things to think about."

Rising, he noticed the disappointment that filled Linda's eyes with his abrupt change of attitude.

Her comment confirmed what he'd seen. "Wait. Where's the fire? What's your hurry?"

"No hurry. I just better go. Thanks for the pleasant conversation. It sure felt good talking to someone without reservations."

"William, what's wrong? What are you running from?"

"It's nothing, really. I just think I should quit while I'm ahead. It was nice meeting you. Maybe I'll see you again sometime."

"Wow, I thought we were having a good time. I was enjoying your company, but you're running away faster than Terrell Owens taking off from the two-yard line with the entire Steel Curtain chasing him."

William stopped in his tracks. "What do you know about T.O. or the Steel Curtain?"

"I know that the Steelers are going to open up a can of whoop-ass on the Cowboys in their pre-season game tonight at six o'clock."

"So you're a Pittsburgh Steelers fan, huh?"

"Die-hard since the seventies when they were winning all those Super Bowls."

"That's a long time to have a problem like that."

Linda's eyes grew wide. "Don't tell me you're a Dallas Cowgirl fan."

"That's Cowboys, Linda," William announced proudly, "as in five Super Bowl rings."

"We have five also, Mister McCall, including two against the Cowpokes."

"One of them was tainted. The official made a lousy pass interference call on Benny Barnes in Super Bowl Thirteen. We all know he didn't trip Lynn Swann."

"Just like a Cowboy fan," Linda mocked. "You guys are forever blaming your losses on the officiating. You should be blaming Jackie Smith for dropping the wide open touchdown. He couldn't catch a cold if he tried."

Breathing in her scent as he sat once more, this time closer, a mixture of admiration and amazement captured William.

"You really know your stuff, I see."

She nodded proudly. "That's right. I used to date an Omega brother in college who was a huge football fan. Poor guy, he was another Cowboy fan. He lost a lot of money come Super Bowl time."

"Just like you did when we beat you guys in the nineties."

"I bet on the Cowboys that game." Linda chuckled.

"You're a smart woman."

William rose once more.

"William, all this sitting and standing you're doing… Are you nervous?"

"Listen, I really had a nice time chatting with you. It's not every day when a man can come to watch water move and find stimulating conversation with such a beautiful woman." He peered, then pointed at the words on her left shoulder. "I really feel Lucky. Must have been the tattoo." He smiled. "Have a nice day."

"Wait," Linda requested. Using his hand as a forklift, she finally stood. "I'm headed your way."

FOUR

"You're not obligated to stay, William."

Noticing the relief that covered his face with her allowance, they both understood. Things like this don't happen every day.

As she locked her front door behind him, Linda replayed the previous five hours in her mind. Then, reality set in.

What in the the hell just happened?

Puzzled by her own question, she moved to her bathroom as Heather Headley seductively crooned "He Is" from the living room stereo. Turning the nozzle to open the shower, the terrycloth bathrobe covering her nude frame fell to the floor. Gazing at her reflection in the full-length mirror on the back of the door, she revisited the erotic drama that had just ended. Absently running her hands across her breasts, she pinched her nipples while studying her thick, shapely physique. Moaning, a tremor seized her for a split second as the memory of what had transpired slipped to the forefront of her mind.

His legs were so solid and almost as hard as the hunger between them that loved me so well. I could feel him swelling with each stroke. Mmm, he had me floating on the Caribbean Sea. Damn, it was good. That was the kind of loving that makes you call into work sick.

A foot up, she was about to enter the stall and wash away the pleasure when her telephone suddenly rang. Cracking the bathroom door about two inches, she listened for the message on the answering machine.

"Hey Lucky, it's your girl Josie. I hope you're not doing anything Wednesday night, 'cause we're going to see Usher in *Chicago*. It's at the Ambassador Theatre. Carl got tickets for us through one of his connections. Call me when you get this message."

Ooh goody.

Smiling at the news and turning back to the stall, *Wait 'til I tell her about... She's gonna trip*, Linda surmised as she stepped under the soothing spray. Once again pondering the afternoon's events that lasted deep into the evening, guilt and justification waged war in her mind.

Why did I even do that?

Considering how everything had transpired, she couldn't say that she regretted her actions. Truth be told, Linda had been without the comfort of a man for months. Her body, craving a trip down a naughty street, needed the expert worship William had supplied.

Mmm, I can still feel him moving inside me, pushing fast and deep, then shallow and slow. Damn, that hook in his dick can get a woman hooked.

Twitching and tensing as if still feeling the aftershocks of an intense orgasm, the memory of it all left her baffled; losing all thoughts as he hit the right spot repeatedly in her mind after wearing it out in a recent reality.

How did we get from watching football, exciting football no less, to my bedroom?

The walk together turned into a casual drink, Linda's treat. Washington Street in Hoboken housed restaurants for everyone's taste, desire or inkling. Selecting a Mexican restaurant, Linda decided to tie one on.

"I don't have any money," William confessed.

"Did I ask you for any?"

Downing a drink apiece only served to lower their inhibitions.

"The Steelers are going to whip the Cowboys' butt," Linda announced, sipping from her drink.

"C'mon. Pittsburgh won't even make the playoffs this year."

"Would you like to bet on that? Put your money where your mouth is," she crowed, then paused. "By the way, where do you plan on seeing this beat down?"

William shrugged. "They have a television at the shelt...where I... I was going to watch it at home."

"I have a fifty-two-inch plasma television complete with high definition and surround sound where you can see and feel the fury of Pittsburgh."

"I'll have to take you up on that offer."

Blushing, Linda smiled as she stared into his eyes. Seeing a reflection of her own curiosity, the Riesling she ordered went down a whole lot easier than the moonshine she'd taught her sorority sisters to make at college.

"Is this a pre-game ritual?" William asked.

"Nah, I'm just feeling good. By the way, you never answered my question I asked earlier."

"About what?"

"Your availability. I don't want any crazy women hunting me down."

A searing pain that William had become accustomed to heated his skin, melting his smile away and threatening the merriment of the moment.

"I'd rather not discuss that," he responded, never bothering to sugar-coat his annoyance with the subject matter.

"Okay, but you need to know this, William. I can't let you come to my house without knowing something. There's a little thing I call respect that means a lot to me, and if you're involved, then finish your drink and be on your way, 'cause I don't do dirt on my fellow sisters. We go through enough as it is with you men."

"People go through stuff, Linda, not just women. Being subjective when discussing emotional injury shows a level of ig..." Pausing, as opposed to escalating the situation with his own pain, he stifled his agitated outburst. "I'm not dating anyone, but I'm also not available at the present time. Is that answer good enough?"

As it turned out, it was. After paying the bill, Linda escorted William through a maze of Hoboken sidestreets filled with bricked buildings, pizza shops, and ma-and-pa corner stores. Crossing a set of light-rail train tracks and climbing a slight hill, they approached her Congress Street home.

Once inside, he found the layout of her railroad apartment quite appealing, beginning with the long hallway leading to her living room. Immediately finding a comfort zone on her sofa, there was no misinterpreting his gratitude.

"Thanks for having me over. I appreciate this, Linda," William said at least three times in a minute as he reached for the gray cable remote. "I owe you one."

After an outfit change, the hostess in Linda took charge. The shorts and body-hugging top that accentuated her sexiness were replaced by black snap down athletic pants, gold slippers and a matching gold T-shirt with the Pittsburgh Steelers logo. Her laid-back attire exhibited a completely different side of her beauty.

"Boooo," William mocked when Linda returned from her bedroom.

"Don't hate. Congratulate and participate." Linda smiled as she moved into the kitchen.

It was only short minutes later that William heard the sizzle of something frying so he got up to satisfy his curiosity. He was amazed when he saw Lucky seasoning two large pieces of salmon, broiling on her George Foreman grill. Next to the stove were additional pieces. The defensive posture Linda encountered an hour ago collapsed under the weight of the warmer one she initially met at the pier hours earlier.

"Why are you doing this?" he asked.

"We need something to eat while John Madden's running his mouth, right? Look in the cabinet over there," she said, pointing, "and grab a can of corn."

William obliged. Placing the can on the table, he started to speak. "Lucky..."

Her slender index finger stilled his tongue when it pressed against his full lips.

"Go watch some TV, Baby."

Submissive to her kindness, William complied.

Linda presented herself about fifteen minutes later along with two plates of appetizing food just as the Cowboys kicked off.

"I hear you guys got that idiot kicker from the Colts this year," she announced. "Let's hope he doesn't choke during the regular season like he did in the playoffs against us last year."

"You guys better worry about your quarterback riding his motorcycle with a helmet on," he teased back, then continued. "What you need to do is enroll him in a defensive driving course against himself."

"Ouch. Good one."

Their respective commentaries throughout the first half were lively and playfully combative, and Linda's knowledge of the wide receivers' pass routes astounded William. Watching Hines Ward stutter-step, "Throw the damn ball," she screamed at the Steelers quarterback. Whenever her black-jersey wearing warriors were on defense, she called for a "red dog," an all-out, blitz alignment where all three linebackers rushed the quarterback.

"T.O.'s gonna burn him, so long as he doesn't take too many painkillers for that broken finger," she apathetically commented when she noticed the controversial figure isolated on a helpless Pittsburgh defensive back trying to make the final cut. "I think he's going to run a chair pattern from the slot."

"What do you know about out and up routes?"

"Just watch." Sure enough, after a pump-fake to freeze the pass rush, the Cowboy signal caller lofted a tight spiral in the direction of Number 81, who ran the pattern as predicted. It was a touchdown for Dallas, right at halftime.

"How did you know that, Linda?"

Linda pointed to her tattoo as she rose. "What's my nickname, William? Now if you'll excuse me, I'd like to get us some nachos and salsa."

There'd been no way to anticipate the fury unleashed after I said this, Linda recalled later. *I guess that I wanted it as bad as he did, and was blind to his lust.* Her hand had been poised to pick up the dish of salsa, but without circumstance, he entered the kitchen, removed it from her hand and placed it on the counter beside her.

Clamping onto her firm round bottom with the tenacity of a crab clawing its prey, instead of being on the defensive when she finally noticed the aroused, famished flicker in his eyes, Linda laid her palms on his chest and softly sighed. "I don't think we should be doing this…"

Her mouth uttered the words, but her actions spoke otherwise. Brushing his lips with a light, tender peck, she deliberately eased her long, flat tongue inside his mouth and poured all of her desire into her kiss, dancing delightfully with his as he eagerly reciprocated. Linda's affection-starved hands became bold, nomadic, touching and feeling the hunger he had for her.

"Mmm, nice and thick," she cooed, tracing the outline of his erection through his pants.

The naughty girl had been paroled from her emotional prison.

Giving way to the sensuous sounds of sexual sensation, Linda moaned melodious tunes of potential pleasure as William cupped her mounds, then languidly rubbed his hands along her flat belly.

Suddenly, he snapped off her sweatpants, delightfully discovering a miniscule thong, then lifted her effortlessly and sat her upon her kitchen counter. Squatting to gain the access needed to carry out his mission, for he was locked in on his target, William forged ahead.

"William, I..."

"Let me see how lucky I am," he said as he pulled aside the thin strip of her thong and kissed the lips of her heavenly haven.

A programmed checklist of insecurities ran through Linda's mind, all by-products of her operation and years of checkered experiences. *Will my scarred stomach scare him away? Will he think of me as neutered, like so many other men have? Will I get wet enough for him to taste me?* Sighing with pleasure as he licked the remnant of her surgery, the first two questions were quickly answered. Quivering, she needed freedom from her last fear.

"Are you lucky?" Linda panted.

"Yes, I am."

Strumming her sweetness like a seasoned musician, William's tongue composed its own score as he flicked his tongue back and forth, and up and down. Lapping her flow like a feline would a saucer of milk, he stuck a finger, then two, inside her cavern as he moved his oral instrument along her swollen outer lips.

Wiping away heated sweat from her forehead, Linda's face contorted into a wonderful grimace as he feasted. Grasping his head like a drowning woman clutches a life preserver, a ragged breath escaped as the birth of a climax commenced within her. Rising fast, the pinnacle would arrive in record time. Linda's voice deepened and while an accent surfaced, the audible aggression of a southern sex partner emerged as he melded his face in her intoxicating wetness.

"Eat that shit, Baby...YES! Ooh, that's good...do that...ooh, I like that... damn, Baby..."

"That's right, Lucky," William panted through magnificent munches.

Linda was on fire. Tossing her head from side to side she encircled his neck with her legs and humped his face in uncontrollable thrusts. Wanting William to taste every drop of her natural nectar as his tongue switched to a circular motion within her watery well, she pressed closer still, trembling furiously.

"Make it cum," Linda ordered as lust-laden screams escaped her. Jerking, her back arched, as if she'd changed her mind and didn't want to succumb to the salacious satisfaction of his exquisite execution; she slapped his bald dome. "No. I don't want to," she begged.

"You will, right now." His response as arrogant as the control he exercised over her body, William continued his passionate escapade. Licking here, there, and everywhere within her pungent, precious folds, William's performance titillated the deepest nerve of Linda, inducing a minor quake. Moving outside, he found her angry, aroused and already swollen bud.

"High libido, huh?" he asked while using his thumb and pinky to tickle and tease her pearl.

Linda, too breathless to respond, felt rolling waves building deep within rise to pleasure's peak as he went from masterfully massaging to sensuously sucking her clit. Shuddering uncontrollably while feebly attempting to quell the rising storm, her eruption was fierce and ferocious like thunderbolts rocking her core. Gulping and gasping for air as she twitched involuntarily, she pulled his head to hers.

"More, later," she breathlessly demanded.

"More is my favorite word, Lucky."

In a passionate scramble, they undressed one another, then brought their tongues together again for a torrid tango. Wandering, while moaning and sighing, Linda's hands began a journey to the center of his earth, caressing the curved length, girth and bulb of the prize she wished to claim.

Pushing him backward, William fell into a wide wooden kitchen chair. Motionless and powerless all at once, his penis stood rock hard, hungry for her warm, wet oral cavern. Lowering herself to her knees in the next seconds, Linda studied his seven-inch erection as she meticulously stroked it, but decided to leave a little something to be desired.

"We're not done, sugar," she announced, returning to her standing position over him. "You have more work to do."

Pulling her into an embrace, William rested his head on her stomach. "It's been a long time since I've been with a woman, Linda."

"How long?"

"Over a year."

"Mmm, that means you have a lot to give me," Linda purred as she tasted his lips. Breaking free from his affectionate hold, she moved into the living room, shut off the television, put on a low light, then her stereo. "It's time for you to score a touchdown, baby." Aaliyah's "Rock the Boat" was a welcome intrusion.

"I hope I'm not scaring you, but I feel so comfortable right now," Linda cooed as she thought of her mother's prophetic words: once ignited, her sexual appetite was enough to satisfy three men. Hips swaying loosely in time to the rhythm, her arousal had her feeling high when she grabbed William's hand. "When's the last time you danced with a real woman?"

Feeling the heat of her advance, William blushed. "It's been a long time."

Floating on the waves of her aggression, William was doped up by her spell. Winding as the lyrics spoke to them, their bodies melded to one. A scintillating power surged through both of them as their frenetic dance of lust continued. Enraptured by the reality of being with her this way, he released his inhibitions. His hands traveled slowly down her torso, massaging her ample breasts, pinching her nipples, before nestling at her opening. Touching her vagina, then inserting a finger into her warm slippery place, the movement suddenly stopped.

"Let's go to bed, daddy," Lucky demanded. "I want to feel you inside me."

Reduced to being a follower, William obliged.

Her bedroom was rather large; two rooms really. One furnished with a solid oak queen-sized bed and mirrored dresser, and the other a treadmill, ab-crunching machine and a black leather recliner from which she could enjoy her twenty-five-inch flat-screen television.

Covering his mouth with hers at the entryway, Linda's hands made their way to the reawakened inferno between his legs.

"I have condoms. I'd let you in bare, but…"

"No, you don't know me, Linda, and I don't know you."

"William, please don't think of me as easy. I've never been this forward before."

"We can stop if you want to."

"No, I need this. And," she sheepishly added, "from the way you feel in my hand, you do, too." Kissing him deeply after she uttered these words, Linda felt completely vulnerable yet strangely safe. Although he'd said nothing, the way he held her sent a strong, silent message. Tonight, William would be her heart protector against lonely, empty moments; the joy bringer if for just a respite; a pleasure releaser of many pent-up emotions; and the caretaker of this rare moment in time where she needed to feel the comfort only the male physique could provide. Somehow, Linda knew all of this before their bodies merged.

After laying her on the bed and covering himself with latex, William entered her from the missionary position.

Feeling the fullness of his rigid shaft, Linda sighed. "That's it. That's what I needed, Baby." Moaning as his thickness circled within, she could feel the pulse of his tool against her tingling, pulsating walls. Clenching her muscles as they danced together, she joined his motion. Sliding in, slipping out, dipping down and pumping up, his hook struck a special spot within her sugar, causing Linda to lose all train of thought.

"Please don't stop," she cried as she met him thrust for thrust. Feeling herself stretch to accommodate his width, she felt his motion become more aggressive and tried to control his pleasure with her own assertiveness.

"You like this, don't you, William?"

"Yes, Linda."

"Mama's got some good stuff, doesn't she?'

"Yes-s-s…"

"You feel lucky fucking me like this, don't you?"

"Yes."

"Then show me," she panted, "show me how lucky you are, Baby. I want it harder."

Complying, William's stroke became demanding as he pounded her wetness savagely. Reaching long, searching deep, the tempo of his passion increased. Penetrating her pleasure, he was retreating and advancing; pushing, pulling, swooping and swerving; in and out, over and over, with relentless, rigorous, rhythmic repetition.

Linda, grabbing her sheets, bit her lips as she fought the animalistic growls emanating from her mouth. Tears formed in her eyes as the knob of his tool discovered a place she never knew existed. Her hands left the mattress, searching for something, anything to take hold of. Finding a special place on his sweaty body, she gripped his cheeks as his energy continued hurting her so good.

A current of electricity, beginning at her toes, made its way through her flesh causing a fire in some places, a flood in others. Continuing its ascent, the erotic jolts arched Linda's back into his sweaty chest, forcing her to capture his lips with her own.

The intercourse was getting personal.

"Shit, yes, yes," she moaned as he pummeled the remaining reserves of her sanity. Explosions going off in her head, Linda yielded to the sexual storm; that inevitable shuddering sensation. Her orgasm caused her body to quiver and quake.

William, sensing her pleasure, held her tightly as another wave of bliss hit her, this one even more intense than the first. "That's it, Lucky," he moaned. His manhood swelling with every deep thrust, it was almost time for him to…

Suddenly and inexplicably, he pulled out.

"William, what's wrong?" Linda panted.

"Nothing."

"Don't you want to cum, too?"

"No, that's alright." Reclaiming his normalcy, he moved from atop of her, finding a place at her side.

Wow, this is a first, Linda thought. *Most guys won't stop until they get theirs.*

"What's wrong?"

"Nothing, Linda. It's nothing, really."

"Weren't you feeling good?"

"Yes, I was."

"Then why'd you stop?"

"Because I didn't come here for this. Listen, I'm sorry if I was too aggressive in the kitchen. I don't know what made me get up and…"

"Shh…" Linda's long index finger stilled his regret. "It's okay. You owe me no explanations."

Did I scare him away with my confidence?

Sitting in her living room some time later, puzzled by his abrupt departure, Linda couldn't rid herself of the thought. Having ventured to her peaceful Hoboken getaway many times through the years, she'd had many conversations with men who'd tried to get close: yuppies and metrosexuals of various nationalities, white and blue collar workers, intellects talking about politics and thugs running game, hoping to catch a vulnerable woman with her guard down. The men came and went and the discussions, for the most part un-memorable, didn't last. On the editing floor of her mind, they lay in her room of amnesia.

But William, buzzing around in her brain with the persistence of a gnat, had not only broken through, but forced her guard down. Although she'd had one-night stands in the past, the momentousness of those engagements had lasted no longer than the reality of them. And as alone as she'd been since Emerson's departure, she wasn't lonely.

Like a comet sighting, her conversation with William had been filled with bright energy, yet succinct in its presence. Recalling the flashing of boyishness evidenced by his dance impersonation in concert with his post-pubescent wisdom, she smiled. Her initial feelings of embarrassment were giggled away with the memory of his skillful technique when they came together in the thoroughly adult dance of the ages.

Mmm, brotha sure knows how to rock that body. Lucky's rumination prompted an involuntary tensing at her core that sent a jolt through her whole body.

Shaking her head, her blissful reflections were disturbed by the shrill ringing of her phone. When her answering machine clicked on, the familiar, good natured voice was a comforting respite.

"Hi, honey, it's your mom. I didn't get your usual Sunday phone call and Davis and I are checking in. Call me when you get in to let me know everything's…"

Linda picked up.

"Mama!"

"You screening your calls, sugar?"

"No, I was just sitting here, thinking. How was Pastor Willis' sermon this morning?"

"Lucky," Mamie Woodson sighed, "there's so much drama going on at that church it's sickening. Ever since that phony list was circulated with the names of women the preacher supposedly slept with, the place has been a friggin' zoo. People in the congregation have lost respect for him and constantly interrupt his sermon, yelling 'sit down' and 'adulterer.' All kinds of stuff."

"Why doesn't he leave? Are the rumors true?"

"I don't know, honey, but you can see the strain in his face. I feel sorry for his wife. She doesn't deserve all of this."

"Mama, why don't you change churches?" Linda asked. "I remember the last time I came home. The tension could be cut with a knife. I felt it as soon as I walked in there."

"Your stepfather's been saying the same thing for months now. He's standing here nodding his head now, like he's on the phone eavesdropping. This man knows me so well."

"Mama, you always taught me that when more than one person is thinking the same thought, it's likely they can't both be wrong. You should leave that church."

"That's easier said than done, Lucky. Our whole family grew up there. Your great-grandfather built that place."

"With all the strife going on there, I doubt Grandpa's spirit is still there. The church is in your heart, Mama, not in the structure."

"I know, Baby. I'll take it up with God in prayer and let Him guide me." She paused, "So how's work?"

"Mama, ever since the death of Nixzmary Brown… Do you remember that case I told you about a few months ago?"

"Yes, honey, regretfully so," Mamie lamented. "If these abusive parents today knew how lucky they are to have children…"

"You had your turn, Mama," Linda joked.

"You know I can't help myself."

"Mama, there've been so many shake-ups in the agency that I'm being considered for a promotion to a position that oversees the Child Safety Task Force. Either that or one of the positions that oversees all the field offices, like the one I work in."

"That's great news, Lucky! I'm so proud of you."

"Congratulations!" Davis yelled from the background.

"Tell Daddy not yet," Linda said.

"Why not? Isn't this what you always wanted, to get away from the everyday grind?"

"Mama, I don't want a position that forces me to judge my colleagues. I mean, the job is brutal enough and my fellow caseworkers do their damnedest to save every child. When a child dies because of abuse, no one feels worse than the caseworker. Unfortunately, we can't save everyone. Besides," she continued, "I feel I serve the department better in the trenches than sitting up in an office like a general giving orders."

Mamie chuckled. "My pit bull daughter, Linda, always wanting to be in the middle of the battle. You have so much of me in you that it's annoying."

"And you wouldn't have it any other way."

"No, I wouldn't," Mamie admitted. "So, how's everything else? Do you still have those pains in the middle of the night?"

"Like clockwork. Today, I had one in the park."

"You should go to the doctor, honey."

"You know how I feel about doctors, Mama," Linda said stubbornly. "If Daddy could be my gynecologist, he'd still be looking at me. No more of them."

"Baby, now you know you shouldn't talk like that," Mamie encouraged. "You need to see about your health."

As if on cue, Linda felt a familiar twinge, then a surge of pain. Starting at the small of her back, it moved quickly and sharply. "Hold on, Mama." She grimaced. Stifling her wail with a couch pillow she placed over her face, she doubled over in agony. Surprisingly, the awful feeling made its stay brief. An excruciating minute passed, although to her it had seemed an eternity. Bravely, she returned to the phone. "I had to run to the bathroom, Mama."

Mamie's tone changed to one of concern. "Baby, what's going on up there? Do Davis and I need to make that long drive? I know we're old but…"

"No, Mama, you and Daddy stay put," Linda panted.

"Davis wants to talk to you. Hold on."

Seconds passed before a distinguished baritone utterance pervaded the phone lines. "Hey, old gal."

"Hi, Daddy," Linda affectionately replied. Even at forty-seven, she felt a blissful sensation whenever she spoke to Davis. For Linda, her biological father, Julian, lived through him. "Mama's not running you into the ground, is she?"

"No, sweetie. She's been good to me, but we've been worried about you."

"I'm okay," Linda responded quickly.

"Are you sure?" Through the years, Davis Malloy had learned to read his stepdaughter as well as if he had known her from her birth. Able to break through her defenses, as a man, he saw things her mother couldn't always see. "You over that Emerson guy yet?"

"Yes."

"Are you dating?"

"Well…" Linda paused. "I had company watching the game tonight."

"Come with it, Linda. You're holding out." Maybe it was the fact that as her physician a quarter century earlier and seeing her through what had to be the toughest period of her young life, Davis seemed to know Linda's thoughts, so much so that he could tell when she was withholding information. Through the years, she had become his daughter.

Like a schoolgirl caught with her hand in a cookie jar, Linda confessed. "I met a guy today, but it's way, way too soon to be thinking about anything serious."

"Do you like him?"

Pausing ever so briefly, Linda remembered William, every inch of his chocolate hue, the warm smile and the shared fondness of music, the laughter when conversing, the guy-like sports chatter, and lastly, his seduction. Sighing deeply, she could still feel the taste of his lips, the caress of her fingertips, and his strong sword injecting love into her with each strong, sensuously symphonic stroke. "He's okay," was her response.

"It sounds like he's a little more than that."

"Daddy, I just met the man."

"How old is he?"

"I'm darn near fifty with my own life and career. Don't you think I'm a little old for this interrogation?" she asked indignantly.

"You're still calling me Daddy, aren't you?"

Linda smiled. He'd done it again. "Well…"

"Gimme what you got!" Davis screamed, impersonating Al Pacino's passionate demand in the movie *Heat*. "Gimme what you got!"

"Daddy…"

"C'mon, sugar, you know us old folk need something to gossip about. It keeps us alive."

"Well, I don't know much about him yet. He seems like he's cool."

"Uh-huh. Honey," he yelled to his wife, "our daughter invites total strangers into her apartment to watch football games. You know you didn't raise her like that."

"Daddy!"

"C'mon, Baby, you know I can't hold water." Davis chuckled.

"I think I'm a pretty good judge of character, thank you very much."

"Seriously, you'll be fine. Just take your time."

"Time is all I have.'

"You'll be okay, girl." Pausing, his proud beam traveled through the communication cables. "You know, I've watched you grow into an amazing woman and if I've never told you before, I'm very proud of you."

"You tell me every time we talk."

"You're right, Lucky, and I'll never stop telling you. Your mother and I want you to find the happiness we've shared for so long. I mean, look at you. You're intelligent, successful, brilliant and beautiful. You should have them banging on that door trying to marry you."

"Been there, done that, Daddy, with Emerson."

"And you'll do it again. Your mother and I are proven examples that love can be better the second time around."

Pausing, Linda sighed. "If it's in God's plan, then so be it, but I'm comfortable with myself. I don't need a man to validate me."

"No," Davis corrected, "but everybody needs somebody to love, Lucky. That's the problem with you damn kids today."

"Kids? I'm almost…"

"You're still a kid to me," he interrupted defiantly. "The problem with everyone is that they're scared to give their hearts completely to anything other than for selfish gain. It's like love has to be proven to them before they surrender."

"My mother didn't raise me like that," Linda countered.

"I know she didn't. But for all your accomplishments professionally and all that you've endured personally, you still haven't learned to overcome vulnerable emptiness."

A pregnant pause.

"I know you don't know what that means, child," Davis continued. "It means you have resigned yourself to whatever direction love takes you. You've accepted, without fight, whatever destiny is dropped at your feet. Because of your past, you won't open up completely, even when you think you are. A good man can sense that and will either exploit it or not commit his heart to nonchalance. You're going through the motions, because you refuse to feel."

"That wasn't Emerson's problem. He wanted kids. I disagree with what you're saying, Daddy. I loved that man."

"With every ounce of your being or were you going through the motions, holding back?"

Pausing once more, Linda reflected on the events that led to her and Emerson's demise: her desire to spend time alone when he wanted to go to sporting events; the fact that she was more knowledgeable than he in most areas and how she let him know this whenever the opportunity presented itself; her half-hearted offers of support when he ventured into his investigative work; the twinges of jealousy when he was feted for his community work, as if she were playing second fiddle to the mayor. Subconsciously, instead of complementing him, Linda had competed with him.

She listened more intently as her stepfather continued.

"You see, learning to overcome vulnerable emptiness really means you leave nothing to chance. You give your all each time out without regrets, expectations or wondering how you'll feel if it doesn't work. You invest your soul in that man and leave all the issues of your past out of it. He has nothing to prove to you and vice versa. Every day should be like Christmas, because both of you have a feeling the deepest of problems can't erase. You become one because you realize it's not about finding something in one another that you already didn't possess, nor does it mean competing with each other for the last word as head of your household. None of these petty issues maters. You simply live to inspire each other every day with something new and fresh. You love without fear of disappointment, and if it doesn't work, so what? You gave it your all and would be willing to do it again. The fact that it didn't work is not your problem; it's the other person's for not appreciating the value of everything you unselfishly offered. All this comes with learning to overcome vulnerable emptiness." A long silence filled the air before Davis continued, "Linda, take the first letters of the words learning, overcome, vulnerable, and emptiness and tell me what they spell."

Pausing, Linda smiled. *I'll be a son-of-a-gun. You learn something new every day.*

The silence only confirmed her stepfather's thoughts. "Learn to love completely, Lucky. I'm going to put your mother back on the line."

"I love you, Davis."

"No sense in changing up on me now," her stepfather responded.

"I love you, Daddy."

"I love you, too, sugar."

"So," Mamie said, returning to the conversation. "Is he done lecturing you?"

"He actually made sense this time." Linda giggled.

"I know, Baby. I was listening. Don't be too scared to care."

"I won't, Mama."

Hearing her mother sigh, Linda knew the sound was filled with deep affection; a point further emphasized by what came next. "I'ma have to give him some tonight," she cooed.

"Mama, that's too much information!"

"Lucky, don't act like you don't know how you got here."

"I arrived by stork."

Together, they shared a laugh only the most precious bond could generate.

"Lucky, I gotta get some rest. I'll call you during the week, sugar."

"I love you, Mama. And give Daddy a hug for me."

"I love you, too, Baby."

Turning back on the television, Linda frowned. Sportscenter flashed the final score of the game. Dallas 31, Pittsburgh 17. "Lucky bastard," she mumbled. "Next time I see him, I'll settle the score."

Moving to an extensive DVD collection, she bypassed Denzel Washington, Robert De Niro, Jamie Foxx and Tom Cruise for *The Desk Set*, another Hepburn and Tracy collaboration.

Like her mother, old-school loving would put her to sleep.

FIVE

Why did I sleep with her? Staring at the moonlit Hoboken sky from the bench where it all started, guilt played mind games with William. Two days ago, he had been on a leisurely stroll along this strip in an effort to eradicate unpleasant memories from mere months ago.

They'd been eliminated, alright. Still staggering from her mind-altering sensuality, ever since leaving her captivating presence Sunday, William had asked himself what triggered the release of his pent-up passion. *Was it loneliness and the need for comfort?* Or had it been the sight of Linda's full, unrestrained bosom as she sauntered by him at her apartment? Had it been their shared affinity for Luther and sports, or the seductive scent of that perfume and how perfect it smelled on her? Could it have been her secure swagger, or, in the alternative, something solely sexual? Dismissing that notion immediately, he knew the feeling had been more than a purely physical one.

Something about her engrossed him but he wasn't quite sure what it was, and the thought of his uncertainty confounded him. Lord knew he wasn't in any position for love or the type of relationship their activity would normally garner, for the remnant of a tortured past haunted him. But there was definitely something about Linda that made William feel free; *Lucky*, he thought with a meager smile.

Appreciating everything that had transpired—the initial laughter and ensuing cat-and-mouse bantering in the park, the trash-talk over drinks, her seductive abilities, and ultimately every single curve, contour and crevice of her anatomy; every breath and blood vessel. The hours spent in her aura had seemed endless. Leaving him enlivened and empowered, the cumbersome weights of life that had been suppressing his confidence were lifted, if but for a momentary respite.

His search for a rationalization of that impromptu moment in time with Linda proving futile, he dialed a number from memory on his cell.

"I was just thinking about you, Black," Steve responded. "Your Cowboys got lucky Sunday."

Damn, why'd he have to mention her name?

At this point, the results of the game were insignificant. "The Cowboys won?"

"Yeah, those chumps won. Thirty-one to seventeen."

Ha, ha, Lucky.

"Did you see that move T.O. put on the corner? He broke his ankles."

She'd called that touchdown. That woman is amazing.

"You there, Black?"

Steve's question brought him back to the present.

"I'm sorry, Steve. I was thinking about something."

"Where are you? You must be in a bad area. I can barely hear you."

"I'm in Hoboken."

"What are you doing there this time of night? Does the shelter have a curfew?"

"No. As long as I don't disturb anyone when I come in, it's cool. Besides, I have my own room."

"A'ight. I don't know how you're maintaining your head under these circumstances but, then again, I remember how we used to ball back in the day. You always gave me more than I could handle."

"But you always won in the end, Steve. No matter what I did, you always found a way. If anything, I picked up that resolve from you in dealing with everyday life. I do what I gotta do." William sighed. "I'm just glad you're a phone call away."

"Now don't get emotional and start crying, Black. You know how you get."

"I'm not, but even if I did, can I help who I am?"

"People see all that sensitivity as a weakness."

"I'm not people, Steve. You know, I happened to be listening to the Love and Life radio show the other day, and the topic of male emotions came out. A lot of men called in proclaiming their sensitivity because of their tears at funerals or when they had baby mama drama. All the women that phoned in afterwards were moved as well. I was, too, but they all missed the boat, Black."

"Why? Are you telling me those things wouldn't affect you?"

"I'm not saying they don't, Steve. Don't get it twisted, but all these women got caught up in instances where things moved those men. *Moments.* Being an emotional man, Steve, is not a moment or an instant, it's a *state of being.* It's not something turned on and off or reserved for funerals and drama. It's who you are all the time. Men confuse those instances with their natural state, then pat themselves on the back for momentary happenstance. That's a joke.

"People will know an emotionally sensitive man from his sure-footed gait to the loving way he communicates with people. Unfortunately, the majority of people see that sensitivity, especially in black men, as a liability. And with that being the case, we have a lot of incomplete brothers out there; brilliantly incomplete, but incomplete nonetheless."

"Yeah, but women still see a brother who's too emotional as a punk. They're always saying, 'I don't want a man who cries more than I do,'" Steve responded. Then, he joked, "Would you care to respond to that?"

"I sure would, dawg. It's a conditioned ignorance because we've been programmed not to show emotion; that's what they're used to. And it's filtering down into our youth. All these teenagers and young adults are walking with 'the screw-face,' mad at the world for no particular reason at all. The girls see this so much from us that they've accepted it, and then those girls become young women. If they see anything other than what they've become conditioned to, it disrupts their belief system, prompting fear and denial. People fear what they don't understand, Steve, and you know how it manifests itself? With ridicule and all kinds of unwarranted labels, names such as 'weak,' 'soft,' 'wimpy,' or like you said, a 'punk.'

"You know, I always wondered why when a white man emotes publicly, it's accepted. Remember Dick Vermeil, the football coach, and how much he hugged his players and bawled in front of the cameras? No one mocked his sensitivity. But let a brother break down and all the bullshit starts, like we're not supposed to have a natural propensity to feelings of joy or pain. That's a crock of shit, Steve, and you know it."

"You have a point there, Black," Steve thoughtfully stated.

There was a pause on the line for the next few seconds.

"I met this woman on Sunday," William mumbled.

"I knew it! That's why you went off on this tangent."

"Shut up!"

After sharing a hearty laugh, William continued, "We watched some of the game together and..."

"And what, Black?"

"Well..."

William's hesitance, speaking volumes, gave Steve the words his friend couldn't say.

"Was it good?"

"That's not the point."

"C'mon, man, was it good?'

"Steve."

"Stop holding out on your boy."

"Now you know, ever since that day back in eighty-five when I lied about sleeping with that chick JoAnne Rivera and you and your brother called me on it, I've been cool with my shit."

"That was then. I know you wouldn't make up stuff up now to impress me at forty, would you?"

"Of course not."

"Well then, Black. Was it good?"

After a pause, "Yeah, Steve, it felt too good."

"With everything you're going through, you needed some. Now, being that it had been a while for you, did you represent?"

"Steve..."

"C'mon, man, give it up."

Pride surfaced within William.

"I never had a problem there, you know that."

"Right. How could I have forgotten; Mr. Five Tool-Player always... ahem...comes through."

"You better believe it," William bragged. "When a woman gives you her body, whether in a one-night stand, or the consummation of a relationship, a man should consider it as an honor. And with that honor comes the duty..."

"Of pleasing that booty," Steve interjected.

"Yup. We have to be the best she's ever experienced. Anyway..." Pausing, he continued, "Sex is sex. I don't have anything else to offer this woman."

"Did she ask for anything else?"

"No."

"Then accept the moment for what it was; two people getting together for a good time."

"I can't do that, man."

"Oh," Steve mocked, "Mr. Sensitivity's feelings got in the way again."

"C'mon, man, I didn't make her any promises."

"So then, accept it for what it was."

"It was more than that, Black. We met right here on this bench I'm sitting on right now and talked; about all sorts of things. When we got to her house, she cooked me something to eat and she didn't know me from Adam, man."

"What's her name?"

"Linda. Linda Woodson. She's from the South and she knows sports."

"C'mon, man."

"I'm serious, Steve. That touchdown T.O. scored, she called the pass pattern."

"Really?"

"Yeah, man, she's crazy cool."

"So then, get to know her, Black. Why are you always putting pressure on yourself?"

William sighed. "I have nothing to offer this woman. Zilch. Nada."

"You can give her a Happy Meal or a quarter-pounder with extra lettuce."

"Steve..."

"I'm sorry, I couldn't resist." Pausing, William's buddy was perplexed. "Man, I can't help you with this one. I remember when I lost my job at the post office, Anita stayed with me through the storm. That's why I married her. Things are so different now."

"Yeah, but you and 'Nita were already hooked up. I just met this woman."

"What does she do?"

"I don't know, man. We didn't really share much personal information, but she's got a bangin' crib that I'm sure she's paying a nice piece for, and I'm walking around without a pot to piss in or a window to throw it out of. What could I do for her like I am?"

"How about being her friend? Think about it, Black. There was a reason she got with you and y'all just met. Maybe she's got some stuff going on, too. Just 'cause she's not in the same place you are doesn't mean she doesn't have her own struggles."

"Yeah, I guess, but things happened way too fast, man. I mean, it was crazy," William exclaimed.

"Crazy cool, right?" Steve said with a smile in his tone.

"You're not helping me, Steve."

"Look, Black, stop making more of it than it was. You always blow things out of proportion. Take it as it is and let whatever's going to happen, happen. You got her digits?"

"Yeah."

"Have you called her?"

"Not yet."

"Why not?"

"I don't know what to say to her, man."

"You've got to be kidding me. How do you know she might not be able to help you out of this rut?"

A warrior's pride surged through William; one constructed from a combination of mule-like stubbornness, anger and pain. "Now you know, I definitely won't be asking for this or any woman's help. Besides, how do I know she's not one of those sisters who expect the ready-made package? Or one who expects a man to pick himself up after he's fallen? She could be a fair-weather friend, a sunshine soldier."

"You're dismissing this chick without even knowing her. That's not only a bad move, Black, but a dumb one, as well."

"Steve, I can't afford to invest time in someone only to be dragged deeper into this hole. Fuck that; I can do dirt all by myself. I'll find a way to rise again, and I'll do it by myself."

Hearing William's emphatic rant, Steve, growing frustrated, sighed.

"Black," he said in a measured, meaningful tone, "has it ever occurred to you that maybe, just maybe, you're not alone in this world? We all need help sometime, and if you don't humble yourself long enough to realize that, you will drown."

Suddenly without warning, Steve stopped speaking. The next few seconds passed in silence.

"Steve, you there, man?"

"Hold on, Black."

Those seconds turned into a full minute.

When he finally resumed conversation, his voice sounded unfamiliar. "I don't want to see you drown, William. When I got that letter from you, I was stunned and scared. No matter what you've gone through in the past, man—even the crap with that Andrea chick that messed you over years ago—I knew you would bounce back. My boy's a fighter, I always told myself; he'll be okay. But the more I read your letter, Black... This time I wasn't so sure. For the first time in our friendship, I was scared for you. You sounded suicidal, William, like your spirit had been broken. I thought all the fight had left your soul and you'd given up on life. My God, you were sleeping on trains and washing your ass in nasty terminals. For crying out loud, you borrowed money to send me that letter!" Angrily, Steve questioned, "Why in the hell didn't you ask for my help sooner?"

When his query received no response, Steve's voice quivered as he continued, "William, if you have to drown, know that you've exhausted every possibility life has to offer. You make sure you've done absolutely anything and everything you can to survive. Don't drown yourself with foolish pride. We all need help sometime and when it comes—in any form—embrace it. Only a fool will push away food when he's starving. Everybody, and I mean everybody, needs somebody sometime."

William heard a sniffle, then silence.

"Steve, you weren't crying, were you?"

"Fuck you, Black."

William laughed. "Welcome to the real world, man. How does it feel to be complete, brother?"

Ignoring the question, his friend continued, "So are you gonna call her, man? She might be your life preserver."

When William didn't respond, Steve immediately recognized his reluctance. "Did you not hear anything I said?"

"Yeah, man, but… She probably thinks I don't respect her since I didn't call her yesterday."

"Lie," Steve countered. "Tell her you had to do double shifts or something. Don't leave her out in the wind wondering."

"I'll think about it."

"Call her, man, or forget about her, but don't spend the next few days pondering what went down 'cause you'll only make yourself miserable, and don't you have enough misery in your life right now?"

William paused, then looked at his cellular. "I'll think about it. Even if I wanted to call her now, I couldn't."

"Why not?"

"Well, for one, I have to get across the river to get some rest; I'm doing a double tomorrow. And reason number two…" William chuckled. "I only have one more bar of phone life."

"I hear you, Black. Handle your biz."

"No doubt, Steve."

Shutting the phone off, William felt the collision of two emotions within his mind. Feeling his friend's passionate plea, for the first time in what seemed like an eternity, he fought hard to control the need for love, attempting to build a home within his heart.

The construction project, however, ran headfirst into the brick wall of a disturbing memory. Reaching into his pocket for change, he inadvertently pulled out the diamond ring that he'd planned to give Anna. Seeing the object sparkle under the moonlit sky brought it all back with supersonic swiftness.

"That's right, Anna, this is my shit right here," the faceless male announced as he pounded his pleasure doggy-style.

"Ooh, I love it when you fuck me hard."

"Whose pussy is this?"

"It's yours," William's intended submitted to her lover. "It's all yours."

"I'm gon' put my name on this shit."

"Ooh, yes, Daddy," she moaned.

"I'ma put my name all over this shit!" he growled as he banged her more ferociously.

"Yes, Daddy, it's…all…yours!"

Inexplicably, this agonizing memory tortured William more than it ever had before. Unable to deflect the avalanche of emotional anguish that accompanied the negative thought, he rushed to the railing that separated land from water and vomited up his dinner.

That phone call to Linda would have to wait.

SIX

"Fries up!" William called as he emptied the extra large basket into the bin at the Times Square McDonald's that had become his second home.

It was rush hour Wednesday evening and the place was packed as usual. Perfectly content to work the skillet, the microwaves in the back or the fryers, he was glad for the promotion from mopping up the messes of others.

As long as I don't have to deal with the customers, I'm cool here, he thought.

The last thing he wanted was to run into someone he knew from his former life. When he'd been informed that this particular location was the only one with a position available, he'd wasted no time and accepted the job. Pure and simple, he'd been desperate for the income. Mission one had been accomplished; now if he could just get out of that shelter.

A consistent dream of his was to once again be a tenant in a place he could call his own, a humble abode where the pillow he rested his head on was his. Despite having his own space at the shelter, he refused to get too comfortable there. While offering heartfelt support and encouragement to many, he witnessed the effects of people who had become complacent, content to remain at the mercy of the state's overseers.

But that was not going to be him. *No way*, he thought. In case he needed further motivation to complete his double-shift, all he had to do was remember the empty room above his own and the voice of a matriarch.

"You don't strike me as the type who gives up... Something very special is about to happen to you... He's getting you ready."

Although she'd gone on to join the angels in heaven some seventy-two hours earlier, the fighting spirit of Alvina Carter had found a safe haven within his soul. Through him, she still lived.

This line of thinking brought to mind the reluctantly treasured memory of someone else who had inhabited his soul since that Sunday. A recollection of that entire New Jersey episode quickly resurfaced of its own accord. Try as he might, William had been thoroughly unsuccessful in dispelling the numerous flashbacks of his rendezvous with Linda Woodson. The woman's image was branded on his mind's eye. Recalling the fire she'd set ablaze with her wit, intelligence and beauty, he also remembered the sweet, caramel taste of her mouth. Perfectly intertwined, their tongues had delightfully danced as one.

I guess I should call her. He didn't want her to think he felt nothing for her or that he had taken their encounter for granted. William didn't believe she was the type of woman who would just pick up any guy and take him home and screw him.

Replaying his conversation with Steve last night, William considered that she might be battling demons of her own. *But she seemed to have it all together. Her confidence was undeniable and unmistakable. It couldn't have been just a show, could it?* He didn't really believe that, but there had to be a reason. There always was.

I've got to stop thinking about this woman. Each time he did, his body reacted as if she were standing in his presence. Still tasting the sweetness of her on his lips as he licked them, an involuntary smile crossed his face. Remembering the feel of her love muscles gripping his steel like a firm handshake, he also remembered the fluidity of her hip motion beneath his, and the arrogant, aggressive sex-talk that simultaneously tamed and turned him on.

She definitely knows how to please her man.

His trip to fantasy land was disrupted by a directive.

"William, put more fries on," the store manager ordered.

Drenched from the cold water dumped on his mental picture, his trip to dreamland was rerouted; its destination, the reality of Big Macs, extra value meals complete with super-sized fries and impatient customers.

It's too bad I can't be that.

Linda ended up having to stay at the office much later than usual due to an especially troublesome report she had to write on a case she was involved in. As a result, she asked Josie to meet her at the McDonald's down the street from the theater to get a quick bite before the show.

Linda thought the fast-food restaurant was extremely crowded, considering the time of day and, as they stood in line, she began to reveal to Josie the events of the previous Sunday. Surprised by her friend's impulsive and uncommon behavior, when she learned that the man had made no effort to contact Linda, Josie exclaimed, "What do you expect?"

"But he didn't seem like the type of guy who even did that kind of thing," she explained.

"He's a man, right?"

"All men are not the same, Josie."

"What man do you know would turn down free food and sex all in the same day?"

"It wasn't like I invited him home for that," Linda indignantly replied.

"But you did invite him home. You can't honestly say you didn't expect that he would be expecting to get some."

"Josie, you had to be there. I'm telling you, he's not that kind of guy."

"How do you know?"

"I can tell. That man was in pain. I don't know what's happened in his life, but I sensed it as real as if it was my own. Besides, we connected right from the start. The conversation was easy; our penchant for sports only solidified the bond. It was like… It was like he was a long lost friend or something. I felt comfortable, like I'd known him forever."

"What was his reaction when you asked him about his girlfriend?"

"He said he wasn't dating anyone, but he's not available."

"C'mon girl," Josie argued, "If that isn't a playa line, then I don't know what is."

"Maybe you're right," Linda conceded. "He did seem evasive."

"Typical."

"But what if it's something more than that? Maybe he's hurting and…"

"Lucky, look girl, I know it's been a minute since you had some…"

"It wasn't about the sex, Josie, although it was out of this world," Linda said with a mischievous smile. "Damn, that man could move his ass."

"You're incorrigible." Josie shook her head.

"Seriously, when he touched me that first time, I hesitated, but only for a second. And truth be told, I don't regret what we did." Sighing, she continued, "I just wish I could talk to him. I'm not looking to start a relationship or anything like that. I just want to understand what's going on inside his head."

As they waited, a group of rowdy teenagers came through the line from the front after having their orders filled. One brushed against Linda, nearly turning her completely around where she stood.

"Sorry, Miss." The teen laughed while the others chastised him for his clumsiness.

Linda, however, had already dismissed the boy when her eyes beheld the face of the man she'd just been discussing. Swelling, they threatened to pop out of their sockets.

"Oh my god, Josie!" she urgently whispered. "That's him!"

"That's who? What are you talking about?"

"William. That's him behind the counter."

Josie immediately turned to see who her friend was speaking of.

"Don't be so obvious," Linda scolded. "He's at the fryer."

"That's him?" Josie questioned incredulously.

"Yeah."

"He works at McDonald's?" The astonishment in Josie's tone was unmistakable.

Shaking her head in disbelief, Linda couldn't believe it either. This was an intelligent man. He wasn't a kid in his twenties trying to figure out what he wanted to do with his life. Why was he working in McDonald's? Granted, it was an honest day's work, but he had to have more ambition than this, she thought.

He's forty years old.

"Did you know he worked at Mickey D's?" Josie asked.

"Truthfully, I didn't know where he worked or what he did before I brought him home," Linda shamefully admitted.

"Do you know where he lives?"

"No."

"Aren't you going to say something to him?"

The women had one customer in front of them in the line. Linda's eyes were fixed on William, hoping to will him to turn toward her but he seemed just as fixed on what he was doing. It was almost as if he didn't want to look out into the restaurant for fear that he would see someone he knew or they might see him.

When it was time to order, Linda spoke loud enough for everyone behind the counter to hear her. Hoping William might recognize her voice and turn toward her, those hopes were dashed when he continued with his task as if his life depended on it.

What Linda didn't know was that it truly did.

Seated upstairs with their dinner, the numbness of the shock just administered slowly began to wear off.

"I bet that's why he hasn't called me," Linda said. "He's ashamed of what I might think."

"You should have gotten more information from him before you…"

"Save the lecture, Josie. Besides, you think any forty-year-old man with sense is gonna tell me that he works at McDonald's?"

"Maybe he's the manager, Lucky. That might explain it."

"The manager wears white. He looked soiled and sweaty, like he'd been over the deep fryer all day." Linda paused and began to rise. "Maybe I should go back downstairs and say hello."

Josie killed that notion with a firm grasp of her wrist.

"Maybe you should detach yourself from the emotions that came with Sunday night. Lucky, the man hasn't called you, has he?"

Returning to her seat, Linda shook her head negatively as Josie resumed her thought. "Sometimes you have to detach your feelings from the moment. Men do it all the time."

"Words spoken by a true playa for real," Linda sarcastically countered while pointing to her best friend's wedding band. "Girl, you know my system doesn't function that way. My hormones govern my heart."

"Stop lying! You've had moments where your pheromones got you in trouble. I've known you since college. I know all your secrets, remember?"

"Dilligas?" Linda asked.

"Dilligas?"

"Yeah, Josie. Dilligas."

Still befuddled, she asked, "What the heck is dilligas?"

"Dilligas is an acronym for 'does it look like I give a shit'?"

"You should give a shit, girl. You better not run for president. You'll have to buy my silence. I can see it now: Ms. Woodson, did you have sex with that male intern?"

"Guilty as charged." Linda chuckled, then sighed a breath, aching for something more than temporary fulfillment. "Back to William. Do you think it was just sex?"

"Did he kiss you while he was inside of you?"

"Yes."

"And you allowed it?"

"Yes."

"You shouldn't have done that."

"Why not?"

"Because it becomes more than just sex when he moves in you while kissing. Were his strokes slow and circular?"

"Josie…"

"Seriously, I need to know."

Hesitating slightly, Linda felt a tingle. Within milliseconds, the shared groans and pleasurable moans of three days ago returned her to a heaven on earth. Then the flashbacks: the intense, hungry way he dined on her, the vibrant vibrating his tongue on her clit, the magnificent motion from his midsection, and the way their bodies danced in unison once she embraced his time. His rhythm still alive after three days, she sighed deliciously, as if his limb had found a permanent dwelling place inside her body.

"Yes, girl, the man had me reaching for things I couldn't even find."

Finishing her meal, Josie laughed. "Hmm… I want to say that he made love to you, but these men play so many games today. He looks younger than forty, Lucky. Are you sure he's not lying about his age?"

"I don't think he would do that."

"How do you know?"

"My goodness! What's with all the negativity?"

"It's not negativity, Lucky. I'm just looking out for you. I don't want to see you getting hurt; that's all. You know, we should talk about this Saturday, with our line sisters at our summer gathering."

"No, we won't. This one stays between us, Josie. I'm serious."

"Okay, soror. Your secret's safe with me. For now."

Rising together, the two emptied their trays. Heading downstairs, before they exited the fast-food joint, they took one last look at Lucky's secret lover. He was still working away on the fries.

He looks tired, Linda thought. *I sure hope he's getting rest.*

Sometimes, the heart doesn't listen to the mind when it tells it not to care.

Outside, Linda looked at her lifelong friend, and saw unspoken words only friends share. Her eyes indicated that she didn't understand, but would accept whatever decisions Linda made, provided the end result was her happiness.

"Let's go scream at Usher," Josie said.

"I can't do that. He's too young for me."

They laughed.

Finding their seats in the sixth row of the darkened theater, Linda felt the electricity in the air. Everybody wanted to see if the man James Brown christened as "the Godson of Soul" could leave his mark on The Great White Way.

Appropriately attired in a black Armani suit and a bowler hat, Usher had indeed been a wise choice to play the fast-talking attorney Billy Flynn, the lead role in the musical *Chicago*. Defending two jazz-singing murderesses fighting for media attention, all of the women—the six on stage and those in the audience—swooned over the silver-tongued prince of the courtroom.

Linda, though, was not weak in the knees. Not even paying attention to the tremendously talented and handsome young man who moved effortlessly through his lines and dance routines, all she could think about was seeing William captaining a fast-food fryer in McDonald's.

What was the story with him, she recalled wondering. *Why hasn't he called me? Why in the world is he working in McDonald's?*

After the play, she decided she was going to confront him and get the answers she coveted.

Her decision to face him took a detour to the backseat of her mind as she felt a twinge, then a pain far worse than any she had ever experienced. The awful feeling tortured her with its games, running up and down her spine, rattling her senses. Then a headache rang in her ears.

Bravely, Linda tried to get up but she couldn't feel her legs. Supplanted in limbo, her body was not responding. She was at the mercy of this pain, and her mind, still functioning and alert to other senses, could not protect her.

She tried to speak but the pain was too intense. Gritting her teeth, she had to concentrate on the pain. Josie, seated next to her, seemed miles away.

I'll make it to the intermission, she thought as her whole body throbbed. *Everything will be okay then. The lights will come on, and Josie will notice something's wrong.*

Closing her eyes against her surroundings, Linda grimaced as she visited a foreign state, a place where the soul and spirit of a person is torn between awareness and the unconscious state. Soon, it would just be the latter.

Linda Woodson passed out.

❦❦

Two hours later, Emerson Perkins arrived at the emergency room of NYU Medical Center.

Flying through the automatic doors, "Josie, where is she?" he unceremoniously asked as soon as he spotted her.

"Emerson, thank you for coming," Josie responded, the relief evident in her tone.

She had tried to contact her husband, Carl, but with his job as a technician for Con Ed, he very often had to work under the streets of New York. When she got no response from him, and still hadn't heard from him after ninety minutes had passed, Josie assumed that was the case, especially since she had put in the code 911.

"What happened, Josie? Where is she?" Emerson insistently inquired a second time.

"She's with the doctors. They're running all kinds of tests, trying to find out why she passed out."

Biting his bottom lip to quell his worry, his face wore confusion and even more concern than when he first arrived.

"She passed out? Where?"

"We went to see *Chicago*. I was sitting right next to her," Josie explained as tears formed in the corners of her eyes. "I didn't even know anything was wrong. Just before the intermission, she basically collapsed onto my shoulder. When I tried to wake her, she wouldn't move." Crying openly now, Josie continued, "I didn't even know what was wrong."

Pulling her into his arms, Emerson tried to comfort her. "Josie, it's okay. You were there with her. That's the important thing. You were there."

"I'm scared, Emerson," she cried against his chest.

"Why?"

"She's been having these pains for a while now. She keeps saying they're nothing big, but they've been coming too frequently, probably more frequently than she's even telling me."

"Has she seen anyone about them?" he asked.

"No. She kept saying, 'I'll be alright.'" Josie moved slowly out of his embrace. Emerson swore under his breath. *Still the same stubborn girl he'd loved.*

"Have you spoken to her mother?"

"No, I didn't want to call her until I knew something definitive. I don't want to get her all upset over nothing."

"Thank you for calling me, Josie."

Moving back to the seat she was occupying when he arrived, Josie told him, "Despite everything you guys have been through, I've always known that you care about her."

"I do and I'm glad you understand that. I wish she did."

"Well, you have to look at it from her point of view. She got the short end of the stick when you guys broke up. You wanted something she would never be able to give you and that, by itself, was painful for her."

Emerson sighed as he took the vacant seat next to her. "I know I should have handled that better than I did. Hindsight is twenty-twenty. She probably won't be too happy to see me when they're through with her, but I want her to know that I'm here for her; that I'll always be here for her when she needs me."

Reaching over to take his hand, Josie simply responded, "I knew you would."

"Mrs. Smith," one of the attending physicians suddenly called out.

"Yes, I'm Mrs. Smith," Josie immediately answered as she rushed over to the woman. "How's Lucky?"

"Lucky? Oh, you mean Ms. Woodson. She's resting now. We've sedated her."

"What's the matter with her?"

Emerson was right on Josie's heels and eagerly awaiting the doctor's diagnosis.

"I'm sorry. What is your relationship to Ms. Woodson?"

"I'm her sister and this is my husband," Josie answered with a snippiness that was uncalled for. Reading the ID badge clipped to the doctor's coat, she added, "And you're Dr. Bricker."

Emerson, cutting his eyes at hearing her reply, remained silent. He knew the hospital staff was not required to give information on patients to anyone outside of their immediate family.

"Now that we all know who we are, can you tell me what's wrong with her?" Josie asked.

Used to dealing with the emotions prompted by fear from her patients' loved ones, Dr. Bricker calmly stated, "We're not sure yet. She did awaken for a short time and told us that she was having intense pains in her back."

"She's been having those pains for a while now," Josie volunteered.

"Have they been this severe in the past?"

"I don't think so. I know she's never blacked out before. She's been taking Tylenol and Advil when they come, but every time I told her to see her doctor about them, she brushed me off."

"Do you know how long this has been going on?" the doctor asked.

"At least a couple of months now," she replied.

Dr. Bricker lowered her head for a moment, seemingly in thought. She chose not to share what was on her mind, however. "We're going to keep her overnight to run some tests and to keep an eye on her. Her blood pressure is lower than we'd like it to be right now, too, which could have contributed to the blackout. We should have more information on her condition tomorrow."

"Will she be able to go home tomorrow?" Emerson asked.

"I expect she will, notwithstanding any unforeseen setbacks."

"Can we see her?" Josie asked.

"Yes, you can see her before she's taken upstairs. A room's being prepped for her now."

"Thank you, Dr. Bricker," Emerson graciously offered. Extending his hand, he said, "Forgive my wife's earlier impatience. We're just worried about Linda."

"I understand," the woman responded, giving Emerson a flirtatious smile as she took the hand he offered. "If you have any other questions, please feel free to call me. Here's my card."

Taking the proffered information, Emerson stated, "Thank you, I will."

When Dr. Bricker had moved out of earshot, Josie tightly scolded, "I didn't need you to apologize to that woman for me."

"Josie, she's trying to help us."

"She was trying to get with you. You think I didn't see the look she gave you when she offered her card."

"But why'd you tell her I was your husband?"

"It was obvious she didn't believe me, otherwise she wouldn't have been grinning in your face like that."

"Why didn't you just tell her I was Linda's brother, too?"

"Look, Emerson, it really doesn't matter now, does it? Let's go see how Lucky's doing."

Emerson shook his head as he watched Josie walk, purposefully strutting away from him. *What is it with these women? Everybody's got attitude.*

Thursday morning, William came awake with a start. Sweat drenched his undershirt and his heart pounded in his chest with a ferocity that frightened him.

The picture had been so vivid, so real. Not the normal one that had been tormenting him in his sleep for the last year. This was a different terror with an entirely different cast.

This one starred Lucky Woodson.

They were together in Hoboken. Their laughter rang in the air like that of children on a playground. The setting was sun-filled; birds, not the usual gulls that populated the shoreline, but beautiful, tropical birds sang a joyful song as the lovers strolled along hand in hand.

They were happy. All of the circumstances that had brought him to the lowest point he'd ever sunk to were wiped away. They were both dressed in white; Lucky in a soft, flowing white dress that moved like silk in the slight breeze from the water, while he wore a lightweight cotton shirt and slacks. They were each shoeless; sand was underfoot.

Lucky suddenly skipped ahead of him and William ran to catch up to her. Her jubilant laughter floated on the air, caressing his senses like a lover of old. Yet to his dismay, the more he tried to close the distance between them, the wider the chasm became.

From out of nowhere, there appeared a precipice and Lucky was carelessly dancing along it. She called to him, "Look, William, I'm on a tightrope."

Suddenly, without warning the sky began to darken and the tropical birds became black crows swooping and swirling around her.

"Be careful, Lucky," he called to her, but her reply was pulled away by the sudden wind.

Finally, close enough to take her hand, he reached for her.

"Honey, come down," he pleaded in a fearful voice.

"Look, William, I'm on a tightrope," she repeated in a childlike tone.

Her arms outstretched as if on a balancing beam, she continued along the edge.

Fear gripped William's heart like a vise when he noticed the large black bird heading straight for her.

She saw it at the same time and William witnessed the trepidation that flashed across her face as he reached for her hand.

Dipping close enough to feel the wind as it whipped by, the bird sped between them, jarring Lucky and sending her off balance.

"William!" she screamed as she began to fall.

Jumping to catch her, he cried, "Lucky!" but all he caught hold of was her dress as the thin fabric ripped in his hand. Tears streamed from his eyes as he clung to all that remained of his love.

Fully awakened from his nightmare, William suddenly realized that the tears were not just a part of his dream.

Is she in danger?

Unwilling to acknowledge the truth that something inside of him had turned on when he met Linda Woodson last Sunday on that bench in Hoboken, William realized that he'd broken the promise he'd made himself, that he would not give in to it again.

But she'd touched his heart.

Recalling his first vision of her, singing off-key to what he now knew was a Luther Vandross hit with her sweet, sensuous hips swaying in time to the melody. The easy conversation they'd shared—despite his frequent attempts to cut it off—and her knowledge of sports combined to pique his interest, inciting his desire to know more about her. Surprised by the generosity she'd displayed in buying him drinks before inviting him to her home where she had actually cooked and fed him, William still could not fathom anyone being so open and honest. That was his play.

He couldn't remember a time in his life when a woman had offered herself— her inner self—so freely without seeking some sort of reward in return, but Lucky had asked nothing of him but that he relax. It was that very openness that spurred his impulsive assault on her. Brushing aside her initial resistance, she had quickly succumbed to what became the most impetuously torrid affair of his life.

As he tried to slow the tempestuous beating of his heart, William puzzled over the meaning of his nightmare.

Call her.

Wanting to ignore the pervasive urging that overwhelmed his thoughts, William knew the only way he would be satisfied was by biting the bullet and making the call.

Returning to his prone position, Lucky stayed with him in spite of all attempts to banish her from his mind. As if she was there with him, he suddenly felt her soft lips brush against his as her flowing locs tickled the skin of his chest. His erection was instantaneous as the memory of her capturing and detaining him while he drowned in her sweet nectar moved to the forefront of his mind. Suddenly she was there, massaging him with a skilled hand, eventually blessing him with a delightful pay-off.

"Damn!" he swore.

Wiping away the sticky solution that escaped him, all he'd succeeded in doing was messing up his already soaked undershirt.

I guess I'd better make that call before I lose my mind was the last thing he thought before falling back into a restless sleep.

SEVEN

Saturday morning, Linda rose with the sun. Having been safely sequestered in the room she had claimed as her own in Josie and Carl's beautiful four-bedroom home in Marlboro, New York, she'd had plenty of time to consider the happenings of the last week.

Not trusting Linda to be at home alone, Josie insisted—brooking no argument or discussion—that she stay with her and Carl for the next couple of days so they could keep an eye on her. After her short hospital stay, Linda was eager to get back to her own apartment, but she knew it would just be easier for everyone if she humored Josie and stayed with them Thursday and Friday nights. Besides, since Josie was hosting their annual sorors summer get-together Saturday afternoon, it was more convenient for her to be there anyway. She'd have one of the girls give her a lift home Saturday night when their gathering ended.

Josie and Carl had only moved into their custom-built Cape Cod–style home ten months earlier. Having gone through much of the planning and building process with them, Linda felt like she was truly a part of the family. Since Carl had left the interior designing and layout of the house to Josie's discretion, Linda had been instrumental in helping her pick the color palette, carpeting, kitchen and bathroom cabinetry, among other aspects of their spacious abode.

Josie had even gone so far as to let Linda select the furnishings for the room she'd slept in. The bleached oak Shaker-style furnishings—four-poster bed, matching side tables, armoire and mirrored dresser accented with brushed steel handles—were highlighted by the beautiful violet, lavender and mint-green hues that dominated the room. From the mint waffle-weave draperies banded with purple satin cord to the tapestry and satin violet and lavender pillows resting atop a mint woven coverlet, textural contrast as complex as Linda herself could be seen throughout the guest room. A polished steel table lamp with a translucent cloud glass shade adorned each of the side bed tables. Plush tightly woven carpeting in a pale purple hue was underfoot.

Standing in a Pittsburgh Steelers nightgown in front of the windows that cornered the room, Linda viewed the spacious backyard, complete with jungle gym and swing set belonging to her two rambunctious godchildren, CJ and Crystal, Carl and Josie's eleven-year-old twins. Usually by this time, although it was still early, the house would have been filled with the sound of Saturday morning cartoons floating up from the fifty-two-inch HD television adorning one wall of the family room downstairs. This morning, however, since the twins were visiting with Carl's parents in Atlanta for the next two weeks, the place was noticeably silent.

Linda didn't want to admit that she was afraid. Although since Wednesday, she hadn't experienced the excruciating pain that had overtaken all of her senses, the looks on the doctors' and technicians' faces as she'd gone through the barrage of tests they'd subjected her to, were no comfort. They knew something was wrong but told her they needed definitive answers before they could reveal anything to her.

Monday was the day when everything would be brought to light. She had a 10:00 a.m. appointment with Dr. Everett, her internist. All of the results from the tests taken during her ordeal would be passed along to him.

Suddenly, her thoughts returned to Wednesday night when Emerson and Josie had entered the cubicle in the trauma center of NYU's emergency room.

"What are you doing here?" she remembered asking him first off.

"Josie called me," had been his response.

She'd wanted to strangle Josie in those few seconds.

Seeing Emerson brought back all the hurt she'd encountered when their relationship came to its abrupt end. She was immediately reminded of her shortcomings—he wanted a child and she would never be able to give him one.

Was it selfish of her to want him to give up his dream of fatherhood, simply because she couldn't make it come true? She knew it was, but it didn't make her sorrow any lighter. Linda had pictured their future together. She had begun to build her hopes around him and he'd brought them all crashing to the ground.

Linda had not missed the sadness on his face that night in the hospital, no matter how much she wanted to disregard it. In spite of their present state, he was afraid for her, too.

When he held her hand and promised to be with her, no matter what her diagnosis turned out to be, Linda was unable to stifle the tears that welled in her eyes. *Why couldn't you be there when I really needed you? When you knew I loved you and ached because I would never be able to bear your child. Why couldn't you be there for me then?* Those questions begged for release from her core, but she couldn't voice them. Emerson had never been a heartless man. Deep down, she knew rehashing their past would only bring him pain, and regardless of her own, she could not callously hurt him.

Thinking of her relationship with Emerson brought another man to mind. William McCall. What was the real story with him, she wondered. Linda couldn't remember much after the theater and before Josie and Emerson appeared at her bedside, but she clearly recalled the sight of William working the fry machine at McDonald's.

Is that why he hasn't called? Is he ashamed of what he does? Is it because he's down on his luck that he has decided to ignore what we shared? Linda surmised that he had to be struggling to be working a minimum wage job in a very busy location in midtown. He was too intelligent, she kept telling herself, to be no more ambitiously inclined.

It was agonizing, remembering the way he'd held her and kissed her and sent her soaring to heights never before achieved during their brief encounter. Her body still aching from his tender yet urgent touch, her loins tingled from the memory of his strong, deep and steady strokes. That man was in pain, too. She knew it, but why? What had happened to him to bring him so low?

Regretting not following her gut and addressing him when she saw him working the fries, that might have been too embarrassing for him, she thought.

She didn't want to cause him any undue anxiety. At the same time, she didn't appreciate his silence either. *It's not like I've asked him for anything.*

His abrupt departure came to mind suddenly. When she'd given him the out, telling him he wasn't obligated to stay, he'd jumped at the opportunity to leave. *Was that because he was sorry he'd let it get so out of hand, or was there another reason?*

The questions piled up, one upon the other, over and over until a mountain of them prompted a heaviness in her heart she was all too familiar with. She'd given too much of herself, too fast, once again.

A soft knock on the bedroom door put an end to her solemn contemplation. Putting on a cheerful face, she called out, "Come on in, Josie."

The door opened slightly at first, but when Josie saw that Linda was up, she pushed it fully opened and walked in.

"You're up early. Couldn't you sleep?"

"Oh, yeah, I slept fine. I'm just enjoying the view. I love my room," Linda said, smiling playfully.

"Well, you should. You decorated it."

"I need to hook up my bedroom at home like this, but I still wouldn't have the great view."

"Yeah, this room gets the most light, too, what with these windows cornering it."

"What time are the girls expected?" Linda asked, turning away from the window.

"About two. I've got everything set up already, too, so we can just take it easy until they get here. I figured we'd have lunch out on the deck, then, if they want to, we could move to the gazebo for coffee and dessert."

"That sounds good. Y'all definitely did the right thing when you added that. I love gazebos. When and if I ever get married or buy a house, I'm definitely going to have one in my backyard," Linda stated.

"I hear you. Carl and I christened it when we got it. The kids were upstairs in bed and we went out there in the middle of the night and got busy," Josie revealed with a wicked grin as she plopped down on the soft queen-sized mattress.

"The bugs weren't biting?" Linda asked.

"That thing's screened in." Josie laughed outright. "We woulda been some bit asses if it wasn't."

"I know that's right," Linda agreed, laughing.

"Hey, Lucky, you still mad 'cause I called Emerson the other night?"

Taking a seat next to Josie on the bed, Linda thought for a moment before responding. "No. I'm glad he was there. He said he'd come with me Monday morning to my doctor's office."

"I'll go with you."

"I can't have you taking off again, girl. You've gone above and beyond the call of friendship, Josie, and I really appreciate it. I don't know what I would've done if you hadn't been with me the other night. I cringe when I think that it could have happened in the subway or even on the street. Emerson owes me. Let him handle this one. Besides, if I pass out from what they're going to tell me, at least he's big enough to catch me before I hit the ground," Linda said with a chuckle she didn't really feel.

"Stop thinking negative," Josie said, fear evident on her face.

"I can't help it. Contrary to my nickname, I don't seem to be very lucky."

"I'm not listening to this," Josie said as she rose from the bed and started toward the door.

"Okay, wait. I'm just kidding," Linda softly intoned.

Turning back to face her, Josie assured her, "You're going to be alright."

Linda's head bobbed, almost imperceptibly. "I'm scared, Josie." When she lifted her head and looked into her best friend's eyes, there were tears.

Josie hurried to her side and wrapped her in a fierce embrace. "We're going to have a prayer circle this afternoon. I'm going to invoke the power of God to come down and handle this, Lucky. The sisters and I will see you through, whatever the case may be, but we're going to think positive, right?"

Linda was comforted by Josie's warm hug. Reciprocating and silently thanking God for her friendship, Linda agreed, "Right!"

❦❦

It was four-fifteen and the sorors were lounging around the impeccably designed family room of Josie's house. They had just finished eating a sumptuous smorgasbord of scintillating snacks ranging from catfish fritters and steamed mussels to bacon-wrapped asparagus spears and sautéed eggplant, to name a few.

Contrary to her plans, a sudden rainstorm prevented them from enjoying their afternoon meal on the deck of her home. And since they would have had to run through the rain to get to the covered gazebo, they opted to take coffee and dessert in the family room.

"Josie, girl, you put your foot in that shrimp salad," Alexis, the robust, dark chocolate sister from Philly, stated while loosening the waistband of her slacks.

"You definitely did," Marcia agreed. This voluptuous, chestnut-colored vixen and Josie had been roommates at SUNY New Paltz.

"Thanks. That was Carl's mother's recipe," Josie informed them.

"So mother-in-laws are good for something after all, huh?" Shari, the tall, lusciously-leggy fashion-plate, said with a smirk.

"Now that wasn't nice, Shari. You're going to be a mother-in-law someday, or have you forgotten?" Josie asked.

"Right, with that fine son you've got, I'm surprised he hasn't been snatched up yet," Alexis chimed in.

"Yes, little brother certainly is gifted in the looks department. Too bad he's so young. I'd have given those little hoochies a run for their money," Elise, the youngest of the group, added with a snicker.

"Y'all better take your minds off my boy. He's too good for all of y'all anyway." Shari chuckled.

"How old is your son, now, Shari?" Lucky asked.

"Twenty-one."

"Little brotha's legal. Woo-hoo!" Marcia cried boisterously.

The women laughed.

"What's he doing? Is he still in school?" she asked.

"No. He graduated earlier this year and accepted a position at a large investment firm in Atlanta. He's making close to forty-thousand dollars a year already," Shari proudly boasted.

"Oh yeah, you know these young hotties are going to be all over that boy. He's fine and he's going to be making big bucks, too," Marcia stated.

"Please, I've already let him know to watch his back. I told him to make sure he doesn't let his libido get him messed up in no baby's mama drama."

"You know, looks and money are not everything," Lucky softly intoned.

"In what world?" Alexis boldly challenged.

"What happens when the looks fade and the money's all used up? If the man has no substance, what are you left with?" she asked.

"A reason to get another man," Alexis answered in a matter-of-fact manner.

Lucky frowned and shook her head.

"You're right, Lucky. A brotha's got to have more going on than a nice bank account and a *GQ* cover face," Elise added.

"You can say that, E, but I noticed that Brian is no slouch in the looks department and if I remember correctly, he hooked you up with those wheels you've got parked outside," Alexis pointed out.

"Yeah, that's true, but when Brian and I met, he was fresh out of college and didn't have anything. I didn't marry him because he looked good or because he had money-making potential. I married him because he has a heart of gold, and I was attracted to him on multiple levels. We connected mentally, emotionally, physically and spiritually before we ever made it financially. I know I've got a gem in Brian, but if he lost his job and wasn't making money anymore, I'd be there to pick up the slack in a heartbeat because he's worth so much more to me than what he's got in the bank."

"Well, give her a gold star," Alexis sarcastically stated.

"I'd want my man to have some money in the bank, too," Marcia said. "A good heart is great, but that's not going to keep food on the table or a roof over my head. Been there, done that…and definitely not interested in replaying the tape."

"Yeah, a man's got to be able to take care of me, better than I can take care of myself," added Shari.

"You know, there's a potential downfall in having a man with globs of money. In some instances, he can be very controlling," Josie warned.

"He can control me any way he wants to, as long as he's footing all expenses," Marcia commented.

"So you're saying that if you knew a good man, who'd fallen on hard times and he couldn't take you out and spend money on you with wild abandon, you wouldn't have the time of day for him?" Lucky asked.

"Not until he got himself back together," Shari answered. "Maybe I'm from the old school. I like to know that a man can handle his business."

"That's right," Marcia agreed. "Why should I have to deal with him while he's going through his hard times? I have to worry about myself. I can't be worrying about him, too; always hitting me up for money and stuff."

"What? Am I supposed to buy his clothes and feed him, too?" Alexis asked with an indignant attitude.

"What's so wrong with doing something for your man that he might not be able to do for himself?" Elise asked. "I mean, I can see if he's not trying to do anything for himself. If he's sitting on his ass till noon every day while I'm busting my butt…No, I wouldn't be trying to take care of no bums, either. But I'm talking about a man who, through no fault of his own, is struggling, trying to get himself back on his feet. You're telling me you wouldn't give him a hand up?"

"That's right!" Josie emphatically stated.

Elise, shaking her head, continued, "That's what's wrong with black people today. We're so busy looking out for ourselves, that we won't even take the time to help one another out. You wonder why every other nationality can open businesses in our neighborhoods and succeed? It's because they insist on helping each other. They won't hire a black person to work in their businesses if one of their own needs a job. Everyone looks out for themselves except us."

"I'm talking about taking care of a man, not black people, per se," Alexis defensively commented.

"What difference should it make if it's a man or a woman? We were made to help one another. Women were made to be a man's help mate. Why do you think there are so many single women in the world today, single black women? Because we're so eager to show the world that we can do everything for ourselves, that we don't need anyone and we're not trying to help anyone who isn't trying to first help us," Lucky countered.

"The problem with most of these trifling niggas today is that too many of them are satisfied with sitting back and accepting help from someone else instead of trying to help themselves. They're always making excuses about the white man did this, and the white man did that. We're in the twenty-first century, for crying out loud. How long are we going to blame the white man for everything that ails us?" Marcia indignantly argued.

"All men don't complain about the white man. There are some brothers who are working hard, trying to get their lives together but no one ever gives them the time of day. And yeah, it may be two thousand six but there's still plenty of racism going on in these not yet United States. Why shouldn't we, as black women, do everything in our power to help our black men make it in this world? Our female ancestors may have been forced to raise their families because their men were taken from them or even killed, but they never just turned their backs on them. They knew how difficult it was for them in this white man's world and they did everything they could to make the men feel powerful, even if it meant taking a backseat to their man's needs. They supported one another. We don't do that anymore. Everyone is out for self and until we, as a people, male or female, figure out that the only way we will ever succeed at anything or be taken serious about anything is when we start sticking together, we will always be seen as the minority," Josie definitively stated.

"Yeah, well, you can believe that if you want to," Shari said with a shrug. "That's why I only date white guys, so I don't have to deal with all that crap. My man's going to always have money in the bank and if he can't take care of me and give me what I want, then he can keep right on walking."

"Your son's father's not white," Linda pointed out.

"My son's father is a trifling, no-good so and so who can't and won't do like he should for his five children. I don't need that. His best feature was his dick and that probably ain't saying much of nothing these days, either," Shari coldly decried.

"What about your son, Shari?" Elise asked. "Is that the way you want him to think you feel about black men. He's one of them, remember?"

"I'm not talking about my son…"

"Yeah, but when you make blanket statements like the ones y'all have made," said Linda, addressing Shari, Marcia and Alexis, "you're lumping him right in with the group. People who hear you speaking that way will never have to wonder why we're always looked at with derision. When you shit in your own backyard, why would anyone else want to play there?"

"Bottom line is this, Lucky," Shari said, "I want a man that has a job that allows him to pay his bills..."

"And yours, too. You can admit it. Your secret's safe with us," Lucky cracked.

"That would be nice, too," Marcia added, eliciting a collective laugh from the sisters.

"All I know is that I'm at a point in my life where I want a man who is bringing as much to the table as I am," Alexis announced. "And I'm definitely bringing more to the table than hamburgers and French fries."

From across the room, Josie and Lucky locked eyes. The expression on their faces spoke the same language.

If only they knew. If only they knew.

EIGHT

It was a beautiful Sunday afternoon and Linda was glad to be home. While her short stay with Josie had been relaxing and enjoyable, she was always happy to fall asleep in her own bed.

Returning to her peaceful haven—the pier at Hoboken—Linda took a seat in the same area she had first encountered William McCall.

Refusing to dwell on what might have been with them, she now had more pressing matters to contend with—her as-of-yet unknown diagnosis. *What are they going to tell me tomorrow?*

Emerson had promised to pick her up in the morning and accompany her to the office. Since he had his own investigative business now, he could make his own hours and come and go as he pleased.

I wish William was coming with me instead.

Where did that thought come from?

It hurt that he'd never bothered to call her, although she would never admit that out loud. And despite his thoughtlessness, she wanted to see him, if only to talk to him; to find out what had happened. By now, she was fairly certain that he must have had some type of life-altering occurrence in the past year or so. What other explanation could there be for a man of his intelligence to settle for a minimum wage job at any fast-food joint? The whole thing seemed bizarre, incomprehensible. It wasn't like he was the manager or something—he was a fry cook. It just didn't make any sense.

This train of thought carried her back to the animated conversation with her line sisters yesterday. Shaking her head incredulously, she couldn't believe how shallow some of their opinions were. These were established, educated women, who, like Linda, were in their mid-forties and pretty much settled. And it pained her to think in some instances, they were still little girls. But then her mother always said, "They don't give diplomas for common sense. If they did, very few people would have one."

Josie had teased her about bringing the subject of William up with them, but Linda was relieved she hadn't. She sensed that Josie, although always keeping Linda's best interests at heart, knew after listening to them, that these women would never understand and might even look down on her for what she'd allowed to transpire between them. The last thing she needed in the midst of her troubles was a cat fight, because some of their comments had really ticked her off.

William had been disappointed that when he'd finally gotten up the courage to call Linda—first on Thursday, again on Friday and, lastly, on Saturday— he'd been unsuccessful in catching up with her. Opting not to leave a message any of the times he'd called, he felt safe assuming she wouldn't bother trying to call him back since the number was a foreign one to her.

He didn't know what he would say to her, anyway. How could he explain the reason for not calling when he was unsure of what that reason was? Conflicted, he couldn't tell her he was afraid of what he felt for her. She'd never believe it, or worse, if she did, she'd think he was a punk. But the thought of her scared the hell out of him. In those few short hours, she had put some kind of hoodoo on him. He could not get her out of his system.

Venturing, once again to Hoboken, he waffled. Hoping their paths would cross, on the other hand, the thought of that had given him pause and he'd actually considered if it was a smart move when he arrived at the PATH station that early afternoon.

Upon his arrival, instead of heading toward the pier, he turned in the opposite direction, down Washington Street. The variety of restaurants, shops and assorted businesses were buzzing with activity. Unable to do anything but window shop, William meandered from block to block trying to build up enough courage to hazard a walk toward their meeting place.

"Man up, Black!" he could imagine Steve saying if he knew how hesitant he was being about confronting Linda again.

Creating an emotional filibuster with his indecision, he should have done just as his friend said, call her or forget about her. The latter, he now realized was not even an option. She was permanently soldered in his mind. At least he could say he called her. But, where had she been? Maybe she was seeing someone else, after all.

Yeah, he decided, that was probably the case. Why should he take her at her word simply because she claimed there was no one else in her life? Hadn't he made that mistake before? *When are you going to learn? Women can't be trusted.*

Convincing himself that it was better with things as they were between them, William turned and started back toward the PATH station.

To hell with Lucky. Like Jay-Z said, "I got ninety-nine problems, but a bitch ain't one anymore."

❦❦

A couple of hours had passed and Linda was strolling down Washington Street, trying to decide whether to stop and get a bite to eat or head straight home when she saw him. He was across the street looking into the window of a jewelry store. He was wearing the same jeans and polo shirt he'd been wearing last week. *Does he live here in Hoboken?* No, she kind of remembered him telling her that he lived in New York. *Could he be here looking for me? Was he on his way to the pier hoping to run into me as he had before?* Well, she was going to save him the trouble.

Crossing the street as soon as the light changed to green, William still hadn't noticed her. He had resumed his stroll, absently window shopping as he moved along. She couldn't help but notice the somewhat downtrodden look on his face. That didn't temper her greeting one bit.

"William!"

Turning immediately at hearing his name, Lucky witnessed the surprise and trepidation that flashed across William's face before he pulled the shade, cutting off the view into the windows of his soul.

"Hello, Lucky."

"Fancy meeting you here. Where you headed?" she boldly asked.

"Nowhere in particular. Just strolling."

"You mean you weren't hoping to run into me here in Hoboken?" Lucky brazenly asked in true form.

"No. Why would you think that?"

He's such a horrible liar, she thought. "I thought I would have heard from you. I mean, you weren't under any obligation to call me or anything, but I thought we had a nice time together. I was looking forward to seeing you again."

"I'm sorry I haven't called. I've been really busy."

"Oh yeah. Busy doing what?" she inquired.

"Just trying to handle my business."

With a cynical nod, "Wanna get a drink?" she asked.

"No, thanks."

He couldn't tell her he couldn't afford to buy either of them a drink.

"My treat," she added.

"You've already done way too much for me as it is."

"I did what I wanted to do. I wasn't forced."

"I know and I appreciate that. Really, I do, but I can't let you spend any more of your money on me."

"Can I ask you a personal question?" Lucky pondered aloud.

Feeling as though his heart was going to explode from his chest in a fireball, William reluctantly replied, "Sure."

"What kind of work do you do?"

"Why?" he asked with a frown.

"Just curious."

"I have a job, if that's what you're wondering," William defensively stated.

"That's not what I'm wondering. I know you have a job. You don't really fit the profile of a bum. I merely want to know what you do. That's not too strange a question to ask, is it? I mean, people ask each other about their jobs all the time, right?"

William sighed. "I work in the food industry."

"In a restaurant?"

"Y-yes."

"How long have you been in the food industry?" she next posed.

"Why?"

"Not only am I lucky, William, I'm also curious. I mean, don't I have some right to know?"

"How do you figure?"

"You've been to my home—I don't just let anyone into my home. You've eaten my food, which I was happy to share with you and you've... well, you've seen parts of my anatomy only a few other privileged folks have had the pleasure to view. I've shared more of myself with you than you have with me. I'm merely trying to even the score."

The insecurity in William rose as high as his wall of mystery.

"Look, I didn't ask you for anything so I don't owe you anything," he stated a bit more contemptuously than he intended to.

Startled, Linda was clearly taken aback by his hostile tone. "Did I do something to you?"

"What?"

"I didn't stutter. I asked you if I had done something to you because you're talking to me like I wronged you or something."

William hissed between his teeth and waved her off before he said, "I don't have time for this."

When he turned to walk away from her, Linda grabbed his arm. "Well, you're going to make time!"

Looking at her as if she had lost her natural mind, William opened his mouth to speak but before he could utter a sound she raged.

"Who the hell do you think I am? No. Who the hell do you think *you* are? I'm not some little chicken-head you can talk to any damn way you want to. If you don't want anything to do with me, William, that's fine, but you will NOT disrespect me. I don't know what kind of women you're used to dealing with, but I am not the one! I know you didn't ask me for anything and I don't remember asking you for anything in return. Forgive me for trying to be a friend to your tired ass!" Rolling her eyes as she sucked her teeth, she lowered the boom. "Food industry, my ass. You work at McDonald's."

Unable to hide the shock at her discovery, William suddenly felt ashamed. His wall came crashing down on top of his fear.

"Yeah, that's right! I *know* where you work, but that really doesn't matter to me. I try to offer you a hand up and what do I get? A kick in the face. Well, fuck you, William, and the horse you rode in on! You won't ever have to worry about me bothering you again. Have a great fucking life!"

With that, Linda turned and started to stomp off.

Feeling every word as if she had been shooting them from a .44 magnum, William was ripped apart.

"Lucky, wait," he called after her, but she didn't slow her pace or turn.

Hurrying after her, he reached for her hand to halt her stride.

Yanking away, she yelled, "Leave me alone!"

But he wouldn't. He couldn't. Stepping in front of her, he noticed her tears. His mortification was complete.

"I'm sorry."

"No kidding?" she spat.

Unable to speak under the weight of his own self-reproach, William's own eyes began to water.

"I didn't mean to hurt you, Lucky. Please. Let me try to explain," he begged.

"Explain? How can you explain why you were so rude to me just now? How do you expect to explain that?"

"I... It was... I was embarrassed."

"Why?"

"Because I hadn't called you. Because I... I don't have anything to offer you."

"I didn't ask you for anything. I just... Ohh!"

The pain that cut through her at that instant was excruciating. Her arms encircled her waist as her knees began to buckle beneath her. In a flash, William caught her in his arms before she went down.

"Linda! What's wrong?" he asked in alarm.

She couldn't even tell him. Her agony was too great.

"Linda!"

Not knowing what else to do, he lifted her in his arms and moved to the unoccupied bench at the bus stop a few feet away. Cradling her against his chest as she sat atop his lap, he held her, rocking her, trying to soothe her misery; the cause of which he did not know.

They sat that way for close to ten minutes without a word passing between them but their communication was crystal clear. Her body was tense, letting him know that her agony had not abated. For Linda, William's touch was compassionate, caring and comforting.

Short minutes later, Linda pushed away from him and tried to stand.

"Are you okay?" William asked with genuine concern.

"Yes," she answered, clearly embarrassed about being forced to lean on him.

"What's the matter with you, Linda? What's causing your pain?"

"I don't know."

"You should see someone about it. That's not normal," he urgently insisted.

"I know it's not normal," she angrily responded. "I should find out tomorrow."

"What do you mean?"

"I'm going to see my doctor in the morning and he's… I'll get the test results then."

"What tests? When did you have tests taken?"

"Look, I don't want to talk about it. I'm going home."

Turning to start away from him, William stopped her by clamping onto her wrist.

"I'm not going to let you walk home alone in your condition."

"What condition? I'm fine now," she argued.

"And what if you get another attack like that? You were going down, Lucky. You think I'm going to take a chance and have you pass out in the middle of the street? No! I won't. Now, you can argue, fuss, whatever… Call me names, I don't care, but you are not walking home by yourself."

"You know you can be a real pain in the ass," she said with a sneer.

"Get used to it. I'm going to be a pain in your ass until you get yourself right."

"Fine, if you want to walk me home you can, but after that you can go on about your business like you wanted to anyway."

"Okay, okay, I was a dick. I messed up. I'm sorry. My issues have nothing to do with you and I was wrong to take them out on you. I hope you'll forgive me and give me a chance to show you that while I may be a little touched in the head, I'm a pretty decent guy," William stated with a smile.

Unable to resist even his minute amount of charm on display at the moment, Linda tried to suppress the smile she felt building in her heart, but it showed in her eyes.

"Thank you for everything you've done for me, Lucky. With the way my life has been going, you're the first bright spot I've seen in over a year." The emotion in William's voice was evident and his beautiful brown eyes revealed a hurt that Linda had only witnessed in some of her worst home care cases.

"Seems we both have demons to deal with, huh?" she softly intoned.

William nodded.

"Maybe we can exorcise them together. I'll let you help me, if you let me help you."

"I don't do 'accepting help' from folks very well. I find that when I depend on myself, I'm the only one who can let me down," William admitted.

"Well, that's just something you're going to have to get over, now isn't it?" Linda brusquely stated.

"You know, you don't always have to be so snippy."

"And you don't always have to be so proud."

He huffed with humor. "We've got work to do, don't we?"

"I'd say so. Shall we get started?"

NINE

"Hello."

"Hi. How're you doing, Linda?"

"Better, thanks."

"What time do you want me there tomorrow morning?"

"Oh. You don't have to come, Emerson. Thanks."

"How are you getting there?"

"I'm taking the train, but I won't be alone."

"Josie's going with you, huh?"

"No."

"Your parents came up?"

"No. I haven't spoken to them about it. They don't know what happened."

"So who's going with you?"

"A friend."

Unaccustomed to her uncommon evasiveness, his pride took a hit. "What friend?"

"You don't know him."

Him? "Where was your friend while you were in the hospital last week?"

"Emerson, I'm not going to do this with you."

"Look, Linda, I'm not trying to tell you what to do or anything, but don't you think it would be better if someone who really cared about you was there with you?"

"Why do you assume he doesn't care? You don't even know him."

"I know he was nowhere around Wednesday night or Thursday, for that matter."

"He wasn't available."

"If he cared about you, he would have made himself available in your time of need. Where'd you meet this cat?" he possessively asked.

"I don't have to give you any information about him or anyone else in my life. You are no longer my man, Emerson, and you're certainly not my father so you can save that tone of voice for your baby's mama."

Ignoring the snipe, he backtracked. "Linda, I'm concerned about you. I just want to make sure everything is okay with you."

You didn't care whether I was okay when you dropped me for someone who could give you children, she thought, but said, "I'll be fine, thank you. Now if you don't mind, I have company. I have to go."

She heard his deep sigh through the line.

"I'll give you a call tomorrow night, okay?" he persisted.

Exhaling deeply, she replied, "Whatever. Good-bye."

Hanging up the phone without waiting for his closing salutation, Lucky shook her head. *Now that he thinks there's someone else, he wants to make sure I'm okay.*

"Are you like that, William?" she asked.

"Like what?" he asked.

"Do you cut a woman off, then, when you think someone else in interested, you want to know the who, what, when, where and why?"

"I guess that was your ex-boyfriend, huh?"

"Very ex."

"It's an ego thing, Lucky. A man always wants to know if the man who follows in his footsteps is good enough."

"Why should it matter to him if I wasn't important enough for him to stick around?"

"I know it makes no sense, but what about love and relationships does?" William asked.

"This is all Josie's fault."

"Who's Josie?"

"My best friend. She called Emerson the other night when I passed out."

That bulletin shocked William. "You passed out? When? Where?"

"Oh yeah, I didn't tell you about that," she said, regretting her slip of the lip.

"No, you conveniently forgot to mention that," he sarcastically replied.

Cutting her eyes at him she said, "There's no need for the sarcasm."

"What happened?"

Linda relayed the events of the previous Wednesday evening, beginning with her witnessing him at work.

"So why would your friend call him? She knows you guys aren't seeing each other anymore, right?"

"Of course she knows, but she was afraid and couldn't get in touch with her husband. She knew if she called Emerson, he'd be there," Linda admitted.

"So what happened between you two?" he wanted to know.

"I don't want to go into it."

"It seems I'm not the only one with a problem letting go."

"I'm not holding on to anything with him."

"Sure you are. He hurt you. I don't know how, but I'm certain he did, and you haven't gotten over it. You're on the defensive."

"How do you figure that?" she asked.

"Your… outward bravado—for lack of a better word—is a shield. As long as you're the initiator, you're in control. You can determine how soon, how much and how far. When you feel your shield slipping, instead of holding on tighter, you let go before they can."

"Is that what you think I did with you?"

"To an extent, yeah."

"But, remember, I didn't have any way to contact you. You're the one who didn't call me."

"I did call, Lucky. I called you Thursday, Friday and Saturday. You weren't around any of those days and I chose not to leave a message."

"I got out of the hospital Thursday and Josie made me stay with her and her husband when I got out. I was there until last night. Why didn't you leave me a message with your number?"

"Honestly, because I didn't know what to say to you. I didn't know what you were thinking about last week or about me, in general. I knew I was in no position to be the man you deserve, and, well…"

"All I wanted was your friendship, William."

"I know that now." An easy silence lay between them for a few minutes. "Does Josie know about me?" he finally asked.

"Yes."

"I guess she must think I'm some sort of loser, huh?"

"No. Why would you say that?"

"She was with you the other night in McDonald's, right?"

"Yeah, but… She's not like that."

Another pause in their conversation prompted Linda to ask, "What happened, William?"

"What do you mean?" Looking into her eyes, he understood without her having to explain. "Oh. You mean why am I working as a fry cook in McDonald's at forty years of age?"

"Yeah."

"I was accused of doing something that I'm totally innocent of, costing me my job and my reputation. With no income, I lost my apartment."

Sensing that he was holding something back, she let it pass, instead asking, "Don't you have family in the area?"

"Yeah, but they've all got their own issues, so I didn't want to burden them with mine."

"Where are you staying?"

William lowered his head in humiliation. "In a shelter in Brooklyn," he answered, barely above a whisper.

Placing her hand tenderly on his shoulder, Linda said, "Oh, honey. You can't stay there anymore."

Looking over at her, he asked, "I have to. I don't have enough to get my own place yet. I'm trying to save up enough to get a room in a boarding house or something, but until then… It's not so bad. I have my own space there. It's not like… like I'm in a barracks."

"William, I work for Social Services. I know what those shelters look like, even the ones with private rooms. They're not much more than walk-in closets."

"That's my only option, right now, Lucky, but I'm cool with it."

"You're going to stay here."

"No, I'm not."

"Yes, you are."

"No, I can't."

"Yes, you can. I have a spare bedroom. It'll be much more comfortable than that little room you have."

"Lucky, I can't afford that right now," William painfully admitted.

"I didn't ask you for rent. You can pay me by helping out around the house. I have some work that I want to do here, but I don't have the muscles needed to do it all. You can help me with that. And it would be nice to have some company around here. I get tired of coming home and talking to myself all the time."

Trembling with emotion, William's eyes began to water. "I can't let you do that."

"Why?"

Lowering his head once more, crystal tear drops hit the carpeted floor. "I just can't."

Moving next to him on her plush sofa, she put a companionable arm across his shoulder and pulled him closer. "Stop fighting it, William. You need me and I need you."

"Why are you doing this?" he asked, unable to stifle the flow.

"I have to. I don't know why, but I have to."

"I've never met anyone like you, Lucky," he told her.

"Likewise, I'm sure. Are you always so sensitive?"

"My one flaw," he tried to joke.

She smiled and said, "It's not a flaw. It makes you very special."

"Yellow bus special, right?"

In her best Hindi accent, she comically replied, "Jimmy no live here! Jimmy no live here!"

Their mutual laughter broke the ice.

"Let's watch a movie," Linda suggested.

"What do you have in mind?"

"Do you like Spencer and Kate?"

William's eyes lit up like a kid. "Tracy and Hepburn? Who doesn't?"

"I'm so glad you didn't say Spencer and Kate, who?" Linda rose excitedly. "I'ma make some popcorn," she announced, pointing in the direction of her vast menagerie of movies. "They're on the top shelf."

Obliging, William moved to the rack and selected *Pat and Mike*. "Should I set it up?"

"Yeah, the popcorn will be done in a minute."

Ninety-three minutes later, the sports promoter (Tracy) and all-around female athlete (Hepburn) realized their unlikely romance; an irony not lost on the odd couple viewing the feature. As the credits began to roll, Linda turned to William and in her best Katharine Hepburn voice said, "What would I have done if you hadn't been around?"

Seamlessly following her lead, William, imitating Tracy, said, "I think you can take care of yourself."

"No, I can't."

"Ah, yeah, I bet you could even lick me," he said.

"No, I can't."

"Sure, you could."

"I need someone to look after me," said Linda, quoting Hepburn's line from the movie.

"What about me?" William said, continuing their charade.

"Why not?"

He paused momentarily, as Tracy did before continuing, "Well, I don't know if I could lick you or you could lick me, but one thing I do know, together we could lick 'em all."

"Do you think we can, William?" she softly stated with a seriousness that took all of the play out of their game.

Pausing again, he smiled with a truth he had never known before. "Yeah, I think we can. You wanna know why?"

"Why?" she eagerly inquired.

"'Cause I'm feeling lucky."

Agitated with a disturbing feeling he never experienced before, Emerson was not pleased about Linda's brush-off last night. Despite the fact that he was in a relationship with a woman who was carrying his child, a sense of propriety had returned when he learned that Linda had fallen ill.

While his concern was genuine—it was important that he know she was alright—he could not quell the jealousy that raged in his heart upon learning that another man was seeing to her welfare. After all, he thought, why hadn't Josie called that man on Wednesday night? If he was so important to her, why hadn't he made the time to see about her?

Emerson knew the way he'd ended things with Linda was wrong. He should have never gone behind her back with Candace, but when she revealed that she was pregnant, he knew he couldn't string Linda along anymore. Selfishly, he wasn't satisfied having his cake and not being able to eat it, too.

That being the case, he found himself parked in a gray BMW on her block Monday morning, waiting to see who this mystery man was that was coming to pick her up and take her to her appointment.

The shock at witnessing Linda emerge from her apartment with a man already in tow was more than he could bear. Using the telephoto lens on his digital camera, Emerson snapped a close-up of the man's face. *I'll find out everything I need to know about this clown. He'd better represent.*

The ebullient high from the previous night continued to surround Linda and William Monday morning. Rising fairly early, Linda cooked a breakfast of scrambled eggs, turkey bacon, toast and fresh squeezed orange juice. While they partook of their meal, they laughed about another movie they'd watched last night. *Adam's Rib*, another Tracy and Hepburn classic, had followed *Pat and Mike*.

It had been a struggle deciding whether to watch a third or just turn in, but when William reminded her that they needed to be well-rested for her visit to her doctor, Linda acquiesced and set William up in her guest room.

Despite their previous intimacy, they mutually agreed that they needed to take a step back to give each of them a chance to regroup and build a foundation for their friendship.

How quickly their bubble of euphoric bliss was burst. Through the years, both separately and for this brief moment together, they had braved and weathered the many storms of life; things that seemed unimaginable to many. Insecurities and fears, both hidden and obvious, were addressed and overcome. It wasn't fate that caused Linda's and William's paths to intertwine. There was a reason these two survivors of grinding times were adjoined. The most challenging time of their lives awaited them.

Like newfound friends on the precipice of something very special, they held hands and laughed throughout the Lincoln Tunnel bus ride. Reaching the other side of the Hudson, they decided to walk across town to the East side.

Halfway across 42nd Street, Linda stopped to catch her breath. "Let's take a cab the rest of the way," she said.

William wore a look of concern. "Are you okay?"

"Yes, just a little winded, that's all."

"Have you ever experienced this before?"

"No, but I'm quite sure it's nothing."

Hailing a Yellow Cab, William responded, "It's probably your nerves. Have you ever had an anxiety attack before?"

"No."

"You're probably nervous about the test results."

Peering deep into his eyes, Linda smiled. Despite his unfortunate situation, she felt safe with William; he was a soothing, secure presence.

Within seconds, a taxi pulled up.

A young brother was at the wheel. Entering the vehicle, the couple was met with the soulful sounds of Mary J. Blige's Grammy Award-winning "Be Without You." Speaking the words of their mutual existence, their chemistry, as the Queen of Hip-Hop stated with an emotional elegance, was crazy from the get-go, their "Hello" in Hoboken. Linda, too strong for so long by herself, felt her heart softening. As easy as it had been to grill salmon for him that special Sunday a week ago, taking care of his needs in the future would be just as effortless. Like her mother preached years ago, most men need nurturers. For him, she'd walk on water, she thought. Though she said it would be nice to have pleasant conversation upon her arrival home, in her language of love, however, the translation was *Let's see where this goes. Maybe we have something here.*

William McCall, smiling as he listened to the lyrics, understood the unspoken. Grabbing her hand, his head bobbed to the rhythm of the groove. Too hard to fake the feeling radiating his soul with warmth and not wanting anything to replace it, for the first time in his life he was "in sync" with a woman. *Better call the radio,* he thought. Her smile tickling his insides, those braids made him want to melt her with a kiss. The thought of it all making him ache with a pleasurable pain, he would remain cool, calm and composed. *We're friends now,* he thought. *But that'll change.*

Arriving at an office near the NYU Medical Center, the twosome saw patients and visitors of all ages and colors entering the facility. That loving sensation Linda felt throughout the morning was replaced with fear.

William, spotting it immediately, grabbed her hand as they entered.

"You're going to be fine, Baby."

Linda smiled bravely. "From your lips to God's ears."

After checking in, they found seats in the fairly empty waiting area. Linda, perhaps haunted by the memory of a quarter-century ago, asked William, "When they call me, would you come inside with me?"

"Are you sure?"

"Yes."

Suddenly without warning she began to tremble in fear of the unknown.

"Baby, what's wrong?"

"I need to tell you something."

Revealing a painful memory, she replayed the scene where she was told she would need a total hysterectomy. Her mother had been seated in the waiting area of her stepfather's office, then her gynecologist, while she bore that horrible moment alone. She couldn't do that again. If for no other reason than to have something to hold onto while Dr. Everett informed her of the results of the various tests she'd been subjected to during her brief hospital stay, Linda needed the reassurance of William that, no matter what, their sun would continue to shine.

To lighten the tense moment, William, with a crooked smile, said, "Let me get this straight. Your mother married your gynecologist?"

Chuckling, through her nervousness, she answered, "Yeah, as you can see strange relationships run in the family."

"What are they going to say when they meet me?"

Laughing openly now, she said, "Well, you could always win them over with complimentary extra value meals."

"Oh, that's cold, Lucky," he said, joining her in joviality.

"Linda Woodson," the nurse/receptionist called out, her stoic tone humorless. "Dr. Everett is ready for you."

The jubilance of seconds ago disappeared in a heartbeat.

Rising slowly, William squeezed her hand to let her know that he was there for her.

Seeing him start to the back offices with Linda, the nurse/receptionist said, "Sir, you can wait for her out here."

"No. He's coming with me," Linda insisted.

Locking fingers, their friendship was venturing into uncharted territory. Upon entering the office of Dr. Everett, the tenor of the moment felt colder, more serious than ever before.

William, sensing the mood swing, put on his game face. Emboldened with an unfamiliar courage, he extended his hand before the doctor could open his mouth. "I'm her husband," he announced. Glancing over his shoulder quickly, his eyes met Linda's and delivered a clear message: *Baby, you bring out the man in me.* In that same millisecond, he saw a slither of a smile. She already knew.

Looking at Linda curiously, "I didn't know you had gotten married," the doctor said.

"We just did it this past weekend. We're brand-newlyweds," Linda lied.

In a skeptical manner that let them know he wasn't buying it, he merely said, "I see."

"Dr. Everett, whatever the prognosis is, don't sugarcoat it. I'm a big girl." The last time Linda had uttered those words, the result had been devastating. Hoping that fate would smile on her this time around, she again rolled the dice with the courage of a gunslinger facing a duel in the Old West.

Sadly, she again missed the target.

Pausing, the stoic physician was silent for a split second. Having knowledge of her medical history and sympathetic to what this woman had already endured in her young life, the news he was about to deliver could not be softened. He had scanned the X-rays prior to her arrival hoping he would see a damaged disk, a pinched nerve, or something curable. But what he found left him silent. Now he had to share his findings, a diagnosis that would change the lives of all in the room for good.

"Linda, I want to show you something," he said delicately while pointing left, to two images on a screen.

A sudden, sick dread spread through her stomach as she rose. Clutching William's hand tightly, they both looked at the X-rays.

The doctor continued. "Let me show you the picture of a healthy spine." In that image, the vertebrae in the back were white. "Linda... Now, look at yours."

The dread that had her stomach churning wrapped around Linda's ribs and throat, momentarily suffocating her.

Three-quarters of the vertebrae in her X-ray were black.

William, in a noble effort to ease the tension, squeezed a joke out. "Maybe you forgot to use the flash, doc."

Linda smiled weakly, but the doctor remained solemn. "Ms. Woodson, this is what we studied in medical school. I'm ninety-nine percent sure this is..."

"That's Linda to you," she barked defiantly. Her world spinning off its axis, she had been too strong for so long, and finally became unglued. The tears falling fast down her cheeks, she knew what the doctor was about to say.

William knew, too. Lowering his head while covering his face, he shook his head but would not cry. Then, with a resolve they both needed, he returned his gaze to the bearer of this terrible news.

"Are you sure it's cancer?" he asked.

Dr. Everett slowly nodded. "Metastatic adenocarcinoma is a very fast-moving strain." The look on his face speaking words he barely wanted to say, told William this cancer was bad, very bad.

Linda, grabbing hold of him, seemed out of it. "I've got cancer. I'm going to die. I don't want to die, William. I wanted to fall in love with you. I'm so sorry. I'm so sorry, Baby."

After pushing away the culture locs that had flown out of control, he grabbed the back of her neck—not too forcibly—and pressed his forehead to hers. "Why are you apologizing to me? We're going to be okay," he responded gently. "We'll get through this, Lucky." Then with a love he never knew before, he kissed her.

Turning to the doctor once more, he searched for a hook they could hang their hopes on. "Is it just there?" he asked.

"At this present time, we don't know if it has spread or not. With the type of cancer we think she has…"

Sobbing heavily, Linda collapsed into William's embrace.

William's face masked his anger. *We think she has? You're supposed to be a fucking doctor! You're supposed to know everything about this shit that might kill my baby, dammit!* His insides raging, that he remained calm on the exterior was a remarkable feat in itself.

"With the cancer she has, there's no reliable way to find its origin or chart its course."

"How will we know if it's spreading?"

"She'll know when it's getting worse by the pain," Dr. Everett told him. Then, as if offering a crack of daylight, he continued, "I'm going to refer you to the best oncologist I know, Linda. Dr. Madge Stewart at Memorial Sloan Cancer Center and will recommend that she start chemotherapy treatment immediately."

By this time, Linda was zoned out, she was in a fog. Recognizing her numbness to the conversation, William knew he would have to reach into his well of strength and summon a courage he never possessed to fill in the blanks later.

He would start when they arrived at the apartment. After holding through the taxi to Port Authority and the hearse-like bus ride across the Hudson River, every time the tears fell from Linda's eyes, he was there to catch them. With a dab, or gentle kiss on each cheek, he was soothing. All the while, he thanked God for sending him to Hoboken the day before.

Alvina Carter had been right. There's a reason for everything, he thought. While he didn't know their fate, he certainly knew his purpose. Gently seating her on the couch, he moved to her stereo. Searching through her music—*gotta find the right song to help us deal with this*, he thought—William stumbled upon her expansive Luther Vandross collection. Into the player went his self-titled contribution. Pressing the random button, "I'd Rather" filled the living room with an aura that had been absent.

His voice comforting and reassuring, Luther spoke of life and love, something both were scared to lose after having searched far and wide for years. Perhaps the words from him were supposed to lessen the blow; perhaps the lyrics were to fortify Lucky with the strength against what was a deck stacked against her survival. She was to confront the disease and conquer it. Whatever the case, it seemed only fitting the song invaded all somber thoughts.

Returning her head to his lap, William's thoughts were jolted by a faint murmur. Linda, red-eyed from all the tears, peered up at him from his lap. Finally, it seemed her numbness had thawed.

"William," she said in a nasally voice, "you're not obligated to stay with me. You're free to go on with your life if you want to."

It was then the chorus of the melody came on. For the first time in hours, the warrior that kidnapped William's body and filled it with an unfamiliar resolve lowered his shield and took a moment off. Bravely, he tried to speak, but he couldn't. Running his hand through her locs tenderly, he let the lyrics bceome his voice. He'd rather go through hell with her, than to be without her, to navigate them through the stormy waters that might result in her death. He could have good times with another, but would he experience the safe warm haven Linda's heart provided? A resounding *no*, was the emphatic answer his soul gave to his mind. He was chosen to be with Lucky, and to the end is where he would be with her. Singing the reason why in a bold, beautiful voice, Luther said it all:

Linda Woodson was the one who held his heart.

Somehow he wanted to say this, but every time he tried, he choked up. Finally, at the song's end, he looked at her.

"Why would I leave you now," he said gleaming through his own tears, "when I'm feeling so lucky?"

TEN

Using the resources and contacts he'd garnered from his years in the District Attorney's office, it took no effort for Emerson to find out exactly who the man was who'd emerged from Linda's house with her Monday morning.

William McCall.

That same day, he learned that McCall had been employed at several law firms in the city, the last being Gallagher, Goetz and Green where he'd been fired from the managing clerk position in that office. Although no charges had been filed, there was talk that he had embezzled funds upward of $30,000 from the organization.

From his appearance, Emerson recalled, *he certainly didn't look like he had any large stacks of cash lying around.*

The man he'd witnessed was average looking and even less averagely dressed. It puzzled him why Linda, who was extremely fashion-conscious, despite being very down-to-earth in her manner and thinking, would be hanging out with this dude. Hell, he knew she could be fully dressed and ready to walk out the door, but if she noticed the slightest stain, pull or other boo-boo anywhere on her attire, she would double back and change her clothes no matter whether she was running late or not. Her companion had been wearing what looked like an old pair of jeans that were overdue for retirement and an even less impressive polo shirt.

Maybe he has a gambling problem, Emerson pondered.

Putting other cases on the back burner, Emerson felt a sense of urgency in that this was very personal for him. He didn't make a habit of abusing his capacity for gathering information from numerous sources, but this time he was calling in favors all over town.

What he found out in the next couple of days was interesting indeed. William McCall seemed to have been the victim of a very cruel twist of fate. After losing his job and being blackballed in the legal industry, Emerson found out that he'd lost his apartment and was currently a resident in a homeless shelter in Brooklyn. An employee on the payroll of a midtown McDonald's, he found it hard to believe the man had been devious enough to have embezzled over $30,000 but wasn't smart enough to keep himself off the rolls of the powerless populace of New York City.

But how had he hooked up with Linda, that's what Emerson wanted to know. Could he have been one of her cases? *I need to call her, to make sure she's okay*, he thought in hindsight. He was annoyed with himself that he'd let his obsession with this guy overshadow his concern for Linda. *She must have gotten her test results by now.*

Putting everything on hold for the moment, Emerson dialed her cell phone number.

"Hello, Emerson," was the way she answered his call.

"Hey, Linda, how'd everything go the other day? I'm sorry I'm just getting back in touch with you. I've been real busy on this new case I'm working."

"It went okay."

"So what did they tell you?"

There was silence on the phone for several long seconds prompting Emerson to call out to her, "Linda. What did they say?"

"I have cancer, Emerson," she stated in a chillingly calm manner.

"Oh my God, no!"

"Yes. I'm afraid so."

"Are you... Linda, tell me what you want me to do. Anything," he pleaded.

"Thank you, but there's really nothing you can do. I'm going to be starting treatment tomorrow afternoon..."

"Do you need me to go with you? I can rearrange my schedule."

"That's not necessary, but I appreciate the offer."

Emerson sighed. "Can I see you?"

"Emerson…"

"Please, Lucky."

"Maybe we can do lunch tomorrow," she acquiesced.

"Lunch will be fine. I'll come pick you up wherever you want me to, okay?"

"Okay. Emerson, I have to run. I have to meet with my supervisor."

"Sure, I understand. So I'll… I'll talk to you tomorrow."

"Okay. Bye."

Cancer. How could she be so calm? Her news had really shaken him up but she seemed to be taking it all in stride. *Maybe she's still in shock.* Aware that people reacted to traumatic events in various ways, he couldn't imagine how he would be able to maintain such a cool demeanor after having received such devastating news.

He knew he needed to step up his investigation on William McCall now and try to gather as much information as he could before he met with her tomorrow. She would have enough on her plate to deal with in the next few months without having to worry about some lowlife trying to freeload off of her.

Later that day, Emerson learned that the man who had replaced William, one Markham Chandler—whom McCall had actually hired—had quite a reputation around the court buildings downtown. Figuring he might be able to talk to this man and possibly get some insight into McCall's character, Emerson ventured to Goetz, Gallagher and Green only to find, to his surprise and chagrin, that Chandler had already called it quits for the evening.

I'll come back tomorrow morning to speak to him, he told himself. His curiosity momentarily slaked, Emerson ventured into Jack's, a chic midtown watering hole nearby on Fortieth Street. Nearly choking, as he entered, from the cigarette smoke of those clustered near the entrance since being banished by state law, Emerson surveyed the establishment.

The place seemed busy for so early on a Monday evening. "Brian's Flow," an instrumental selection by Brian McKnight, added an urban, upscale feel to the predominantly black after-work crowd. Finding a seat up at the bar, he ordered a gin and tonic while continuing his scan of the surroundings. Spotting a group of four at the other end of the L-shaped bar who were obviously enjoying themselves, closer to him—actually three stools away—

was a man who looked no more than thirty years old, entertaining two very attractive females.

Although he was in a relationship, the ego-posturing competitor in him surfaced. His instincts brimming with fire, Emerson thought, *why the hell should he have all the fun tonight?* Motioning to the bartender, he ordered a Cosmopolitan for the spectacular sister sporting streaked blonde hair and black hiphuggers with a navel ring peeking from under a white blouse unbuttoned at the bottom.

When the drink arrived in front of her, the young man looked coldly in Emerson's direction, his face twisted in a frown like the women belonged to him and he wasn't willing to share either of them with an outsider.

"Chill, brother," Emerson shouted over the music. "I sent it in peace."

Minutes later, a shot of tequila appeared in the investigator's face. Looking in the direction of the young man, he saw an arrogant smile. "Man up, Pops."

Having developed a high tolerance for tequila, vodka, and numerous other hard liquors through drinking games Emerson had played while in law school, in addition to the fact that he'd been at it for probably twenty more years than the young pup, he tossed the shot straight back. His face remained expressionless as he slammed the glass down onto the bar. Again, motioning to the bartender and with a subtle wink, the fellow delivered his second offering.

As the music shifted to the guitar riffs of Carlos Santana, two shots of Cuervo 1800 went in the direction of his immature counterpart. Acknowledging the drinks from his elder, he downed them both with ease, then gulped a large portion of the Long Island Iced Tea he had in front of him.

"Good lookin' out," the younger said admiringly and motioned him over. Emerson pulled up a stool.

"Brother, ain't no fun if the old man can't have none," he joked as he greeted the women and offered a handshake to the young man. "Emerson Perkins."

"Markham Chandler."

Really? Thinking Christmas had come in the twilight of summer for him, Emerson remained composed, although on the inside he was slapping high-fives because he'd hit a bull's-eye when he stopped into this spot. Now if he could only sink William's battleship with some dirt, this impromptu sidebar would be quite fruitful.

"Now this is a coincidence," Emerson told him. "I was trying to catch you at your firm a half-hour ago."

"I had a half-day today," Mark announced in a defensive tone. "I needed a half-day today because I worked this weekend."

"I feel you, man. Me? I own my business but sometimes I need a quick get-away."

"I envy you that, bruh. So what did I do to have the honor of your visit?"

"I was trying to find out some information about the man who preceded you in the managing clerk's position at Goetz. William McCall."

Mark shook his head and snickered.

"Something I said amuses you?"

"Nah, man. Ladies, could you excuse us for a few? We gotta talk man talk." Obliging, the women took their drinks and started to move away. As they did, Markham swatted one of them on her behind. Believing that he and Emerson were on the same page, Markham winked at him, not even noticing the look of disdain the offended woman shot him or the apathy from Emerson.

Once they were out of earshot, Markham continued, "So, do you want the politically correct answer or something off-the-record?"

"Why not give me both."

"Okay, on the record, I'll say that William McCall lacked professionalism and deserved to get terminated. Off the record…"

The ringing of his cell phone interrupted his flow. "Hold on, man. This is my trick. What's up?" Markham impatiently said into the phone. "Yeah, yeah, I'm coming out tonight. What? Bring a bottle? Shit, the liquor store is right down the street from you. Get off your lazy ass and go get one yourself. What? Now why you ask me such a stupid question?" He winked at Emerson again. "Don't I always hit you off proper? Is that right? Look, I know it's been a minute, but I'm bringing the good wood home, Baby. You just make sure you can hang wit' me. I don't want you passing out on me again." To Emerson he whispered and laughed, "I spanked that ass so well last time the bitch passed out."

Damn, that's foul, Emerson thought as his already sinking opinion of Markham took a nosedive. He didn't know who the woman was, but he felt sorry that she had no more self-esteem than to hook up with the arrogant twit in front of him. Analyzing him in nanoseconds, Emerson's investigative sense told him that he was going to get a lot more than he'd bargained for.

Tuning back into his phone conversation, Markham continued, "What? Look, Anna, I just left the job. I'm outside and a damn Explorer is blaring its stereo. What? Listen, I'll call you later. Yeah, yeah, you, too," he concluded. Closing his flip phone, his eyes rolled skyward with sarcasm. "I'm sorry, but that old broad is strung out on this," he bragged, grabbing his genitals. "She's forty–seven and needs the young stuff."

Fuming at his lack of respect, Emerson mused, *this clown has a managerial position?*

"Where'd we leave off?" Markham asked.

Giving away no inclination of his contempt, he coolly replied, "You were about to tell me something off the record about McCall?"

"Oh, yeah. That moron got fired for embezzlement. I mean, how stupid is that?"

"Pretty stupid."

"Yeah, right? They said he stole over thirty thousand dollars in four months."

Emerson arched an eyebrow. *But he's homeless. That sounds a little fishy.*

"Do you think he did it?"

"Yeah, why not?" he announced without hesitation. "We were always hanging out and he always picked up the tab. That chump even had box seats at Yankee Stadium."

Gesturing to the bartender to refresh their drinks, Emerson asked, "You ever consider that he might have earned the money to do what he did?"

"Please, a black man doesn't get box seats at Yankees games without doing something grimy."

"I have them," Emerson countered. "I'm a season ticket holder."

Markham paused considering Emerson's admission. "Yeah, well, that might be, but I know he did it," he defiantly stated. "And all his wrongdoing caught up with him."

"Yeah, well, it usually does."

The new drinks were placed in front of the men.

"Thanks, man," Markham said, as he unceremoniously tossed down the shot and took a big gulp of his fresh Long Island Iced Tea.

"So, what was your relationship like with him?"

"Man," Markham said, "I couldn't stand his ass." The alcohol was clearly beginning to take its toll, Emerson noticed, so much so that he began to use an entirely different vernacular. "That bitch lost everything."

"He's not a bitch, Mark."

"Yes, he is, and I got him good. D'you know he's working in McDonald's now?"

Tequila shots and Iced Tea, the perfect truth serum, Emerson thought. His premonition held true: he was getting all the goods and probably a little more that he'd bargained for. A few more questions and he would be done.

Suddenly, Markham stumbled unsteadily off his stool. "Damn, that shit just hit me. Um… what'd you say your name was again?"

"Emerson."

"Yeah, that's right."

"You were saying something about you got him good?"

"Yeah," Markham sneered. "I took… everything from him. His job and, because he was such a punk-ass bitch… I even took his… woman!"

Emerson, stunned by this revelation, was unable to hide his emotion.

"Yeah, that's right. I took 'is woman, too. That bitch… Anna, I was… talking to. He wasn't fucking her 'cause… he was out… of town all the damn time. He… shoulda been taking her on… his business trips, like I do. All she wants is… is…"

"What does she want, Mark?"

"Uh… What?"

"Anna. What does she want?"

"She ain't want no punk-ass, das for sure. William… ain't got no spine. He's too damn… nice. Bitches need a bad boy, a rough… neck every now… and then. Know… know wha' I mean? No… all da time. Iss dat… simple!"

Lifting his glass and downing the remainder of his Iced Tea, Markham shook his head and waved to the bartender for another shot.

Interceding, Emerson stated, "He doesn't need anymore."

"Eh, man… you can't tell… me what… I… need. I'ma… man!"

"Yeah, you might be one day." Spotting the bartender a C-note, Emerson told him, "Take his check out of this."

Helping his staggering parakeet out the bar, Emerson flagged a cab. When one stopped in front of him, he tossed the drunk into the backseat, "Where do you live, Mark?" he asked.

"Strong Island, dawg," he slurred, then fell over onto the cushion of the backseat.

Emerson handed the driver a crisp one hundred dollar bill. "Take him to Long Island, then wake him up and ask him where home is."

As the driver sped away, Emerson stood where he was and reflected on his conversation with Markham Chandler. Although his research had cost him two hundred dollars, it had been well worth the cost.

He wondered now, however, if this fellow, William McCall, was, in fact, the lowlife freeloader he'd initially assumed him to be. From what Chandler had revealed, Emerson concluded that he was somehow involved in what had gone down. He didn't find it farfetched believing that Chandler may have even been the embezzler himself, and had set McCall up. But how could he ever prove that? Since no charges had been filed against McCall when the whole thing was exposed, the firm had probably filed the episode away in their cache of embarrassing moments, hoping the incident would never again come to light.

Emerson also wondered how much Linda knew about McCall's background. Would she knowingly associate with someone living in a homeless shelter, to the point that she would invite him into her home? Because he had been parked outside of her building before the sun came up Monday morning, Emerson assumed that McCall had not arrived that day, but had instead been an overnight guest.

Was she sleeping with this dude?

Well, he thought, the only way to put his concerns to rest was to ask her and tell her the truth about what he'd learned today. Maybe his information could help lighten the load she'd have to carry in the days ahead.

❦❦

Linda was not looking forward to lunch with Emerson. His reaction to her news yesterday was as she'd expected it would be, but the last thing she needed was one more person feeling sorry for her.

As much as she loved her girl, Josie, in the days since Linda had broken the news to her, Josie would call, several times a day, questioning her about how she felt, if she needed her to do anything, and the like. While Linda truly appreciated her sister-friend's love and concern, she didn't want to be fawned over like a fragile piece of fine china.

She still hadn't told her mother and Davis about the cancer. Linda felt this was news they deserved to hear in person, not through the telephone lines. Lacking the courage she needed, she did, however, let William talk her into driving down to Spartanburg this coming weekend, but only after he agreed to take the ride with her. Afraid for her mother, Linda knew that her disclosure would be cataclysmic for her.

The only presence Linda had been able to bear since she'd learned the depth of her illness was William. He'd been a calming influence during these turbulent days. She looked forward to coming home now, knowing he would either be there already or coming soon. The past few evenings had consisted of dinner where one or both cooked, a movie—usually one of her classic titles—or a board game. Learning that he loved to play Scrabble, Tuesday night they'd competed until almost one in the morning with her winning two games to his three. If, by chance, she had one of her excruciating attacks, William would hold her tightly in his arms and rock her until the pain subsided.

Up until this point, they hadn't revisited the intimacy they'd shared on the first day they'd met, but William slept in her bed every night and Linda's slumber was peaceful and calm, as she nestled safely in his arms.

It was her turn to feel lucky.

Agreeing to let Emerson pick her up from her office, she met him at noon; earlier than she usually took lunch, but she wanted to be done with him well before William came to take her for her treatment.

Undeniably handsome in his monochromatic tan attire—collarless shirt, slacks and sandals—Emerson's smile, while sincere, was conspicuously sympathetic.

"Linda," he tenderly intoned as he pulled her into his arms. "How're you feeling, Baby?"

"I'm good, Emerson."

"You look great."

She smiled up at him. "I feel pretty good."

"Listen, I know you don't have much time, so I thought we could go to that Spanish joint around the corner. Is that okay with you?"

"That's fine." She shrugged.

Seated across from him in the dimly lit restaurant minutes later, Linda wanted to inquire about Emerson's girlfriend—the one he'd dropped her for—but decided, she really didn't want to hear anything good he might have to say about that.

After they had placed their food order, Emerson asked, "How's your mother handling this situation?"

"I haven't told her yet."

"Why not? Don't you think she'll be upset that you're keeping this from her?"

"I plan to drive down there this weekend and tell her. I didn't feel this was something she needed to hear over the phone."

"Yeah, I can understand that. You're not driving down there alone, are you?"

"No."

Eager to know if her companion was to be William McCall, he asked, "Who's going with you?"

"A friend."

"The same mysterious friend who wasn't at the hospital last week?"

"If this is why you invited me to lunch, Emerson, I should just go now," Linda said and made a move to rise.

Stilling her before she could leave, he said, "Linda, I'm not trying to run your life, or anything like that. I know I gave up that privilege, but I'm concerned about you. I care about you, whether you believe that or not."

"I know you care, Emerson, but what I do with my life now, is really not your concern."

"You're my friend, Linda. Concern and friendship kinda go hand in hand."
She sighed.

"I know who he is," Emerson admitted.

"You know who who is?"

"Your friend."

"Who is he, Mr. Know-it-all?"

No longer interested in beating around the bush, he boldly stated, "His name is William, right?"

Linda's face became a mask of indignation. "Have you been spying on me?"

"Look, when you told me... I'm not proud of it, but yes, I have."

"Emerson!"

"Listen, before you get all bent out of shape, let me explain something. When I found out who he was and where he lives and how he came to be in the situation he's in, I did some checking since I noticed that you seemed to have taken him in. My inclination was to protect you from him..."

"Why are you playing Dudley-Do-Right after the fact?" Linda interjected.

Sighing, Emerson continued. "It's because I thought he might be trying to take advantage of you. I saw him come out of your house with you Monday morning and I knew he hadn't come that morning to pick you up."

"You were sitting outside of my house?"

"Yes. I took his picture. I found out that he's working a minimum wage job at McDonald's. He lives in a shelter in Brooklyn. I found out that he was fired from his old job and I made arrangements to speak with someone from that firm to get additional information. But I happened to run into, purely by accident and maybe divine intervention, the person who took over the position your friend was in. He told me some things about William that gave me a completely different perspective of him."

"Like what things?" Linda asked, barely able to contain her rising ire.

"Did he tell you he was fired for embezzlement?"

"No," she haltingly admitted.

"Supposedly, he stole over thirty-thousand dollars."

"I don't believe he would do that."

"Yeah, well, I'm not so sure he did either. I think your friend was set up, and although I can't prove it, I think I know who set him up. This guy I spoke with told me some things about William that, from his mannerisms, seemed a bit vindictive. He even confessed that he'd stolen William's fiancée," Emerson said.

"Why would he tell you all of this?" Linda wanted to know.

"Because aside from him being an arrogant, no-count son-of-a-bitch, he was drunk. He seemed to revel in the fact that William had lost everything he'd ever worked for."

"Well, for your information, Emerson, aside from knowing that he might have been purposely set up, I knew about everything else, because William told me. He may be down on his luck, right now, but one thing I know is that he's not a thief. He's a good man, with a good heart…and I'd appreciate it if you would stop following him around and stop spying on me," she said while trying desperately to stem the rising tide of her tears. "I have enough on my plate right now."

Reaching across the table and taking her hand, he earnestly swore, "Linda, I know, and I'm sorry. Like I said, I was only trying to look out for you. If there's anything, and I do mean anything, I can do to help you, please tell me. You have my numbers; they haven't changed. Don't be afraid to call me, okay?"

ELEVEN

When William emerged from McDonald's at the end of his shift Friday evening, he was eager to get back to Jersey City. He and Linda were planning to start their drive to her mother's home in Spartanburg, South Carolina around midnight and he knew he needed to get at least four hours of sleep before they began the trip.

His journey, however, was halted by a man who approached him as he was about to cross the street on his way to Port Authority to catch the bus.

"William McCall?" the man asked.

Not recognizing the man from anywhere, he responded, "Who wants to know?"

"You got a minute?"

"That depends on who you are and what you want?" William cautiously intoned.

"My name is Emerson Perkins. I'm a…"

"Emerson. I know who you are. What do you want with me?"

"Oh, so, Linda's told you about me?"

"I've heard some things," William stated as he squared his shoulders in challenge.

"Yeah, well, I've heard some things about you, too," Emerson responded.

"Is that right?"

"Yeah, that's right," he stated, sensing William's justifiable antagonism.

"What do you want with me?" William asked.

"Listen, I'm not here to cause you any grief. I'm just concerned about Linda."

"If you're so concerned about her, why aren't you more integrated in her life? I understand you had that privilege and gave it up. You can't be that concerned about her, brother," William said coldly.

"Look, I know where I messed up, but that's neither here nor there. This is about what's best for Linda," Emerson said.

"And what makes you think I'm *not* what's best for her?"

"What do you really think you can do for her on the salary you get from that place?" Emerson asked, gesturing to the establishment William had just vacated.

Taking a challenging step closer to Emerson despite the height difference, William said, "I can give her exactly what she needs; someone who's thinks what's important to her is paramount. Linda is a beautiful woman who deserves a man who's going to put her needs before anything else, including his own selfish desires. Yeah, I know all about you, brother."

Accepting the low blow for what it was, Emerson conceded, "Look, man. You've got me all wrong. Like I said, I'm not here to give you grief."

"So what do you want?"

"I want to help you, if you'll get that chip off your shoulder and take a minute to listen to my proposal," Emerson stated.

"Your proposal?" *Who the fuck does he think he is*, William thought, *the cavalry?*

"Yeah. I spoke with your buddy, Markham Chandler, and learned a few things that piqued my curiosity."

"Wait a minute? Who exactly are you? I mean, I know you're Linda's ex, but what are you not telling me?"

"I'm a private investigator. I own my own business."

I don't believe this crap, William thought. *He's John Wayne, the cavalry and the CIA all rolled into one. How's that possible?*

While William's mind was working, Emerson continued, "When Linda's friend Josie called me to the hospital last week after she passed out in the theater, I was all set to take her to see what was wrong. But she put me off, telling me *a friend* was going with her. I wanted to know who this friend was who was so important that they never showed up when she needed them most."

Defensively, William said, "I didn't know she was in the hospital."

"Yeah, well, Josie called me and I was there. Despite what might have gone down between Linda and me, I still care for her and I only want what's best for her. That includes anyone who happens to be in her life. She seems to think you're a decent guy."

"When did you speak to her about me?" William asked.

"Yesterday. I met with her to tell her what I'd learned about you from your buddy, Markham."

William felt his blood boiling over. "What does Markham have to do with any of this?"

"I don't know but after our little chat, I have reason to believe he might have been instrumental in setting you up for your fall."

"When did you talk to Mark?"

"A couple of days ago. He's quite the character."

"What makes you think he had something to do with my termination?"

"Look, I told you I don't have any proof, so it really doesn't matter. I have a proposition for you. Are you interested in hearing it?"

Shaking his head incredulously, William had to take a moment to consider this guy's motivation. *Why would he be so eager to help me? This isn't* Let's Make A Deal. *This is my life. It's obvious he's still got a thing for Linda. If this clown thinks he can play me like a piano, he's going to be in for a rude awakening. But what if he's on the level?*

"I'm listening."

❦❦

Too much was being thrown at William. In a little less than two weeks he'd met a woman who had revived what had lain dormant within his core for a year, become her unofficial caretaker after receiving tragic news, then met her ex-boyfriend who through either genuine compassion or a hidden agenda, had offered to help him get his life back on track.

As crazy as the scenario appeared on the surface, only a person with the fortitude William possessed could make sense of it all. Somehow, someway he knew by the time this journey had run its course, he would be a better man.

After Emerson's intrusion, he needed to walk. While strolling up Broadway in the direction of Central Park, William, by chance, noticed a black T-shirt with white lettering hanging in the window of one of the many souvenir shops lining that strip. *Something good's about to happen to you*, it read. Immediately recalling his dear departed mother-friend, Alvina Carter, saying much the same thing to him, William smiled, picturing her laughing and saying, "I told you so."

Shaking his head in amusement, he said, "Shut up, Alvina."

Reaching into his pocket, he removed his cell phone as he took a seat at the fountain in the midst of Columbus Circle.

After checking on Linda and making sure she was resting for their long trip south, he decided another call had to be made.

"Yo, man, where have you been?" Steve asked with a concerned voice.

"I'm cool, man."

"Well, don't stay out of touch! You had a brother all worried."

"My bad, Black." After a pause, William said, "Steve, you will never believe what just happened to me."

"Let me guess, you saved money on your car insurance by switching to…"

"I'm serious, man!" William shouted.

"Okay. You're lucky you caught me home. Monday I'm supposed to be headed on a trucking route to Denver."

There's that name again.

"I'm glad you're there, man. You know, I'm really beginning to believe I have one of those lives." Sighing, he continued. "Steve, Linda's ex-boyfriend Emerson came to see me and…"

"Wait," Steve interrupted. "You called her?"

"Oh, yeah, Steve, I finally did."

"So, what's up with that, man?"

"Cancer, Black. That's what's up."

"Whoa, rewind. She has cancer?"

William sighed hopelessly. "Yeah, that small word with enormous consequences."

William felt Steve's shock in his thirty-second silence. "Is it malignant?" he eventually inquired.

"Yes."

"I'm sorry, man. What are you gonna do?"

"What do you mean what am I going to do?"

"I mean, are you still gonna kick it with her?"

"I'm not going to leave her, if that's what you mean."

Silence.

"Yo, Black, this is some serious stuff you're getting into. You sure you wanna do that?"

"This woman literally picked me up off the street, Steve. In the two weeks I've known her, she's done nothing but give, never asking for a thing from me. There's a reason we're in each other's lives."

"If you say so, William. You know I'm here if you need me."

"I'm sure I will, Black. This one's gonna be tough."

"Hold up, man. Back up a minute," Steve said, remembering the commencement of the conversation. "What were you about to tell me about this Elliot dude?"

"Emerson, Steve. Linda's ex."

"Linda's ex? You hangin' with her ex, man?" Steve continued with disbelief in his tone. "What… What the hell's going on up there?"

"If you shut up, I'll tell you." Relaying the whole story without edits, William told the details of his conversation with Emerson and how he'd offered his assistance in finding him a job. Emerson knew of a position as an Assistant Managing Clerk at a firm in Rockefeller Center, near Radio City Music Hall. The position was currently filled by an alcoholic, he'd told William, and the firm had been looking to replace the man for a while but had found no viable candidates for the position.

"Are you sure you want to return to the legal field?" Steve asked.

"Well, I could use the money, Black."

"But what if they find out about that crap that happened at the last firm?"

"I can't concern myself with that," William responded. "All I can do is hope that things work themselves out."

"I hope so for your sake." Shifting gears, Steve asked, "What's your take on this guy Emerson?"

"Well, he knows about what went down at Goetz, and if he's putting in a good word for me, then it's all good as far as I'm concerned. At this point, I need to be able to do everything I can for Linda."

"You love her, don't you?"

Sighing, "Let's just say I'm going to be for her the man I should have always been."

Another pause. Steve, with emotion, eventually said, "We ride together, we die together, Black. We're boys for life. Whatever you need, call me. I love you, man."

"I know. I wouldn't be here if you didn't. I love you, too, Black."

TWELVE

Laughing, singing and sometimes sharing a comfortable, companionable silence, made the thirteen-hour drive to Linda's childhood hometown of Spartanburg, South Carolina seem to whiz by. Stopping only twice, once for gas and another time breakfast, they saw the giant peach that signaled their arrival.

"Do you know that BMW North America is here," Linda said, referring to the automotive manufacturing company.

"Wow," William said "And I thought you grew up with Andy Griffith in Mayberry."

"Mayberry's in *North Carolina*," Linda shot back. "Stop hatin' on my birthplace. Besides, I think you would have loved it down here."

"Yeah, right."

"I'm serious," Lucky insisted. "When I was a little girl, I used to go to Milliken Park, not too far from here. It was so much. I mean, ducks of colors and sizes would come from the water, and I literally placed pieces of bread in their mouths. And schools of fish would fight for the pieces we tossed in the pond. It's so peaceful here."

"So why did you leave?"

Sighing, "Big-city curiosity. I should have never left," Linda lamented.

"But if you stayed here, we never would have met."

"You're right, Baby. So I guess leaving had its benefits."

Happily, Linda suffered no more discomfort than being stuck in a sitting position for all those hours. For most of the way, William had been at the wheel, but when they got closer to her parents' home, Linda had taken over.

The weather that day was beautiful. The sky was a peaceful cerulean blue with not a cloud to be seen. As they drove through the residential streets leading to the neighborhood of Ashley, William admired the majestic-looking homes with perfectly manicured lawns and lush landscaping decorating them.

"These folks around here are rolling in dough, huh, Baby?" he said to Linda.

"Not really. Most are middle-class earners. The cost of living down here is much lower than in New York."

"Yeah, but that's the case everywhere."

"True. Mom and Dad have a beautiful home, though. My mother has a great eye for decorating and she's a huge fan of that cable station, HGTV."

"What's that?" William asked.

"Home and garden television. If she could, she'd watch that channel twenty-four seven and be redecorating at every opportunity. Davis had to assign her a certain number of hours a day that she can watch it." Linda laughed.

"I'm sure she's not that bad," he commented with a smile. "Oh, do you think we should stop at McDonald's?"

"For what?"

"I could use my employee discount to get those extra value meals you suggested," he laughingly responded.

Shaking her head, Linda said, "You're stupid."

Minutes later, they turned left onto Elana Street and pulled their rented black Ford Taurus into the driveway of the Malloy home.

"Wow, this is a nice house," William commented.

"And the nicest people live inside." Sensing his apprehension about meeting her folks, Linda reached for his hand. "They're going to love you."

Emerging from the car, William reached for the duffel bag in the backseat. Since they were planning to drive back to New York tomorrow, they'd only brought one change of clothes apiece.

Upon standing erect and closing his door, William noticed Linda's sudden hesitation.

"You okay, Lucky?"

"I don't know why, but all of sudden I've got butterflies in my stomach."

Walking around to the driver's side of the car, where Linda remained, he placed the bag on the hood of the car. Taking both of her hands, William pressed his forehead to hers. "If you need to lean on me, Lucky, do that. I know this is going to be tough, but we're going to do this together, okay?"

Nodding, Linda stared into his eyes until the strength and resolve she saw there became contagious. "Thank you for everything you've done for me, William."

"I haven't done anything I'm not supposed to. You, on the other hand, have saved my life."

Pressing his lips to hers in a tender peck, they embraced. After several minutes, Linda stepped back and said, "Okay. I'm good."

Walking to the front door, Linda said, "They must be in the back. I'm surprised no one's come to the door already."

She rang the bell.

"Do I look okay?" William suddenly asked.

She smiled and said, "No, you look amazing."

"Liar."

When Davis opened the door for them, Linda and William were laughing.

"Hey! What is this? Why didn't you call and tell us you were coming down?"

"Hi, Daddy," Linda said, walking into his waiting arms.

"Baby Girl." He kissed her cheek and squeezed her to his chest. "How you doin,' sugar?"

It was then that Linda's composure seemed to slip. Looking up into the eyes of the man who'd, twenty-five years ago, been a pillar of strength in her life when she thought her world was falling apart, Linda's eyes revealed her pain. "Is Mama home?"

"No. What's wrong, sugar?" Davis asked, reading Linda's sorrowful expression as clearly as if it were in a book.

Linda sighed and stepped out of his embrace. "Daddy, I want you to meet William. He's the guy I was telling you about. Well, sort of."

"I was gonna say, 'cause you were bobbing and weaving around the issue, as I recall it." Then addressing William, Davis offered his hand and said, "How are you, son? Come on in."

"I'm fine, thank you."

"Where is she?" Linda asked as they moved into the living room.

"At Home Depot, where else? She wants to remodel the upstairs bathroom so she went to price stuff," Davis said with a wave of his hand.

Taking a seat in her favorite easy chair, Linda laughed. "What did I just tell you?" she said to William. Then to Davis, "I told him Mama was an HGTV junkie."

Davis chuckled. "She's gotten worse."

William took a seat on the sofa, while Davis sat opposite him on the loveseat.

Studying Linda's face as she made small talk and alternately, William's as he watched her, Davis surmised that something very serious was afoot. He and Linda shared a special bond due to his intimate knowledge of her as her gynecologist since the age of eighteen, and stepfather since the age of twenty-four. Unwilling to wait any longer for the news she'd obviously thought was serious enough to take the thirteen-hour drive there to tell, Davis cut her off.

"Come here, Lucky," he softly insisted.

Hesitating briefly, Linda rose from her chair and went to sit next to him. Davis put his arm around her shoulder and in a tone she liked to call his physician voice, he said, "What's going on, Linda? Talk to me."

When she didn't immediately respond, Davis looked at William.

Leaning forward in the seat, "You want me to tell him, Baby?" William asked.

Lowering her head, she replied, "No. I'll tell him." Linda took a deep breath and began. "Wednesday before last, Josie and I went to see Usher in that play *Chicago*." She paused momentarily. "Maybe I should wait until Mama gets here."

William and Davis both noticed her voice crack when she said, "Mama."

"No, sugar, tell me," Davis gently urged.

"I... I passed out during the play. I got a really bad pain in my back... all across my trunk, really," she softly relayed as her eyes began to water. "I'd been having them off and on for a while. I woke up in the emergency room. They kept me overnight and ran all these tests."

"Why didn't you call us?" Davis asked.

"They didn't tell me anything and I didn't want y'all to worry for nothing.

I had to wait until Monday to see my own doctor and he told me what they'd found."

"You know I could have gotten that information from the hospital the same day, sugar."

"I know. I was scared of what they were going to tell me. I wanted to wait as long as I could."

"What is it?" Davis asked.

Looking into his eyes, she revealed, "Late stage metastatic adenocarcinoma. It's all over my spine and maybe elsewhere. They don't really know where it started."

For the first time in her life, Linda saw fear in Davis' eyes.

Speechless after her revelation, he tried to blink back tears but was unsuccessful. "Oh, Baby." Suddenly, he wrapped her in a crushing embrace. "Linda. Oh, Baby, I'm sorry."

His tears were flowing freely now, but Davis knew he had to check them. She didn't need him falling apart on her.

Feeling like an intruder at that moment, William rose and started out of the room.

"Don't go, Will," Davis called. "Have you started treatment?" he then asked Linda.

"I had my first treatment Thursday."

"Were you with her?" he asked William.

"Yes, sir."

"He's been there from the start, Daddy."

"Thank you."

"Thanks aren't necessary, Mr. Malloy. I owe Lucky big time," William admitted. "I'd do anything for her."

"The name is Davis, Will. How'd it go, Baby?" Davis asked as he tenderly caressed her cheek.

"It was horrible. I knew I couldn't do it again without you and Mama. That's why I had to come."

The three of them sat in silence for the next couple of minutes, each trying to absorb the gravity of what lay ahead for Linda.

"I'm scared to tell Mama," she suddenly said.

"Let me tell her," said Davis. "How're you feeling now?"

"Tired. We've been driving since midnight. I didn't really sleep much on the way down."

"Why don't you go upstairs and lie down. Get some sleep. Your mother won't be back for a while anyway. She's only been gone for about a half-hour."

"Yeah, I could use some sleep," Linda agreed.

Davis and Linda rose from the couch. Wrapping her arms around him, she cradled her head against his chest. "I love you, Daddy."

Tenderly rubbing her back, Davis replied, "I love you, too, sugar. We're going to get through this together, right?"

She nodded.

"Go on, Baby. We'll wake you when Mamie gets home."

Once Linda had left the room, Davis said to William, "I need a drink. Can I fix you anything?"

"I'll have whatever you're having."

"Let's go downstairs."

Leading William through a sparkling kitchen, fully laden with the most modern stainless steel appliances and marble countertops, Davis opened a door near the exit to the back porch and headed down a flight of stairs.

Emerging into the softly lit basement, William took in his surroundings. *Now this is the kind of room I want in my house*, he thought.

In the far left corner was a handsomely carved pool table. On the wall behind the table was a rack that held six cues. Opposite that, to William's right, was a full bar. Six highback stools were positioned in front of it and bordering the mirrored wall behind it seemed to be every type of liquor known to man.

"I'm having scotch. You sure that's what you want?" Davis asked.

"I'll take a vodka with tonic, if you have it."

"Sit down," Davis offered.

William looked longingly behind him to the plush chocolate brown leather sofa that faced a fifty-three-inch plasma television, but headed toward the bar and sat on one of the stools.

Placing a drink in front of him, Davis asked William, "So, what's your story?"

Unprepared for the lightning-fast change of climate, William responded, "Excuse me?"

"Look, Will, I know you and Linda just met two weeks ago, and she's not too long out of a relationship that she'd been in for almost three years. Now, there's not much a person can learn about another in two weeks, so I want to know why it is that you made that declaration you did upstairs."

"Mr. Malloy..."

"Davis."

William didn't feel like he was companionable enough to call this elderly man by his first name, but he could also see that Davis Malloy was no one to play with.

"Lucky saved my life, sir."

"How so?"

William proceeded to reveal to Davis everything that had transpired in his life in the past year, from his heartbreaking discovery of Anna's betrayal to his wrongful termination from Goetz, Gallagher and Green. Withholding nothing, including relaying the details of his and Linda's relationship, with the exception of their intimacy on the day they met, William felt a cleansing sensation overwhelm him.

"I'd been so afraid of letting anyone get close to me ever again, but Lucky just came along and knocked down all my defenses, refusing to let me wallow in my own self-pity. She opened her home and her heart to me without asking for anything in return except that I allow her to be her loving and giving self. When I realized that she was sick, there was no way I was not going to be there for her. Davis, I'm here for the long haul. Whatever she wants, whatever she needs, if it's in my power to get it for her, she has it. No questions asked."

"She is an amazing woman; much like her mother. They are two of the strongest women I've ever known, and by virtue of my profession, I know a lot of women," Davis added.

"How do you think she's going to take it?" William asked, referring to Mamie Woodson.

"Not good at all, but she'll do whatever she needs to do for Lucky. They're extremely close and each would go to the ends of the earth for the other. Sometimes they take on more than they can handle, what with their pride and all, so we just have to make sure we're there to catch them when the load gets too heavy."

❦❦

When Mamie entered the bedroom where Linda was resting, she stood over her daughter for a long moment watching her as she slept. *My baby's got cancer.* Deeming her fate unconscionable and unfair, she didn't want to believe it. Linda had been through so much already, why this? Why now? Wanting to rail at God for the cruel hand He'd dealt her only child, she thought, *Linda was a good girl*, she thought. *What has she ever done to deserve so much pain in her short life?*

Moving closer to the bed, Mamie sat down, leaned over and gently tucked a loc that had fallen across Linda's face behind her ear. *She's my miracle baby. How can you take her from me? Oh God, why are you doing this?* A solitary tear fell from her eye, belying the agony she felt in her heart.

Suddenly, Linda began to stir. Turning over onto her back, she sensed a presence in the room and opened her eyes.

"Mama."

"Hi, Baby." Mamie tried to smile but it appeared more a grimace of pain than anything else.

"Daddy told you?"

Nodding her head while fighting to control her emotions, Mother Woodson knew she had to be strong for Linda, especially now.

"I'm gonna be okay, Mama," Linda lamented as her own eyes watered.

"I know you will. We're going to get through this, Baby. Just like last time." Mamie reached out, then, caressed Linda's face, "My beautiful girl. Oh, my beautiful girl."

Unable to contain herself, the dam of restrained tears broke. Weeping, she pulled Linda into her arms and held on for dear life. "I love you so much," she cried. "Oh, my baby."

"I love you, too, Mommy. I'm scared," Linda sobbed. "Mommy, I'm so scared."

"I know, honey, but I'll be with you every step of the way. Okay? Every step of the way."

The women remained clutched in each other's arms until their tears had run out.

"We've got some plans to make," Mamie finally said. "I want you to come home."

"I can't, Mama. I can't leave William. He needs me."

"What about you, Baby? You don't need to be concerning yourself with anyone else right now. William will understand. I've met him and Davis has told me everything he's done for you and I appreciate that. But you need to be with your family. Davis and I can see to your care…"

"Mama, you don't understand. I need him, too. We're a team, William and me. I can't abandon him now. We have too much to do," Linda explained.

"Honey…"

"No, Mama. There's no compromise in this. I won't leave him."

Mamie studied her daughter's face. The fear she'd seen there only moments ago was replaced by a fierce determination. Remembering her own courage, she couldn't help but smile.

That was her Lucky.

"Okay, Baby. Then we'll be moving up north. I refuse to stay in the waiting room this time."

THIRTEEN

Two months later...

Her eye sockets were a little deeper and the beautiful copper skin that covered bones and blood vessels, once loose, wrapped a little tighter around her skull. The twenty pounds she'd lost since her initial treatment made her appear trim and fit, like she was able to run miles around a track any time she pleased. Her eyebrows had thickened in a special way and her magnificent locs, against all medical logic, had survived massive chemotherapy. Linda Woodson, still optimistic, was existing in a world where every day could be her last. It was a place where many of God's courageous vanished when terminally ill.

Alternately accompanied by William, Josie, Mamie or Davis, Linda remained upbeat even as she fought her worsening state. Often times, she was a source of encouragement for them. When the devastating effects of the poison injected to kill the spreading cells took their toll on Linda—physically and mentally—her supporters were often at a loss for what to say. And although she consistently tried to assure William and the rest that she would make it through, many times she ran out of things to say, as well. Words held little meaning after undergoing the strenuous treatment she hoped would be her salvation.

During these times, she would become angry. *I'm a captive of this dreaded disease; at the mercy of this damn cancer. They stick me with these God-forsaken needles, injecting venom that would ordinarily kill a bear, to wipe this crap out. I can't believe it. I feel like a fuckin' freak. Just let me die!* These thoughts would invade her soul every time she went for treatment, and the one thing she could always look forward to upon her return home was curling her body against a toilet, retching in agony while vomiting the remnants of her hopeful savior. But she refused to put a voice to these negative feelings and speak a worse fate into existence.

"I'm hangin' in there," was her usual response to the many who showed their concern for her well-being.

"Keep fighting," her friends would say. And like Queen Nzinga, an independent woman and leader who had determined never to accept the Portuguese triumph over sixteenth-century Angola, Linda carried on.

"That queen won," she would say, clutching William for support as her body bent as though hit with a two-by-four. "And so will I, Prince William. Just for you."

"I know you will, Baby. I have faith," he'd respond. Turning his face away, however, he would conceal his tears. He, too, was a fighter, and despite the fact that every pore of him reeked sensitivity, somehow he would be strong in a way he'd never been before. Venturing into unfamiliar territory, there was no blueprint to follow.

Even as they endured all of this difficulty, William McCall felt lucky to be with her; especially after the chemo. This particular Thursday morning, as she had every two weeks since her diagnosis, Linda walked into the oncology center at Memorial Sloan Cancer Center. Taking her place with William among the hundreds of people whose empty stares spoke volumes about their common predicament, she waited about two hours before she was called.

For some reason an elderly Caucasian man stood out from the others. His skin pale and ashen, he looked as if he was at the doorway to the other side and check-in time was only seconds away.

Feeling a surge of pain run through her from her own agony, Linda smiled through gritted teeth. "Let him go ahead of me," she told the doctors.

Many of the other patients, all unknowing about what tomorrow could bring, yet hopeful for today and any day God blessed them with above ground, witnessed this noble act. As such, there wasn't a dry eye amongst them.

Leaning on William for support as she warded off her excruciating agony, she whispered, "I don't care how much pain I'm in. I had to let him go before me. This disease has no face, color, religion or gender, honey. We all get equal time with this demon."

William was stunned into silence. Thinking of his days prior to taking residence at the homeless shelter, his woes of yesteryear paled in comparison to what Linda was experiencing.

At that instant, her name was called and as usual, he accompanied her into the area of "medicine."

"Veins or port?" the nurse asked.

"Port," Linda said, which meant her veins had collapsed from being pierced with so many needles. The four vials of fluid would be drawn from a lump just to the left of her spine. Removing her shirt, Lucky looked at William. Her thoughts unspoken, bravely, she smiled as the nurse swabbed the lump with disinfectant, numbed it, then drew blood. Sending them back to the waiting room after the procedure, in an effort to liven the mood for others, together they recited a favorite comedy.

"Hey, Lucky, I'm looking for a man," William started.

"What man?" Lucky responded.

"The man with the power."

"What power, William?"

"The power of hoodoo."

"Hoodoo?"

"You do."

"You do what?"

"I'm looking for a man…"

As they repeated the skit taken from one of their favorite oldies *The Bachelor and the Bobbie-Soxer* starring Cary Grant, Myrna Loy and a teenaged Shirley Temple, some of the patients, needing a lift of any kind to their spirits, smiled. Others, still in their world of nothingness, just maintained their blank stares. Together, thinking of others, they tried to offer encouragement to nearby patients, oftentimes with comedy, other times, conviction. Feeding off the love they had for one another, they tried, in their own way, to share the feeling.

An hour passed before Linda went into the office of Dr. Stewart. Lying down, she was injected with Velban, a cell killer pushed into the veins in the hopes that it would eradicate more cancer cells than healthy ones. Limping out of her office as if struck by a baseball bat, she clutched William like she never wanted to let him go.

Bravely, Linda fought on, not only for herself, but for Rebecca, a five-year-old Jewish girl she had befriended during her treatment. Looking forward to seeing her ever-smiling face, Lucky made sure to bring a Charms lollipop for her to every visit. Upon receipt of her tasty candy, the little girl smiled with wattage that illuminated the treatment center.

Bald from her own radiation, Rebecca cried happily every time, running to Lucky with an innocent, heartfelt embrace. Her parents, saddened by the inevitability of losing their child, encouraged the bond.

"It's keeping her alive," they'd told her.

The relationship warmed Linda's heart, as well. Having her ability to conceive stripped away, she had taken to the young girl, sometimes unconsciously picturing her as the daughter she'd never had. Together, reading *The Little Engine That Could* before they underwent their therapy, both of them, laughing heartily, would shout, "I think I can," repeatedly, each time more lively than the previous. Not long after that, some of the other patients would chime in.

Feeling Lucky Linda's love of life, they all believed they could lick this thing.

Sadly, many in the room didn't.

And neither did Rebecca.

One Thursday morning, Linda and her mother arrived a half-hour early. Waiting all day for Rebecca and her parents, when she was finally called to receive her treatment, Linda grew worried.

"Where's Rebecca?" she asked a nurse.

Pausing, the nurse sighed deeply. Knowing how close the two had become, her exhalation gave Linda the answer; one she had not wanted to know.

Holding back her tears, Linda didn't want to cause a commotion among the other patients; her release would come later, she decided. Somehow numb to the chemo radiation this day, she was thawed to her own reality. Medicine can prop a human being up, even temporarily make them feel alive, like their old self. But it's all just a lie when it comes to a terminal illness like hers. Hope against the deterioration of strength and resistance is only optimism replacing common logic.

Linda Woodson was dying.

❦❦

Traveling through the Lincoln Tunnel after a long day at his new job, William McCall felt great. In the first month as an assistant managing clerk at Mayer, Mendel and Shaw, he immediately established a positive relationship with the attorneys who depended on his knowledge of the judicial system. Attempting to reestablish court contacts with some of his old friends, he found a few to be apprehensive about their association with him. Others, knowing his character, listened to his struggles before rendering judgment, and came to the conclusion that William couldn't have embezzled any money. Welcoming him back with open arms, they offered to do whatever they could to help him regain his footing in the legal community.

One of the first things William did while at his new job was get in touch with Juan Roldan, the director and principal of Reliable Clerical Services. The news William discovered about Markham Chandler disturbed him.

"Why didn't you call me before hiring this dude?" Juan asked.

"Well, I trusted him. And I figured I'd give a brother a shot."

"William, every brother ain't a brother. Man, I could have told you all about this clown."

Juan then relayed his own history. Markham had come to him looking for a job and while, at the time, he'd had no openings, he'd given him a job off the books paying three hundred dollars a week with the opportunity to continue his search for better positions with employment agencies. Believing him to be an invaluable asset, Juan had been on the precipice to offer him a piece of his partnership when it was revealed by one of his staff that Markham was actually trying to get money from the agencies by raiding his staff.

William was stunned. "Word?"

"It gets better, man." Continuing his story, the timbre of his voice changed as a rage rose in his chest as though the incident had just occurred. Juan told William about the moment when he confronted Chandler.

"All he kept saying to me was, 'Man, it's about the money. It's about the money, man, nothin' else.'"

"So, it was about the money, huh?" William asked.

"Yeah, Will. He was willing to take food out my families' mouths just for the paper. Man, after he said that, I was ready to kill that fucker, but I chilled and cut him a check through week's end and told him if he ever saw me in the courts or on the street to keep it moving."

"Damn, Juan, I bet he railroaded me, too."

"I know he did. When I heard about what happened at Goetz, I knew it was him. It's a shame we can't prove it."

Sighing, "Juan, I can't worry about that. He'll get his. God don't like ugly," William said.

"Next time," Juan reiterated, "check those references."

"Good looking out."

"If there's anything I can do, give your boy a holla. My business is reputable," Juan added.

"I know. Your legal company has all the retrieval business on lock. You'll definitely be one of my vendors."

"Remember, every brother ain't a brother."

"Tell me about it."

Recalling that conversation, his innocence had been validated. At this juncture, while the memory of the nightmare remained in his mind as a reminder of the ashes from which he'd risen, Linda was now at the forefront. *The road to recovery started with her love*, he thought. Wishing he was the one stricken with cancer so that her life would be serene, tears fell from his eyes as he privately worried about her. The feelings she'd given him enlivened his soul and restored his faith that there were positive women only wanting to show love to a man sans expectation or remuneration.

His tears of anxiety would stop once he reached what had now become *their* Jersey City Heights home.

I have to be strong for my queen, he thought as he turned the key.

As usual, his courage would be tested by Linda's recent development.

"Rebecca died, William," she said an hour later.

"That's the little girl you always took the lollipops to, isn't it?"

She nodded.

They were seated on her sofa. Linda's legs were stretched out across the length and covered with a down-filled throw. Resting her upper body against William's, she was fatigued from the chemo treatment, yet comfortable; this despite her spirit being a bit downtrodden.

"I'm sorry, sweetie. I know how special she was to you."

"Why do I even bother with this?" she asked dishearteningly. "I'm not getting any better and all it's doing is making me sick to my stomach. I'm going to die. Nothing they're doing is going to stop that."

Suddenly overcome with emotion, Linda began to cry.

Unable to think of anything to say that would alleviate her mental anguish, William remained silent.

Allowing her tears to run their course, Linda composed herself and eventually suggested they partake of what had become their favorite pastime. "Do you wanna watch a movie?"

"Which one?" he asked.

"This feels like a Spencer and Kate night, don't you think so?"

"Yeah, let me set it up."

Linda leaned away from William, affording him the freedom to move to her movie case.

"*Guess Who's Coming To Dinner?*" he suggested.

"Perfect."

But was it a perfect choice? The next hour and forty or so minutes screamed a resounding *no*. Viewing this cinematic treasure and knowing the depth of the Hepburn/Tracy union, both were cognizant of the fact that the underlying current on screen ran much deeper than the backdrop of interracial relationships in the sixties.

This landmark film, although featuring Sidney Poitier in a breakout role, was the very last professional pairing of Spencer Tracy and Katharine Hepburn. Anyone who knew their background would know that throughout the film, they had relayed personal feelings of love for one another. Reel life meeting real life, twelve days after the filming, Tracy died, thus concluding their imperfectly perfect union. For the duration of the movie, one got the feeling that the loving sands of their wondrous hourglass were running out, as was the case with William and Linda.

Both of them had gotten this message. Holding hands during the entire movie, they watched as Tracy, cast in the role of Matt Drayton, delivered a powerful speech at the film's climax. Boldly declaring, "In the final analysis, it doesn't matter what we think; the only thing that matters is what they feel about each other."

Linda, delivering a message that words could not articulate, grabbed William's hand with all the strength she could muster from her chemo-ravaged body. As Spencer continued declaring his love for Kate in character, tears formed in her eyes, then began a sad journey. Running down her cheeks, Linda barely fought the sniffles of uncontrolled bawling. Knowing that the only thing that mattered was what she felt for the brave warrior who was standing by her side and what he felt for her, in Spencer's dying words, that was everything.

Linda Woodson was saying goodbye to her king.

In sync with his soul mate, William, noticing her reactions, understood the moment clearly. Gazing lovingly at Linda, at movie's end he reached into the pocket of his gray slacks. Pulling out the engagement ring he'd been carrying around every day as a reminder of the pain he'd endured by his ex-fiancée's betrayal, William smiled.

"I realize the mistake I made, Linda." Placing the diamond bauble on her once fleshy but now sickly thin ring finger, he too, began to cry. "I should have waited for you."

"Oh, William, I love you so much," Linda said.

"I love you too, Lucky."

Composing himself moments later, William watched as several emotions crossed Linda's face. Obviously something was on her mind. Finally, she spoke.

"William, there's something I need to tell you." Looking away for an instant, she was nervous about how he would take her revelation, fearing his rejection. "I should have told you this a long time ago… I don't know why I didn't."

"What is it, Baby?"

Slowly, she began. "I've told you about Emerson, what happened between us."

"Yes." William realized, in that moment, he would probably have to tell her that Emerson had been instrumental in getting him the job he presently held.

"What I didn't tell you was that he came to see me the day I had my first treatment. I met with him for lunch. He seemed so insistent and since he'd come to the hospital, I felt I owed him at least a little bit of my time. I was taken aback, though, when I found out his true intentions."

"He wanted you back, huh?" William interjected, knowing that had not been the case.

"No. He told me that he'd been spying on us. He was jealous, that's for sure, but I believe he was genuinely concerned, too. He told me he'd looked into your background, including your firing from that law firm where you worked, and that he believed you might have been set up. He said he'd spoken to a guy you worked with. I can't remember his name."

Sighing, "Markham Chandler," William announced.

"Yeah, that's it. He told me a lot of things, but I'd rather hear your version of what really happened."

William shook his head, then huffed in mock amusement. Sighing again, he started, "I don't know how he did it, if indeed he had something to do with me getting fired, but I told you, Linda, I didn't steal any money."

"I know you didn't, but that's not what I meant."

"What?" he asked, unclear as to what she wanted to know, if it wasn't that.

"Tell me about Anna."

As if triggered by her words, William winced, closed his eyes and revisited a painful memory.

"Ooh, I love it when you do it that way…"

"Do you want it harder?"

"Yes, Mark, yes," Anna screamed. "Harder, dammit! Harder!"

Trembling, he tried to speak but William couldn't. Rocking, William covered his face with his hands.

"Whose pussy is this?" Mark asked.

"It's all yours, Baby…"

"That's right, you greedy bitch! This is my shit here! Now say my name!" he barked.

"Mark… Mark!" she submitted.

Shaking his head, William's mind watched the culmination of the horrid visual. Trying desperately to maintain his cool, the recollection of her taking his semen in her mouth again made him vulnerable and small, just like that fateful day. He moved to get up.

Linda, using strength only God could have given her, grabbed him.

"Talk to me, Baby. I'm here for you."

Looking deep into her eyes, William cried, but there were no tears. He cried out the truth. "Linda, Markham Chandler not only took my job from me. But…"

"It's alright, William," Linda encouraged.

Warding off pain's attempted takeover of his soul, somehow he regained his power. "I lost everything to him; my fiancée, then the very next day, my job. In less than twenty-four hours my life, as I'd known it, was over. Look at your finger, Linda," he directed, pointing to the engagement ring. "I went to her house to give her that and saw them in bed."

"How did you respond?"

"I didn't. I just left. My plan was to fire him the next day, but I got fired instead. The whole thing sent me spiraling, Linda. Every day, for almost a year, I got high on weed trying to incinerate the memory. Running back and forth to landlord-tenant court, I tried to save my apartment, but couldn't. There were times I thought about killing myself, but my faith wouldn't let me. Somehow, someway, I knew that I would be okay."

Sitting up, Linda shook her head, over and over. Tears rolling down her cheeks, she felt angry for him.

They were wiped away by the hands of her prince. "But that's all over now, Linda," William said. Bravely, a smile escaped the corners of his mouth. "The storm I experienced brought me to you. Lucky, you've been so good to me, so good for me. Being with you has brought me new life. I feel alive, like I've been born again. I never thought I could live again, I mean really live and be happy again. Even in the face of this, your cancer, you've changed all of that."

Linda took a deep breath and gazed into his eyes. "Can you do something for me?" she pleaded.

Curiosity got the best of William. "Sure, Baby. What? Anything you want."

"Can you...can you just hold me?" Seeing the question in his eyes, she explained, "I need to know, need to *feel* what it is to be held by someone who truly loves me. Can you just hold me and show me what it feels like?"

"Sure, Baby. I'll do anything for you." Peering into her eyes as he caressed her face, their tongues collided in emotional passion.

Suddenly, Linda pulled away. Crestfallen, she was sad that she couldn't make love to him. The tears she valiantly tried to control came in the form of an uncontrollable sob.

"I'm so sorry, William," she weakly apologized.

"Did I ask for anything, Lucky?"

Shaking her head *no*, she cried, "I'm gonna miss you."

"Don't you say that, Linda," William defiantly responded. "Don't you say that. You're going to beat this thing so that we can grow old together."

She laughed weakly. "I sure hope so, my king. I sure hope so."

What neither of them realized was that the end was frighteningly near.

FOURTEEEN

Two months later…

While her chest rose in a steady rhythm, each seizure she experienced brought her closer to home. Every time she passed out, her body was in limbo. Torn between the conscious and unconscious in her queen-sized bed, Linda would remember the promise she'd made to her Prince and open her eyes.

I will make it to Valentine's Day, his favorite holiday, she told herself. Weakly touching her "wedding ring," the object William had placed on her hand after watching Spencer and Kate, *the paper don't mean diddly if there's no love*, Lucky bragged through her pain.

Dr. Stewart had called her into her office in early November and Linda had limped there with her man in tow. Each attempt to quicken her pace that day had been unsuccessful. Her right leg wouldn't let her. Every part of her ached—her hips, back and knees. Her stomach churning from the massive doses of chemo, the countless Advil tablets and prescribed pain medication had her wanting to give up, especially after hearing the doctor's fatal prognosis.

"There's nothing more we can do," the oncologist told them.

Despite the finality of those words, a brave smile emanated from both of their faces.

"I guess it's time to start looking for that man," she joked, tapping William's leg.

On cue, William asked, "What man?"

"The man with the power."

"What power?"

"The power of hoodoo."

"Who do?"

"You do."

"You do what?"

"Start looking for that man," Linda finished with a weak smile.

Love would see them through the valley of death, they both realized.

Only in the privacy of their home, when having to break the news to Mamie and Davis, did Linda lose her composure. Never forgetting her wail of despair, seeing her mother inconsolable was like a stake in the heart. *No parent wants their child to leave the earth before them*, she thought as Davis held her.

Daddy was a champ about it all, Linda recalled, *but even he lost it.* She remembered him watching a television commercial that showed a dad accepting a gift from his little girl, a Rolex watch, hugging her and saying, "I must be pretty special for you to bring me this." The warrior who'd protected her heart for so long let his guard down. Crying outwardly, it was then he noticed Lucky.

"Whether on earth or in heaven," he said, "you'll always be my little girl."

"I know, Daddy," her mouth said, but inwardly, she wept.

Josie, her lifelong friend, was devastated, so much so that Lucky, out of concern for her, suggested that her visits be minimal. "No offense, Josie. But I need all my strength to fight this thing."

"I understand." Josie nodded.

"Tell my line sisters that I love them."

Remarkably, the person she worried most about, her prince, William, provided Linda the fortress of strength she so desperately needed. On the good days, he crawled into bed beside her. Gently wrapping her in his arms, William would hold her through the night as they talked about life. On those really bad days when the pain wouldn't surrender its hold on her, Linda would curse him and he willingly took the abuse. Never leaving her side after arriving home from work, William would fall asleep on the hardwood floor next to her bed, his head resting on a pillow.

Christmas morning came and Linda was greeted at her bedside with love. Her sorors, Marcia, Alexis, Shari and Elise all dropped by, bringing all the love and good cheer they could muster.

Pointing to Shari, Marcia and Alexis, Linda pulled William close.

With a smile, Linda told him in a stage whisper, "Those three, you should give them complimentary fries."

William agreed. "I should, right?"

Sharing a laugh, it was another of their perfect moments within their imperfect world; one of the last they knew they would ever share.

By now, all of the line sisters had heard about *Lucky's secret love* and upon finally meeting him expressed a degree of remorse for their close-minded opinions.

William, fully aware of their comments, put them at ease. "It's all good. It's always wise to look at the fabric of the man as opposed to the fabric of his suit."

Placing a pajama-attired Linda in a chair, the Deltas instructed William to hold her hand as they formed a circle around them. Together, their voices became one as they proudly sang their "sweetheart song," a song normally reserved for weddings.

Once completing the tune, they embraced Linda, one by one. As Elise, the last of her sorors hugged her, tears came as they all returned to her for a final bonding moment; the last they would share together on earth.

Even in the face of death, sisterhood refused to lost its luster.

Watching the snowflakes fall to the Jersey sidewalk, Mamie Woodson sat coatless on Linda's porch. Numb to the winter chill raking against her cooca-colored skin, the winter chill paled in comparison to the reality of her daughter's present state. Feeling helpless, it was difficult watching Linda's brave fight against the inevitable. Seeing her convulse every time her body shook from her seizures, she wished it were her that were in that bedroom fighting death. *A mother never wants to see her child suffer,* she thought.

Feeling a coat being draped around her shoulders, she looked up and saw William.

"I thought you might need this," he said.

"Are you always this attentive?" she asked.

"I try, ma'am." He paused before continuing, "You know, I feel awful that we know each other under such difficult circumstances. In a perfect world..."

"There's a reason for everything, William," Mamie consoled as she turned to face him. "Son, with all my heart I want to say thank you."

"You don't have to thank me for taking care of Linda. I'm only showing the love she's shown me from the very second our lives connected. Ms. Woodson, that fighter in the bedroom is the best thing that ever happened to me. And looking at how calm you've been tells me where it all comes from. So no, I say 'Thank You' for raising such a beautiful woman."

For the first time in recent months, Mamie beamed. "William, I was so scared that my Linda would never know the feeling of real love. Not the stuff that you kids call love today. But that real love, that true love, that lasting love. That shared energy that starts with nothing and builds together; the meeting of spirts where worlds are complete with each other's presence. The passion between two that never dies when there are problems, that 'till death do you part' love."

"The love that you and Davis have," William murmured. "I can see the fire in your eyes."

"Precisely, honey. I thought she was never going to find it in a man. But she found it in you, and I am so thankful."

"She's the one that holds my heart, Ms. Woodson. I just wish..." Trembling with emotion, William lowered his head so that he wouldn't bawl.

Linda's mother picked his chin up.

"Son, no matter what happens, you will get through this. Linda wants you to. Behind all that sensitivity you possess is the heart of a lion. And you need to continue showing that strength. Not just for you, but," she said while pointing in the house, "for your wife in there. It's keeping her alive."

"I will, Ms. Woodson."

FIFTEEN

I t was a struggle for Mamie to remain composed during Linda's last days. Watching her *miracle baby* deteriorate right before her eyes was more than she could bear, but she saved her tears for when she was alone or with Davis.

Doing everything in her power to ensure Linda's comfort, Mamie would read to her, much the way she had done when Linda was a child. It didn't matter if she was asleep or not either; she felt that the sound of her voice would be soothing to her daughter, even if she couldn't personally take away her pain.

During one of these sessions, as Mamie read one of Linda's favorite books, *Their Eyes Were Watching God* by Zora Neale Hurston, Linda opened her eyes and smiled. Interrupting the melodic tone of her mother's voice, she said, "You should have been a schoolteacher, Mama."

Putting down the book, Mamie responded, "No, I wouldn't have lasted two minutes in a room full of kids."

In a weakened tone, Linda said, "Yeah, you would've. All you'd have had to do was read to them. You know how they say music soothes the savage beast? Well, I'd say, 'My Mama's voice will give you peace.'"

Mamie smiled lovingly at her brave offspring. "You amaze me. Here you are, fighting through all of your pain and fear just to brighten the lives of me, Davis and William. Do you know how special you are?"

"Oh, Mama, don't."

"No, Baby. You need to know if you don't already. What you have done for me... You've given my life so much meaning and joy." Mamie sighed in satisfaction. "God blessed me beyond comprehension when He gave you to me. You are a treasure. Every life you touch, you change for the better. Look at William. You never told me everything about him, but he did. He told me what you did for him; how you picked him up and brushed him off and gave him the confidence and the will to get his life back on track. Only a very unselfish person could do something so beneficent. And Davis…" Mamie lowered her head and paused momentarily. "He loves you so much, as if you were a child of his own loins."

"I love him, too, Mama."

Mamie reached over and caressed Linda's skeletal face. "I'm so proud to be able to call you my daughter."

"Mama, I don't want you to be sad. You'll go on. You have to. Just do me one favor," Linda asked.

"What, Baby?"

"Promise me you won't forget about William. Promise me he'll always have a place to call home," Linda pleaded with watery eyes.

"He's my son. Of course, he'll always have a home."

❦❦

When Linda opened her eyes the morning of Valentine's Day, all she could see were the heart-shaped balloons and bouquets adorning her room.

Noticing William at her dresser with a vase in hand, she called out in a weak voice, "Did somebody die?"

Turning to her, he smiled. "Hey, gorgeous, Happy Valentine's Day."

"Is it really V-day? Oh good, I was scared we were at my funeral."

William moved to her bedside. Taking the seat that had become a part of the room's décor, he leaned over and kissed her lips tenderly. "I love you, pretty girl."

"Now you need to stop lying to me, 'cause I haven't even washed my face yet."

"Don't you know you're beautiful even with mud on your face," William whispered close to her ear.

"Yeah, I noticed you said that so no one else could hear it though. They might think you're a little touched."

He chuckled. Gazing lovingly at her, he asked, "How're you feeling, Lucky?"

"Just like my name." With effort, she reached up and caressed his face. "Thank you."

"For what, precious?"

"For everything, William. For those beautiful balloons and those, my beautiful flowers. Are those lilies?" she asked of the vase he'd placed on the dresser.

"Yes."

"I love lilies. No one's ever given me any before. Would you bring them closer?"

Without hesitation, he rose and retrieved the vase, placing it on the table right next to her bed.

"They're beautiful. Thank you."

"You're welcome, my queen."

"Baby," Linda said, "please put on Luther for me."

Obliging, William turned on the CD player that lay on the night table. "Never Let Me Go" filled the room.

Sitting on the bed, "Mrs. McCall, may I have this dance?" he asked her.

Smiling weakly, "I'd love to," Lucky said.

Although she barely had the strength to sit up, Linda summoned the courage to raise her arms just enough for William to fall into her feeble embrace. Holding her gently, he made sure his movements were slow and steady. At song's end he returned her to a comfortable resting position. Noticing her tears, he turned his face away so that she wouldn't see his.

"I'm gonna miss you so much, William. You're gonna make someone a very happy woman one day," Linda whispered.

Ignoring her words, he smiled, then reached to the floor. Up came two plastic champagne flutes, then a bottle of sparkling apple cider. "Honey, this isn't *Cristal*, but it'll do." Pouring her a glass, he fed her the drink slowly.

Linda sipped from the flute, despite the fact that her sense of taste had diminished long ago. "Mmm," she sighed.

Luther's "I'd Rather" came on. Linda, offering another weak smile, reached for William's hand. "Remember this song, sugar?"

"I sure do, Lucky."

"When we found out I had cancer, I was so scared you were going to leave me."

"Oh, Linda, don't think negative thoughts now. You know what I actually thought?"

Contorting her face in puzzlement, she didn't have the strength to ask what. So William continued. "I wished it were me, so you wouldn't have to suffer one day."

Taking a deep breath, "I haven't suffered, Baby. You wanna know why?" she asked.

"Why?"

"Because my love for you has me feeling no pain. I knew from the minute we started talking that I loved you."

"You know what I thought when I first saw you, Baby?"

"What?"

"That you couldn't sing a lick."

"You still have jokes, huh?" Too weak to laugh, Linda again smiled, then drifted into a deep sleep. Clearly more fatigued than normal, she slipped in and out of consciousness throughout the day. Willing herself to live through William's special day, Linda wouldn't have it any other way.

The next day, the sun was shining brightly on Linda as she opened her eyes. Realizing that her vision was gone, but knowing her mother was in the room when she heard the shades being raised, Linda's voice was barely above a whisper.

"Hi, Mama."

"Good morning, sugar," Mamie said.

This was not a good day for Linda. In addition to her loss, experiencing intense pain, she grimaced. Turning her body left toward her mother, she got her attention.

"Mama," she calmly called out, "Please get William for me." Obliging, Mamie fulfilled her daughter's request.

Immediately entering the bedroom, William's face, as usual wore a smile of love.

"Hello, darling," he said in a radiant tone. Sitting at the head of the bed, he grabbed Linda's left hand.

"Hey, Baby," Linda whispered.

"How are you?"

"Other than this blurry vision, I feel great." She wouldn't tell him the true extent of her blindness; that she couldn't see him at all. Her body was shutting down. "Honey, I have a taste for ice cream. Would you mind getting me some from the store?"

"Anything for you, Baby. Vanilla Swiss Almond?"

"Sure." Covering his hand with both of hers, Linda said, in her most pleasant tone, "Hurry back, sugar. I love you, William."

"I love you too, Lucky," he said, kissing her forehead. "I'll be right back."

"Honey?" she called as he started from the room.

"Yes?"

"Thank you."

Not realizing that she was saying good-bye, William smiled and replied, "Anytime, sweetie."

Mamie, witnessing all of this from the entryway, knew what was transpiring. As William passed her, she turned and watched as he walked to the door of the apartment and exited without a second thought.

Moving to Linda's bedside, Mamie took her daughter's hand.

"Mama?"

"Yes, Baby. I'm here."

"I'm ready to go."

Tears flowed unchecked from Mamie's eyes. Leaning over, she pressed her lips to Linda's forehead and whispered, "I love you, Baby. I will always love you."

She felt a slight pressure on her hand as Linda, with the minutest bit of strength, squeezed it for a brief second.

Then it was over.

As William stood at the counter of the corner store waiting to pay for Linda's ice cream, he suddenly had a sense of foreboding much like the dream that he'd had with the crows.

Immediately, without regard for the pint he'd removed from the store's freezer, he turned and ran straight for home. Upon his arrival, one glance at

Mamie Woodson as she stood in the hallway just outside of Linda's bedroom and he knew but refused to accept it.

Finding a place at her bedside, he grabbed her hand. Trembling while holding her warm, yet lifeless limb, he whispered, "Hey, Baby. I wanted to get your ice cream, but something told me to come back and check on you." The tears flowed freely as he struggled with his words. "I know, I haven't told you this, but Linda, I want to thank you for everything you've ever done for me. I love you so much. You saved my life, Baby. And, oh, how I wish I could save yours. Lord knows, I'm trying…"

By now, Davis had joined Mamie at the doorway. Too numb to speak, they couldn't summon the courage to disturb him. Not just yet.

Bravely, William talked on. "You know, I never told you how deep my love is for you. I would walk through fire for you, take a bullet in the heart and die for you. That's why it hurts so much seeing you suffer. There's not much I can do, except hope and pray for some miracle. You saved my soul from depths I couldn't comprehend and I wish I could save you. Baby, please don't leave me. Please don't leave me in such a cold cruel world. Lucky, please don't die. We still have so much to do.

"We're a team, remember, with the power of hoo-doo…" Rambling while crying, he wasn't ready to accept the finality of it all. Life would somehow, someway have to go on without Linda. While she lived she had taught him many lessons, but she couldn't teach him this painful one; how to survive the loss of the love of your life. He'd have to figure this one out on his own.

When the coroners came, he still refused to let go. "Put a blanket over her, she's gonna get cold. I don't want her to get cold," he said to them.

Unable to remain silent any longer, Mamie Woodson wrapped her arms around him. "It's alright, son. She's in a better place now, she's not suffering anymore."

Finally thawing to the reality of it all, the truth came crashing down on him. Collapsing in her embrace while sobbing uncontrollably, his body became unhinged as he finally accepted the awful fact.

Linda, his angel, his everything, was gone.

EPILOGUE

One year later…

William McCall had entered the world's most famous arena many times, but never to play in it. Having witnessed everyone from Walt "Clyde" Frazier and Michael Ray Richardson to Patrick Ewing, Allan Houston and Stephon Marbury adorn the blue, white and orange, the thought of playing on the Madison Square Garden floor for the Lawyer's League Basketball Championship had him grinning with anticipation.

His merriment lasted all of five seconds; the time it had taken for him to look toward the Seventh Avenue end of the arena.

I don't believe this shit.

Over the years, fate had played many games with his mind, however, none crueler than today's. The Runners' opponent for the trophy would be Markham Chandler and the Goetz, Gallagher and Green Pacers.

That was only a portion of the irony. In the stands watching them warm up was personification of the agony that nearly swallowed him whole. Beaming at the athletic muscularity of William's former assistant was his former fiancée, Anna Daniels.

She never came to any of my games, he thought as the pre-game horn sounded.

The mind games continued as William and Mark went to center court to listen to the referee's instructions.

Normally, intimidating stare downs were exchanged between pugilists before a boxing match, but the recitation of the rules of the basketball game were oblivious to both as heated glares were reciprocated.

This motherfucker took my whole life away.

Resisting the urge to choke him, William pursed his lips. He knew on this day, there would be a game within a game. This wasn't merely a contest for a basketball trophy; rather, it was a one-on-one for manhood.

That became evident once the referee finished, as both walked away without acknowledging each other with so much as a handshake.

As the teams lined up for the tip-off, Mark gave William a sharp elbow to the chest as a welcome-to-the-game introduction.

"This is my bitch right here," he announced to the occupants of the world's most famous arena.

The referee immediately blew his whistle. "That's a technical foul on number twenty-four red!"

Without a word, William fired the first salvo. Only after sinking both free throws did he speak. "Does my dick taste good when you're eating her?" he mumbled.

The game and the war had begun.

Trash-talking at William, although his former boss was checking someone else, Mark and the Pacers broke ahead early. Exciting those in attendance with scintillating shakedowns, Chandler scored ten of his teams first twelve points.

"Time out, Runners," the ref called upon noticing the captain's hands.

"You're the only one who can check him. Do you want to go box-and-one and take him?" one of his teammates asked William.

"Not yet. Trust me. I'll shut him down when I have to."

Nothing changed after the break, as Chandler scored from everywhere seemingly at will. After each made basket, he flashed a menacing look at William as if he had stolen something from him, when, in fact, he'd been the offender.

With two minutes left in the first half and his team comfortably ahead by twenty, Mark used a screen and was isolated with William. Using his dribble as a yo-yo, he executed A.I.'s killer crossover, right to left, drove baseline and saw someone coming at him. In mid-flight, he switched the ball from his left hand to his right and dunked on both defenders.

The place went bonkers.

"Take that!" he snarled.

His taunt was muted by the Pacer bench and its supporting fans.

Anna led derisive, rhythmic cheers. "Can't stop Markham," she chanted, clapping in a two-three rhythm as William brought the ball up court.

The crowd, comprised of attorneys and other ballers who had games following theirs, joined in. "Can't stop Markham." *Clap-clap, clap-clap-clap.*

Trying to respond street ball-style, William froze the opposing guard checking him with a behind-the-back dribble, leaving him swooning. Driving to the basket, he encountered Mark, who pushed him hard out of bounds.

Incredulously, the refs didn't eject him; from their angles on the court, the foul looked legit.

Hitting a metal chair head-on, there was William McCall, bleeding from his chin and stretched out.

Chandler, worked up in a lather now, stood over him.

"Yeah, you think that's something, I'll do it again! I took your woman, then I took your job! You ain't nothin,' you faggot! You ain't got nothin' for me!"

Soon after, the first half ended. The score was 52 to 28, in favor of the Pacers.

Walking slowly to his bench, he noticed that Anna had left the stands and engaged her boyfriend with a kiss.

William's attention was distracted by an attorney on his team.

"Number twenty-four is making this personal, huh?"

"Yeah."

"You know," the thirty-something partner said, "there comes a time when you have to plant your feet firm and kick some ass. The only way we'll win this is if you take over."

The message was delivered. In case it hadn't registered, ten other teammates came and patted William on his back.

As if given the green light to reckless abandon, the inner fury that simmered within him boiled over. Essentially being told to put the game on his back, the old man was going to do it all by himself in the second half.

Rationing his energy, the eruption started slowly as William hit a couple of jumpers. Because he hadn't played with such intensity in a couple of years, his hamstrings were tightening, so he relied heavily on his follow-through. The deficit, with twenty minutes to go, was at eighteen.

"We need you to check Chandler in a box-and-one," someone yelled from the Runners' bench.

Clearly fatigued, William nodded. There would be no rest for him defensively, so he wondered if he would have enough left on the other end.

Dribbling across half-court, Mark laughed at the match-up.

"He can't guard me!" he announced. "He can't even keep a woman, much less check me!"

William's rebuttal was a brilliant, open court pick-pocket and driving lay-up.

Sixteen, he thought as he returned up court. *If we can get it to ten with five minutes left, then we have a chance.*

He would do even better. Next trip down, he would hit a three-pointer. Then, after a spin move right to left, a la Kenny Anderson, a driving lay-up.

And one, he thought after being fouled.

With sixteen minutes left, he was halfway up the mountain. They were down ten, 64 to 54.

Trading baskets for the next ten minutes, Mt. Everest seemed insurmountable at the six-minute mark. Using their next to last time out, he crossed paths with his former protégé.

"You have nothing left!" Mark screamed.

He was right. William had exerted all the energy a forty-one-year-old man could muster. Breathing heavily through his mouth as his chest burned with over-exertion, he slumped to the bench, draped a towel over his head and closed his eyes.

Suddenly feeling an odd sensation, all he could see was her smile. Next, a feminine tone jolted his subconscious. *I'll always have faith in you, William,* the voice in his mind whispered.

No matter what it entailed, he knew Linda wanted him to handle his business.

Like a sip of ginseng, he found his resolve. William McCall, a man entering midlife whose goatee was speckled with blood from a busted chin; a man tortured by two decades of emotional heartbreak, fired from a job after a bogus embezzlement charge, spurned by a fiancée for a man eight years his junior, homeless for a minute, and finally, having to grieve over a dying love, was determined to stop giving Job a run for his money.

He drove and scored on a twisting floater, then next trip down, launched a twenty-footer with Chandler running at him.

"Don't look back," William said.

His tormentor showed ignorance, turned his head and saw an orange sphere snapping nylon.

Swish. The mountaintop was five points away, but time was running out. Three and a half minutes remained.

Mark temporarily lost him with another well-executed crossover, then rose for a jump shot in the lane.

Thwack!! "C'mon, Mark... You can do better than that."

A teammate recovered William's block and drove to the goal.

It was down to three.

Mark stemmed the tide with a three-pointer, giving him forty points on the evening. William quickly responded with one of his own, giving him forty-four of his team's seventy-four points. But his team was still three behind with one hundred twenty seconds left.

Those last two minutes of the game would be "high noon" at the Garden; a young, cocky gunslinger with a stolen fiancée in tow versus a battle-scarred warrior of life.

The hundred or so in attendance yelled words of encouragement as if the place were standing room only.

"Bring us home, William," the Runners' bench yelled.

"You can do it, Mark," Anna screamed from behind the Pacers' bench. Her voice was almost hoarse from all her screaming.

"If he gets by me," Mark instructed his teammates, "knock him on his ass. No free lay-ups." Sure enough, after a turnover William sprinted by him and got slammed to the floor, but not before hitting the lay-up.

With his weariness apparent to all that watched, his body ached as he rose from the hardwood. Ambling slowly to the free-throw line, he hunched over for a second, tugged at the bottom of his shorts, collected himself and sank the continuation free-throw.

Game tied, with a minute and a half to go.

Then, he gathered another loose ball and crossed mid-court. Stutter-stepping as if he were twenty, he lost one defender, squared up in the face of another one and let fly from three-point range.

In and out! The game was still tied with a minute left.

As the Pacers called time, William's face was expressionless as he peered over at his former love.

Her stunned expression indicated that she felt his thoughts.

I hope you're happy with your choice. I had a ring in my hand, ready to spend forever with you. You two clowns deserve each other. He's a thief, and you're a nut. Scream all you want, it still won't be enough. You want to know why? Because he has no heart. And you don't either!

His train of thought was stunted by a response by Mark, who promptly buried a three-pointer as William arrived a split-second too late.

"Face, motherfucker!" he screamed. Leaping from the behind the Pacers' bench, his baby met him at his bench.

"You did it! You did it!" Anna screamed.

Time out, Runners.

The clock showed thirty-eight seconds left, which meant a miracle was needed. William, resting on the bench, wiping his face with a towel while peering skyward for help, could feel Linda's strength inside of him. She'd restored everything: his life, his sanity, his heart through emotional nurturing, his faith in love, and he knew her spirit would carry him through.

She was with him all the way. "I got this, Baby," he said under his breath to his angel.

As they broke from their final huddle, William was calm as he received the initial inbound pass. Moving leisurely to his right, he quickly went into attack mode as he drove to the basket, laying the ball high and soft off the fiberglass and through the net.

It was a one-point game with thirty-one seconds left.

"Don't foul yet," he screamed at his team. "Play tough defense."

The clock whittled down to twenty seconds when an attempted pass was made into the post for Mark. William saw the play coming and poked the ball away for the steal.

As he glided up court, he looked at the clock in front of him. Sixteen seconds were left when he crossed the timeline and veered left. Everything seemed to unfold slowly, as if everything in life had prepared him for this moment.

He was feeling Lucky.

Fearful that William might pass to an open shooter if they double-teamed him, the Pacers played straight up, man-to man defense. Suddenly, the loneliest man in the arena was Markham Chandler, out there isolated on William McCall.

His right-handed dribble echoing through the roar of the arena, William smiled with the confidence of a survivor of life.

"So, you think you can take me, Mark?"

"Yeah."

"This is what you wanted, son."

Carefully letting the game clock run down, at eight seconds William made his move, going right as if he were driving into the lane. Mark lunged at the ball as he stopped on a dime while going behind his back.

Chandler went sprawling.

The ballers in the stands, waiting to play the divisional championship games, yelled, "Broke."

One hard dribble back to his left and William was in the clear.

Squaring up, he let fly and made sure to follow through.

As the ball was in mid-flight, he looked to the hardwood at a fallen Chandler, who was peering up at him. Seeing the anguish on his face, the certitude of defeat, his former assistant turned traitor knew the shot was going in. He had not only lost the game to an older, wiser player, but to a better man.

In that next millisecond, he searched for Anna and saw her first extend her hands as if to will the ball from going in, then to cover her face as though grieving. Peering upward, he saw Linda smiling with her hands raised, as if flashing a victory sign.

The ball hit nothing but net.

81 to 80, Runners.

Time-out, Pacers.

The Garden rocked.

Five seconds left.

Moving gingerly, William collapsed on the team bench, physically exhausted. Bloodied chin and all, he turned back the hands of time to score fifty-one points, including his team's final eleven. His incomparable will had taken the Runners to the brink, but there was one more step.

One last stop remained.

Everyone on the planet knew Mark would take the final shot and he didn't disappoint. Driving right, he took two hard dribbles and rose and got his shot returned to his waist.

As promised, Chandler was stopped when it mattered most.

The buzzer sounded.

Punching the air with a clenched fist, William was mobbed by his teammates.

"You did it, man! You kicked ass!"

"No guys, we did it," he muttered.

Placing a towel on his open wound, William smiled weakly, dressed quickly, sat down, and buried his head in the absorbent cloth. Already knowing he needed stitches to close the gash, the hospital trip, he decided, would come tomorrow.

"Yo, man, good game."

Glancing upward, Mark hovered over him in a blue windbreaker, extending his right hand.

William rose from the bench and, without a word or an acknowledgment, walked away.

"Oh, so you don't want to speak? You're not going to say anything to me, man?" Mark asked.

William stopped in his tracks, then looked over his shoulder. "Dilligaf?" he asked.

"Dilligaf?"

"Yeah, Mark. Dilligaf," William yelled. "Do I look like I give a fuck about you?"

Smiling while following his teammates off the floor, his path inadvertently crossed that of Anna's.

"You played a good game, William," she cooed.

"Not as good as yours, though," he said without missing a beat and continued on his course.

As he was about to leave the arena, from the corner of his eye, something caught his attention. Pausing briefly, he turned his head and looked right into the eyes of a beautiful woman wearing a Pittsburgh Steelers jersey. Acknowledging her seductive wink and her flowing braids, he couldn't help but smile.

"I know, Lucky. I know."

A TRIBUTE TO

LUTHER VANDROSS

Forever and Always the Voice of Love

My House is Still a Home
Written July 4th, 2005

It's been three days, and it still hasn't sunk in. God, I miss him. But he's home now, dancing with his father. Smiling from heaven, he's no longer suffering the effects of his stroke, in fact he's in full body and spirit singing in front of Barry White's Love Unlimited Orchestra. I can't wait to hear that duet with Phyllis Hyman. (It's ironic how we lost them all on or around the July 4th Weekend.)

Do you remember where you were when you received the news that a friend to some and lover to all was gone? I was in a car that Friday afternoon at 5:30 p.m. when the bulletin stunned the airwaves. Letting out a scream, I was hoping the Bad Boy of radio would allow listeners to see how much our friend impacted his life.

"I don't want to talk about death on a Friday," was the disc jockey's terse response.

Angered to the point I couldn't see straight, a deep feeling within my core told me we would have been fighting had I been in the studio.

He just didn't get it.

"You'd be celebrating love and life," I countered.

Immediately, I turned the dial to a more compassionate deejay.

As the numbness thawed and the tears came, I thought of his legacy as his talent was the cornerstone, the foundation to everything positive with regards to God's most precious energy.

And oh, that voice. Smooth as velvet, as powerful as a hurricane of love, he was quality personified. No one will ever replicate, or even come close to his vocal artistry. Now I know how people felt when moved to tears by a Nat King Cole, Sam Cooke song. Luther Vandross was for our generation what they were for my parents.

As I listen to the *Dance With My Father* compilation, "I Think About Him." Feeling blessed to have seen him in concert seven times, the last time he touched me live was at Long Island's Westbury Music Fair in May of 2002, a year before the music stopped. Even better on stage, Luther never cheated us. Ladies, how many of you stood up and either, 1) sang his lyrics in tears, or 2) received spiritual chills, as if feeling the Holy Ghost? Us men? While sometimes jealous that Luther enveloped your woman in passion while serenading her, how many of you were fortunate enough after words to be thanked in the most amorous way imaginable after his shows? "If Only for One Night" of the year, you thanked him profusely, because she gave you some of the best lovemaking you ever had after his shows.

After making love to us by way of song for two hours, we were selfish, for we always wanted more. Obliging, if Luther could have sung for ten hours, he would have. And ten hours later, the arena still would have been standing room only. Can I get an Amen?

Ladies, Luther Vandross was my man. Now before you get it all twisted, let me explain: When I couldn't summon the guts to tell you those three words, I spent many a lonely night under red lights in my Brooklyn bedroom making Valentine's Day packages for special friends I hoped would get the message. Two-pound chocolate hearts, big cards, a little stuffed animal or trinket, and…ahem… "pause button slow jam tapes." Every single one I ever made culminated with a powerful Luther song. He always knew the right words to say, the words I felt shy in expressing to you.

He sure had a way of making love feel so good, didn't he? "A House Was Not a Home" without him. "Love Wouldn't Let Him Wait;" he coveted the "Here and Now." After telling us to "Buy Her a Rose," he and Gregory Hines "Gave Me a Reason" why: "There's Nothing Better Than Love." From "I Who Had Nothing" he wanted us "If Only for One Night." When caught "Creepin,'" we had to forgive him, for "He Really Didn't Mean It." "Searching" for the truth, he had the "Glow of Love" on a joyful countenance when singing the damn songs. "Anyone Who Has a Heart" would, if they believed in love.

"Wanting the Night to Stay," I got "The Rush" when he encouraged me to "Never Let Go" of my quest for "Any Love." Cast under a spell, the strong, seductive, sensational sound of his tone was "Never Too Much" to listen to. And to think: this was a man who lost Talent Night at the Apollo four times (!) and was known for doing KFC and pizza jingles.

Stop and think about that for a tick.

KFC jingles.

Pizza jingles.

It boggles the mind, doesn't it?

KFC jingles. I'm still shaking my head incredulously.

My tears have dried again, for I am grateful that he left behind so much of him. All weekend long, his songs told the story of my life, my search for the right one. Crying, dancing, singing, burning CD's for my mother, thinking of his live performances I captured—often going alone, sometimes not—I realized my house is still a home, because his love for song and love itself will live inside me for the rest of my days.

I love you, Luther. Thanks for being you.

William Fredrick Cooper

Goodbye, Luther
Written July 9th, 2005

His casket is made of gold. I can imagine the warmth he'll feel as he travels home. In some uncanny way, we all feel the same time of love today, listening to that one-of-a-kind voice. It'll keep you near, to ease away the tears that his physical departure from us leaves.

But the memory of him remains in his music. The voice will live forever. Trying to convince myself of such last night, I ventured to the Frank E. Campbell Funeral Home to say goodbye to a man I never met, but who touched my life in so many ways. Awaiting the northbound Madison Avenue bus, before I could put a Luther CD in my player, the dam of tear ducts spilled over.

A woman, sixty-something and graying, handed me a napkin. Peering into my grieving eyes, she was comforting.

"I know, baby. He touched us all."

"I didn't know it would affect me so deeply," came my sniffle-filled response.

"Sometimes, love does that, sugar." That woman was a nurturing angel sent from above at the right time.

I knew that Luther sent her to me.

The journey to 81st Street was a trip down memory lane; Vandross Street, actually. Remembering how I stole my mother's cassette of his first album so that I could play "A House Is Not a Home" all the way to high school, I also recalled the many lonely Valentine's Days where I longed to hold a special someone. Luther "Made Me a Believer" in that true love exists. Just "keep holding on," he said in "Any Love." My wedding day? "Here and Now" played through the systems as bridesmaids and groomsmen walked to me. In retrospect, I wish I would have kept the promise Luther encouraged me to do in song. I should have loved her faithfully. My only hope is when Luther arrives at the pearly gates, his initial request to God is to send me another queen whose first words will be I came here "For You To Love."

By the time I reached the line of thousands who also experienced a similar loss, "I'd Rather" was in my ears. That song reminded me of a time where, in an attempt to salvage a foundering relationship, I walked into Houlihan's with two dozen red roses, a diamond ring, and that song on the jukebox expressing every word I felt at the moment. Although another heartbreak followed, it was Luther who told me I was a lucky guy and instructed me not to fall "Too Far Down."

Perhaps I should have conveyed that message to the many in the grieving area. Though we were instructed to move through, many collected themselves in the pews. Sensing, feeling and comprehending their tremendous loss, the tears flowed anew as I viewed the rose-adorned gold casket. Though closed, I saw him, and remembered him singing to me many times over. To the left was a video montage, the right were more flowers, and the many iridescent jackets that illuminated my soul along with that incomparable voice. Smiling as I recalled him actually moon-walking like MJ during one of his concerts, he *Gave Me A Reason* to dance with his mid-tempo cuts.

That it rains here in New York City today, the day of his homecoming, is one last symbol of his love. Waterfalls from heaven to welcome him home, he wants us to cry *If Only For One Night*, heal our hearts from all negativity, then resume our quest for the very thing he wants us all to share: *Any Love*. The skies, while overcast today, will be a generous blue tomorrow. The grieving will cease once God welcomes his prince home, but the gift of song he left behind will bring warmth, compassion and love for all eternity.

Goodbye, Luther.

One Year Later ...

Inspired by "Luther Vandross Live—Radio City Music Hall 2003."
October 16, 2006

One year later, the memory of his voice still sends chills through my frame. Never deviating from the lyrics, nor the trademark ad-libs, in his death, Luther Vandross remains the singular voice of love we have, Forever and For Always. One year later, I'm still shaking my head in disbelief. I just know that in a few weeks, our lives will be enriched once more with something new, something special. Then, the tour will come, and the tickets will go...QUICKLY. The roses I'll share with someone special, as well as the well-dressed dinner at a favorite restaurant will serve as a back-drop to what we'll both cherish. Who cares about the opening act? Not us. The Sultan of Seductive Song doesn't mind our late arrival, unless of course, if we miss his first note.

Let me hear your voice, if only for another night. Many say this, a year after the music stopped. Sure, he has left a legacy of love with that ageless sound. But what we wouldn't give to hear the directive "19 more..." during *Creepin'*, or the melodious mixture of rhythm and words during *Never Too Much*. We know about the killer songs—ALL ACTUALLY—so there's no need to recite, now is there? The ladies in the crowd, were they dressed for us under those red concert lights, or were they decked to the nines for him? I know after dark, in the privacy of our homes, they revealed all to us in a sensuous, seductive manner because of him. To that, many brothers give the heavens hugs and hand-pounds.

As I sit here and listen to this live CD, recorded two months before the beginning of the end (his stroke) I wonder if he knew this was it. Perhaps he and God decided they blessed us enough. Perhaps God wanted him home to serenade HIS and HIS SON'S heart as they decide what to do with the many of us that don't know the true meaning of his most precious energy, that being LOVE.

Here's what I'm thinking: He and his maker had a pact; to loan us that incredible vocal instrument, his affectionately adored, tantalizingly tender tone. We were to have this voice all to ourselves for a half century, just to see how much we treasure love and romance. Then, once Luther made us believers in this spirit and its conditions, he would leave us. Maybe that's it.

Maybe his legacy was defined by our future. Maybe we're supposed to gain bravery in giving our hearts time and time again, renew, recharge and replenish our batteries, escape our emotional insecurities by listening to a Luther Vandross song. Maybe through song, he'll smile from heaven whenever a couple clasp hands while gazing in each other's eyes with a look they only recognize. Maybe he'll give Phyllis Hyman and Barry White high-fives when two people solidify their bond by saying "I do" as "Here and Now" plays in the background. Maybe the love Luther possessed for us still lives within us, with every good deed we do, every time ladies nurture their men, every time kings stand strong for their queens. As he sang so beautifully, we should, to those we cherish, your love is all we need.

When Marilyn Monroe passed away, Joe DiMaggio ordered fresh flowers on her grave every week until he passed some forty years later. Through his magnificent melody, Luther still brings us roses from his heart, but gives them to us while the breath of life remains in us. Why don't we, one year later, show our thanks to him by showing love; to our loved ones and family or strangers in need of a pick-me-up. I think God's noble courier of love would appreciate that.

I miss you, man.

ABOUT THE AUTHOR

William Fredrick Cooper. An ordinary guy trying to make a difference in life, he was in Brooklyn, reared on Staten Island, and presently resides in the Bronx, New York. An Assistant Managing Clerk at a New York City law firm, he is the proud father of a lovely daughter named Maranda. Mr. Cooper is a teen mentor with the Brother 2 Brother Mentorship Program in conjunction with Harlem Hospital; a member of Harlem's Abyssinian Baptist Church; a coordinator of the Well Read Reading group, a Brooklyn based literacy initiative that connects with African American teenagers; and the Acting Secretary of Brother 2 Brother Symposium, Inc., a program that encourages black men and young adults to read fiction literature. (http://theliteraryevent.com/symposium)

Affectionately known as "Mr. Romance," not only is Mr. Cooper known for his enlightening radio interviews throughout the United States and Canada, he has served as host, executive producer, guest speaker and moderator/facilitator to many literary events, including the 2004 Harlem Book Fair, the 2004 Disilgold Unity Literary Awards Show, the Bring Your Book To Life seminar/music concert in Philadelphia, Pennsylvania and the 2006 Erotica Lounge and Lingerie show in conjunction with the African American Literary and Media Group Seminar, held in Reno, Nevada.

His first novel, *Six Days In January*, was published in February 2004 by Strebor Books. A groundbreaking piece of literature that explores the heart of an African-American man damaged by love, the novel received rave reviews in major periodicals in the United States, Canada, Bermuda and the United Kingdom.

In 2006, Mr. Cooper and his novel *Six Days In January* appeared in "After The Breakup: Get Over it and Get On With Your Life," a feature article in the July issue of *Ebony* magazine.

Mr. Cooper is a contributing author to several anthologies. "Legal Days, Lonely Nights" appeared in Zane's *Sistergirls.com*; "Watering Cherry's Garden" was a story for *Twilight Moods—African American Erotica*; "Snowy Moonlit Evenings" was composed for *Journey to Timbooktu*, a collection of poetry and prose, as compiled by Memphis Vaughnes; and "More and More," as well as "Sweet Dreams," were in included in *Morning, Noon and Night: Can't Get Enough—A collection of erotic fiction*. "Te Deseo" was a contribution to Zane's *New York Times* bestselling anthology *Caramel Flava*, published by Atria Books in August 2006. "Dear Zane: A Lust Letter From A Fan" will appear as an extra piece in the forthcoming Zane nonfiction title *Dear G-Spot*, scheduled for release by Atria Books in July 2007. He is also a guest in *Unfinished Business* by Jessica Tilles (February 2007).

William can be reached at damaged06@yahoo.com; www.williamfcooper. tripod.com, and www.myspace.com/wfcooper.

His third novel, *How Come, How Long* will be published in the fall of 2010.

Six Days in January

BY WILLIAM FREDRICK COOPER

AVAILABLE FROM STREBOR BOOKS

Chapter One
SNOWY MOONLIT EVENINGS

Day One

He didn't know which was worse, the bitter cold raking against his dark skin or Della's icy words just moments ago. Echoing softly in his heart, and though wishing the wind would blow them away and the winter chill along with them, he couldn't deny their truth.

Nothing's worse than getting put out at one in the morning on the coldest night of the year, he decided while making his way to the subway station. Face stinging and ears burning from the extreme weather, William McCall wondered how he had gotten there in the first place. Della wasn't supposed to forgive him this time. She'd been "through with his shit" over a month ago after calling his Brooklyn apartment one morning in early December and hearing the voice of another woman—a woman whom she insisted was his ex-wife, a woman he'd divorced two years prior.

"But it wasn't her," he'd persisted, "she's just a friend."

Although honest that time, the issue hardly mattered to her anymore. Fed up with all the crap she'd ingested at the hands of this man, she no longer had the strength to weed through his lies in hopes of finding the truth.

But this was a snowy, moonlit Thursday evening in mid-January, one of those blustery, sub-freezing days in New York City where a cold, empty bed is so hard to bear alone. Doing computer consultant work at a midtown

Smith Barney office, nothing awaited Della Montgomery at her Bronx apartment except post-holiday bills. So when William called her office that morning sounding desperate—as though he'd learned his lesson—she'd accepted his invitation to have drinks after work.

Heading to an after-work watering hole in lower Manhattan where they'd first met a year ago and had frequented often since that fateful night, William found her sitting at a dark, red-bricked bar nursing a Heineken. Della was dressed provocatively in a blue dress, revealing a tight, aerobically carved frame. Her thin braids complemented an unblemished tan shade, making her appear younger than her thirty-nine years. *She still feels as if she must impress me. That's a good sign*, he thought as he approached her with flowers in hand.

"I'm so glad you decided to meet me," he said, handing her the bouquet while offering a kiss that she accepted with her cheek.

"It must be a new year," Della replied, aggressively grabbing the arrange-ment as she crossed her sculpted stems. "You actually made it here at the time you said you were going to. I'm surprised you were able to find such beautiful flowers on such a cold day. Then again, you're at your best when you're being cold."

Grimacing at her bluntness, he thought, *maybe this wasn't such a good idea*. "Ouch, that hurt. You didn't decide to meet me here just to read me my rights, did you?"

Della offered a sarcastic smile. "No, it's because I missed you so much."

"Well, I'm glad to see you, anyway." William ogled her and her beauty filled him up. Her full, inviting lips were sensuous and her eyes, although serious, were warm, sparkling and dove-like, soaring with radiance. "You look extraordinarily beautiful. I'm really glad to see you. Did you get my package last month?"

"I did, but I didn't open it." Della wasn't being truthful at this point. At first she'd thought of sending it back but after the holidays, she'd given in. Upon reading the card, she'd played the accompanying love tape every day for a week, but there was no way she was going to let him know that. Just last night, she'd held the teddy bear and cried, wondering why William couldn't be so sweet and thoughtful all the time. Acknowledging his tender side, it seemed he only showed how much he cared when he'd hurt her, and was tender only when they made love.

Still, the thought of his December package softened her to the point of wanting to strip this slim, athletic thirty-four-year-old man from his blue double-breasted suit. As he looked away to get the bartender's attention, she detected disappointment in his tone when he ordered a Long Island Iced Tea. Realizing that she was supposed to be annoyed with him, she guarded her own vulnerability once he returned to her. "I meant to; I've just been busy," she explained. "I went away over the holidays, and…"

"Where'd you go?"

"To the Bahamas, with my girlfriend, Toni."

"Where'd you stay?"

"At the Nassau Marriott Resort. You know, the hotel with the casino."

The sparkle returned to William's eyes.

"Did you meet Dexter?"

"Plenty of them, but I wasn't looking for one. I was actually trying to figure out why men are so fucked up."

Like a drop of water lingering on the tip of a melting icicle before falling to the ground, William paused ever so slightly, then, prepared for the confrontation he'd briefly sidestepped upon his arrival. "Della, I don't know how else to say I'm sorry…"

"I don't want your apologies, William. I just want to know how you can be so fucked up? Be totally honest with me. Do you enjoy playing games with people's emotions? Do you find pleasure in hurting women?"

"I was honest with you. That wasn't my ex-wife."

Sipping from her beer and realizing that she was being drawn in, Della wanted to resist the temptation to question him. She couldn't. "Well, who was it, then?" Before his lips formed an excuse, "No, forget it, don't tell me. I don't even want to know. It doesn't matter if she was your ex-wife, or your friend. You lied to me, William. I thought I was the only one, and maybe I was a fool to think that. But you proved me wrong."

During the ensuing silence, William tuned in to R. Kelly's "Down Low" on the jukebox. *Everyone's talking about creepin', having sex on the DL, fuckin' on the sneak tip*, he thought. Amused at the irony, he mumbled, "Maybe I shouldn't listen to the radio so much."

"What did you say?"

"Nothing."

The bartender finally returned with his drink.

"You can't think of anything to say?" Della's tone jolted him.

"What else is there to say? I tried calling you. I sent you a package explaining everything and you ignored me. What am I supposed to do? I never said I didn't have a past or a life outside of my life with you. I'm really sorry about what happened that day, I really, really am. But I can't apologize for you not being the only one in my life."

He turned away from her to take a swallow of his drink.

Della crinkled her forehead. Her emotions rising, she began regretting the agreement to see him, having heard his, "I got divorced recently, so I don't want to be tied down" speech too many times before. "Look. I'm not asking you to marry me or anything. I just want to be loved and respected and that means honesty about who you're dealing with. But it seems like that's too much to ask from you, or any man, for that matter."

"That's not true. What do you expect me to do, make a mad dash to the phone just in case it's you who's calling? What was I supposed to do? You have a right to be upset, and while understanding you may not have liked what happened, there are some things that just go with the territory."

"Is honesty part of your territory? Or am I just supposed to accept being disrespected by some heifer? What's her name, anyway? The fuckin' wench!"

"Now, why does she have to be all that?"

✪✪✪

As he crossed the Grand Concourse and made his way down the icy streets, William thought of the hodgepodge of truths, half truths, untruths and deceptions that had painted a murky picture for Della hours earlier—an illustration that became more blurred with each question, each answer and each drink. As candid with her as he could be, but not at the risk of what he wanted, in short, he'd told her what she needed to know.

The woman he'd been with was "a friend," but he was no longer seeing her. In fact, he hadn't seen her since the day she'd spewed venom at Della over the phone. He liked her, he conceded, but she was too demanding and insecure. Reminding him of his ex-wife—in a bad way—he'd stopped seeing her because what he shared with her wasn't worth the loss of Della's companionship.

Having spent the holidays alone, he'd been really down about having hurt her. He was fairly certain that he'd really lost her this time, a point emphasized as the conversation continued. "And I just wanted to see you to let you know all of these things, for whatever it's worth. I know I'm almost out of rope when it comes to my word, for it means almost nothing to you. But I still have to speak my peace, because no matter what happens, I still care about you."

The words rang familiar to Della; they echoed the ones in his holiday card. Already knowing the details of his alibi, she wanted to hear it directly from him. Anyone could write a letter. But probing his eyes that night at the bar, she remembered the heartfelt words he'd expressed to her in his card. Della never questioned William's ability to treat her right, only his willingness and commitment to doing so. Maybe staying away had been just what he'd needed to see what he was risking. Still, the fact that she feared what he'd say if she asked for a commitment from him created an uncomfortable silence as they sat together; William, not knowing anything else to say to mend fences, and Della, trying to resolve questions and issues that his presence provoked. William breached the quiet with a truce.

"Look, Della. I'm just glad to see you. Let's not dwell on what happened anymore. I know it was wrong. I just wanted to see you, share some memories and have a good time. I missed you."

They continued to talk things out, drink after drink and eventually, they tired of the back and forth waffling and began to enjoy themselves. Knowing he was glad to see her—he could hardly take his eyes off of her— Della felt soothed by his presence. After another drink, the night continued with a dinner filled with steamy flirtations at Jezebel's, an old-fashioned Cajun restaurant in midtown. From there, they took a cab to her second-floor Bronx apartment on University Avenue. Then, after some wine and listening to Will Downing, she was ready to forgive him.

❂❂❂

"Get off of me, you fucking bastard! Get your dick out of me!" Della pounded on William's chest and shoulders until he backed off.

"Della, please, I'm so sorry. I don't know what I was thinking. It must have been our conversation earlier," he continued. "Please forgive me; I didn't mean anything by it."

"You are one fucked-up individual, William!" Della screamed as she stormed around the bedroom in a fury. "How could you? Every single time I give in to you, I feel more and more like a fool for listening to your trifling, sorry ass. But, not anymore. Get the hell out and stay the fuck out of my life!"

William stood by the bed, naked, his erection subsiding. "Baby, please, don't get hysterical. Calm down. You need time to think this over."

"Hysterical? You've stepped over the line too many times before…but to call me another woman's name! Is Barbara the bitch you told me all about? Your friend? Well, she can have you, because you can't do shit for me!" Della made her way to the dresser, turned on the bedroom light and started emptying belongings he had left at her house on the floor.

Watching her in silence, he couldn't stop his eyes from blinking as Della's tirade moved from the dresser to her bedroom closet. A pile of clothes, underwear and toiletries from prior visits was accumulating on the floor. *The sex with Barbara wasn't even that good*, he thought. When Della was finished, she slumped to the floor and started crying.

Up to this point, he hadn't moved. But now, still naked, he staggered over to her with drunken tears of his own forming in his eyes. "Della, I'm sorry. I don't know what else to say." Now seated next to her, he tried to rest his head on her shoulder.

Della angrily moved away and began stuffing his belongings in a blue duffel bag. "That's the problem with you, William. You never know what to say. Then again, you always seem to know exactly what to say. But you know what?" She paused to sniffle and wipe the tears from her face. "I just wish this had happened before, because I should have done this a long, long time ago. This past year has been such a waste of my time, trying to get your black ass to act right and treat me the way I deserve to be treated. All I wanted from you was honesty and respect, and you can't even give me that. You never have. You're a fuckin' dog, like so many of you sorry-ass black men." She started sobbing again.

"Della, I care about you, you know that. I'm just going through a lot, right now. That conversation we had earlier had me thinking about her, that's all. You have to believe me when I say she doesn't mean anything to me."

Blankly staring off and ignoring all pleas, Della recounted an incident she'd observed earlier that day while traveling to work. She saw a teenager outside the D-train station trying to get this young sister's attention while attempting to be cool in front of his boys, communicating his attraction to her with all of this "Yo, baby" shit. The young girl had ignored him, so he called her a bitch and threw a snowball at her.

"Later on in life she's going to run across guys like you; always full of shit," she continued. "Always looking for that next piece of ass. Never knowing how to treat a woman, only trying when things go wrong." She paused, shaking her head in disbelief. "I don't believe some of you brothers today." Lifting herself from the floor, Della sorted through the remains of the heap to find his suit. "Just looking at you is starting to repulse me, William. Please hurry up and leave."

"But you can't believe how sorry I am," William implored, as his clothes were being thrown at him. "It will never happen again. I promise."

"You're right about that. You are sorry, and you're damned straight, this shit will never happen again. Now, hurry up and leave." Della left the bedroom, refusing to let him see her cry anymore.

William got dressed and picked up his briefcase, leaving the duffel bag she'd packed in the middle of the floor where she left it. Entering the living room, he found her on the couch, her knees pulled up to her chin with her arms wrapped around them.

"Della, please accept my apology."

"Let me give you some advice, William. Stop apologizing so much and start acting like a real man. Now, get out."

"Please, can't we just start over? Nothing like this will ever happen again. Della, please. Look, I can start here." Pulling a Tootsie Roll from his coat pocket, he remembered how she loved the small chocolate candy.

The peace offering would not work tonight.

Della rose and walked to the front door. "Start by learning how to love someone besides yourself." She opened the door. "Good-bye."

Drunk, defeated and dejected, William walked past her without turning around and made his way to the elevator.

Della stepped into the hallway.

"And you can continue by learning how to fuck!" The door slammed.